Command
of Silence

Paulette Callen

Spinsters Ink
2009

Spinsters Ink
P.O. Box 242
Midway, Florida 32343

Printed in the United States of America on acid-free paper
First Edition

Editor: Katherine V. Forrest
Cover designer: Linda Callaghan

ISBN: 10-1-935226-08-8
ISBN: 13-978-1-935226-08-6

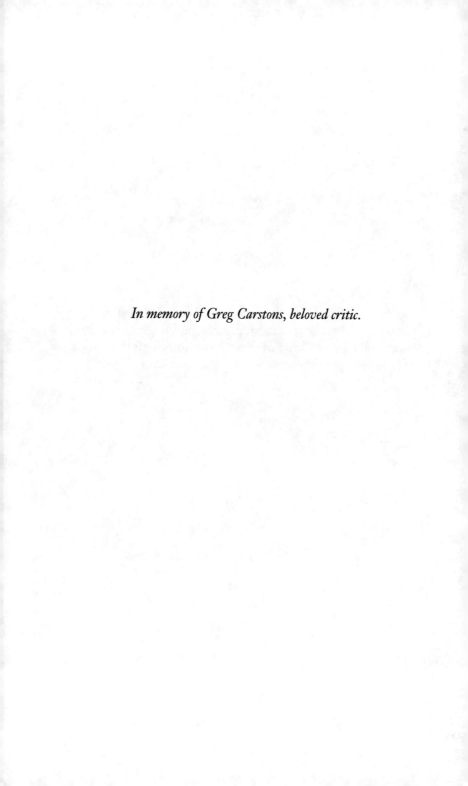

In memory of Greg Carstons, beloved critic.

The Upper West Side of New York is a real and lovely place; however, the specific addresses, buildings and institutions mentioned are products of the author's imagination, as are all of the characters, without exception.

Acknowledgments

Thanks are due to the Every-Other-Monday-Night-Brilliants who, with good cheer, wit and critical eyes and ears, have tried to make me a better writer: Gary Reed, Suzanne Heath, Jonathan Fried and Mary Burns. Thank you, Susan Lycke, for the title. Covers don't always make a book, but titles often do.

Turning and turning in the widening gyre

The falcon cannot hear the falconer;

Things fall apart; the centre cannot hold;

Mere anarchy is loosed upon the world,

The blood-dimmed tide is loosed, and everywhere

The ceremony of innocence is drowned;

The best lack all convictions, while the worst

Are full of passionate intensity.

from: "Second Coming" W. B. Yeats

Prologue—Friday

The day Hawk killed our father was not the first day I'd ever been locked up; it was just the first day I'd ever felt relief at being locked up. I say "our father," not because she is my sister—she's not—but because he begat us both as surely as a struck match begets fire. But why do I think of her now? Oh, yes, because I am confined here among these familiar strangers and feel no relief, only terror, and because, this time, she is not saving me.

I feel the knife, see the smile dawning on Dora's face and realize the bargain we made—not exactly a bargain—we engaged to play the game where she stabs me and I die. Too many realities for the mind to grasp come to a point in that smile as she cuts again, deeply this time—the killing cut, for the blood gurgles like muddy water up through the neck of a slim pipe, warm, spilling over my hands as I try to hold my abdomen together. I lose feeling in my feet, my head floats free from my body, as blank spots yawn and crescents shimmer in my visual field. I beg Ray, "Call an ambulance. Game over. I give up. I want to live. I'll tell them I did it so you won't be blamed." And I think of the pain when they will move me and sew me, stick me and fill me with foreign fluids; I'll feel the pain in every part of me, but I'll live, and I feel myself going under and the medics will get here or they won't; I'll wake up in pain or I won't wake up at all.

People in robes, like medieval religious, gather, and someone lets a child run into the room. My bed is slick with blood. My blood, this time. The child screams and screams and runs back out. I am angry they have been so careless. My anger floats.

I am still conscious, still not on a stretcher. No one is sewing me up. But I am now connected to an IV. Rose-colored fluid drips into my vein. Not enough to save me, just prolong things. Why bother with it? Now, Ray is angry. At me. The others watch, all smiling, smiling, watching me die.

How did I come to this? At what moment did this become inevitable? Not with the well-kept priest's deliberate smile and plea for help, "Two children are missing." No, it has always been.

(the previous) Wednesday

Chapter 1

"Two children are missing," he said, and bells went off in the Company, echoing far back in the gyre. Was Ray serious about referring this guy to us? Voices clamored. Simmer down, Sugartime commanded so we could listen.

The priest, whose name was O'Hagan, was observant. "Are you all right?" he asked.

"Yes." I began with the standard question. "Was there a ransom demand?"

"No."

"Why do you need me?"

"The police are going to arrest an innocent person."

"How do you know?"

"It's the questions they ask, and how they keep coming back to—"

"No. How do you know this person is innocent?"

"She couldn't be responsible."

I let it go and asked how he had come to me. Sent by a friend of a friend, he said. "Who is this friend of your friend?" I asked.

"Ray Martinez."

Ah. The first cut—the razor so sharp, at the time I didn't even feel it.

I nodded to the chair in front of my desk. The priest hitched his trousers and sat. He fidgeted—a man unused to being unnerved.

"Your fee will be generous."

Hester trilled, *Oooh! How generous?* at the same time as Olive inquired, *What's his definition of generous?*

He smoothed his wavy brown hair and checked his pocket again. In a moment he'd be biting those well-manicured nails and wouldn't even know why. Ray says I have this effect on people when they meet me for the first time. She even coached me in small behaviors to alleviate their discomfort. "Shiloh, a little smile would go a long way toward making people feel more at ease." I tried, but that only made her laugh. She said my smile is the kind a cat gets before she steals the liver off the counter. We tried a few other things, but in the end, she said, "Just be yourself. It's better than the alternative." And that was so funny, almost everybody laughed.

I asked the fidgety priest, "Who's paying this generous fee?"

He explained the entire situation, talking on and on. He was handsome, in a tall Irish kind of way, and knew it. He made it part of his persuasiveness, but we had already decided. Still, we listened. Charlotte, a missing infant, and Anna, a missing three-year-old. The baby's mother was Claudia Keating, recently widowed. Anna was the daughter of Charlotte's nanny, Miriam Stern, a Russian immigrant sponsored by the Keatings to work in this country and attend an American university.

Only a small chance remained of finding the children alive, but I knew why Ray suggested me. I might be the only one able to exploit that one small chance. Police have their methods and with them, limitations. My methods are different.

The priest reached into his inside pocket again. This time he drew out a check and placed it on the desk between us. It was already made out to me and was indeed generous. The check was drawn on the account of, and signed by, Claudia Keating.

"Why is Mrs. Keating so worried about the nanny? She just lost her husband and her own child."

"She feels responsible. It happened here. In New York. Miriam and Anna were under her care, you know. Strangers in a strange land and all that. She wants to find the guilty party, and the police won't do that if they settle on Miriam. She is sure Miriam is innocent. Mrs. Keating is a tough woman. You wouldn't think it but..."

He looked at the check and then at me. I didn't care about the money. It was the children—the second cut. My own children wailed softly like little banshees from the mouth of the gyre. Couldn't the gatekeeper keep them out of hearing of this conversation?

"Will you help us?" The priest seemed worn out by his own restlessness and was finally still.

I asked, "What do you know about Ray Martinez?"

"Nothing. My friend just said he trusted her judgment, and I trust my friend."

"Who's your friend?"

"Bishop Cassidy."

Ray socialized in rarefied circles, but I was surprised she knew a Catholic bishop. "I work on my terms."

He nodded, somewhat eagerly. He had no idea.

"Let me tell you about Ray," I began.

Chapter 2

As soon as O'Hagan left my office, we dialed the phone. A pleasant female voice with a note of Latin music in it answered, "Dr. Martinez."

"Yo! Ray-Man-a-danna! Are you freakin' nuts?"

"Cootie! How nice to hear from you."

"So, you knew this is a missing kid case and you send the padre to us? I gotta tell you—the weepin' and wailin' and bawlin'—we couldn't hardly think in here. Whaddaya doin', girl?"

Ray's voice was calm. Her voice was always calm. "Sugartime kept you all clear, though? Isadora stayed conscious?"

"Well, yeah. But—"

"Then it will be all right. This is a case I think you can help on. Believe me, Cootie, I wouldn't have suggested you if I had thought otherwise. I also thought you could use the fee."

"You are really so sure of us, Ray?"

"Hello, Isadora. Yes, I am very sure of you. And you must be too, or you wouldn't have taken the case. You did take it?"

"Um-hm. I gave the priest permission to talk to you."

"How did he respond?"

"Better than average. I think he's had more than Psych 101. A little jarred, but he'll get over it."

"Until he meets Hawk."

"Let's hope he never does," I said.

Chapter 3

The priest was to return in four hours to escort me to the Keating residence. He thought that would be enough time to bring the family together and brief them. How much he told them, I left to his discretion. In the meantime, I wanted a look at the police file.

O'Hagan had been surprised to learn that I knew the lead officer on the case. It wasn't such a big coincidence. Leo Gianetti is head of the mayor's special task force on missing and abused child cases. At the time of its formation, Ray Martinez was already a prominent authority in the city on the most abhorrent forms of child abuse, so it was no surprise that she was asked to help educate this fledgling group of officers, handpicked from various precincts in the five boroughs. It was a coincidence that Gianetti was headquartered in my neighborhood stationhouse. But sometimes a cigar is just a cigar, and a coincidence is just a coincidence.

I walked the four short blocks south and three long blocks east to the police station.

I think you should deposit the check first. We need new clothes.

"Our clothes are fine, Hester," I muttered. "First things first." One of the good things about New York City for a person like me is that everybody talks to themselves on the street. I'm not special.

Never you mind about clothes, Missy, snapped Olive. *We can pay the rent and the phone bill and put the rest in the bank for the next time we are between cases.*

You are always such a killjoy. Can't we live a little?

If it were left up to you we wouldn't live at all. We'd be in debt up to our pierced lobes.

I have learned to more or less tune Olive and Hester out when they go at each other, which is most of the time. None of us bothers to play peacemaker anymore.

The air was cool, the trees just popping their buds. Jonquils bloomed on every patch of dirt: around trees, in the center islands along Broadway, in scattered beds throughout the parks. Alongside them, tiny crocuses valiantly displayed their deep purple. Hester loves flowers and will rhapsodize *ad nauseam* about yellow feeding the soul after a long, drab city winter. But Aurora, deaf and mute though she is, is more eloquent. After our sightings of the first signs of a New York spring, she will produce paintings of flowers or barely budded tree branches that will either take your breath away or soothe your soul. Sometimes both. Her style is deceptive in that at first it seems to be a realistic rendering, but on closer study, it is not. Her colors are alive, her plants seem to breathe and have sentience. I know nothing about painting, but I'm glad that, inexplicably, she does. The SoHo gallery that buys her work pays more of our bills than do SHILOH & Co.'s detective and consulting fees.

"The two of you can it for awhile and give me some peace. That's not a request." When we are working, I'm in charge, no questions asked. That is in our contracts. I invoked my contractual privilege now as I crossed Amsterdam Avenue.

The stationhouse was ahead of me in the middle of the block. I know where it is and still it always appears just before I expect it to. Tucked between brownstones, whose stairs rise to heavy wooden doors, the station's street-level entrance has a cave-like feeling, its glass doors notwithstanding. The laminated poster of a blown-up letter from a local grade school thanking the police officers for their sacrifices during 9/11 has been hanging on the red brick front of the building so long it is tattered; so is the yellow banner expressing the precinct's appreciation for the neighborhood's support. The vestibule is tiny. Just an air lock to keep winter's chill out and air-conditioned air in. Its only ornament is a poster commanding cheerfully: Get to know your local police force! depicting an absurdly handsome officer hand in hand with a worshipful child. Inside, the décor is standard New York Institutional Shabby. Our city is lucky to scrounge up enough money to pay the police and fire department—there's nothing left over for interior decorators. In fact, the place hasn't changed much from the first time I went there with Ray fifteen years ago. The same dusty green on the walls, the inadequate lighting. The rows of dark benches and metal chairs. What is here now that wasn't back then is the bulletproof glass shielding the front desk.

I don't like it here.

Why not, Bethy-June? The officers were always nice to us.

It's dark. It's dark in here.

Not that dark. Now quiet so Isadora can work. I'll tell you a story. Lance began to speak, not sing, the lyrics to "Puff, the Magic Dragon."

Lance's voice is like background music and doesn't distract me. I needed him to keep Bethy-June quiet. She is too young for contracts. "Hello, Rudolfo."

Rudy is a long-term cop with a short neck and eyebrows that qualify as a fire hazard. He's a cop who loves and excels at his desk job. Early in his career he was shot in the leg and instead of disability, he took the front desk. He looked up at me from some papers he was scribbling on. His eyes have a piercing, ice-blue brilliance. His mouth was full of gum and has been since he quit smoking two years ago. He grinned broadly, continuing to chew. "Shiloh! How's it going?" He spoke loudly. He seemed to think he had to shout through the barrier although it was hardly soundproof.

"Okay. How're you?"

"No complaints." Chew, chew. "Here to see Gianetti?"

I nodded.

"I think he's in but you never know with these guys. They like to sneak in and out the back." There is nothing much that Rudy does not know about the goings-on in this precinct. He hasn't sat in on any of my sessions, but he still knows all about me. He has always been kind, and never condescending.

Grinning his full-faced grin, chewing ferociously, he picked up the receiver and punched in a couple numbers on his phone. "Yeah, Lieutenant, Shiloh's here to see you. Right." He nodded toward the back staircase. "Go on up. We got a new coffeemaker. It brews poison." Chew chew.

"Thanks, Rudy."

I took the steps two at a time up the stairway that spiraled inward so that as you disappeared from view to the first floor, you appeared with the railing on the other side on the second. I made my way to the back of the long narrow room through a clutter of desks, filing cabinets and chairs and the ambient noise of ringing phones, voices, shuffling papers and drawers opening and closing. A couple uniformed officers nodded in my direction. I nodded back.

Gianetti was standing, waiting for me, at the back of the room. "Hey, Shiloh!" In the fifteen years since I first met him, Leo Gianetti has begun to show the effects of his job. The burdens of what he's discovered about the dark side of human nature weigh heavily all over him. He's gained weight, his face is lined and starting to pouch. "What's doin'?" He pointed to a metal chair that was orphaned in the aisle.

I placed it squarely in front of his desk and sat down. "Couple of missing kids. Charlotte Keating and Anna Stern."

"Oh." He sat down heavily. Hester teases him about his added weight sometimes, but we really are not amused. We don't want to lose him to a heart attack or a stroke. He's one of the good guys. Tough, not mean. I have watched him work his way up from a junior member of the task force to its head, guiding it from an experiment to an established and respected unit. He has seen us go from a quivering mass of fearful, sometimes hysterical amnesiac jelly to a functioning group with almost total collective memory. I've been consulted on a couple of cases, but only tangentially; Ray is the task force's main resource. She is frequently called upon to interview victims and perps for the police and for the DA. She is often the expert witness in child abuse cases. Occasionally, she asks me to sit in on interviews. I have an uncanny knack for knowing when somebody is or is not telling the truth. Ray says I'm better than a polygraph because I don't need a yes or no answer to spot a lie.

Leo slid a file across the desk toward me. "You can look at it. You can't take it with you."

We knew the drill and didn't need to take it with us. Cootie has a photographic memory. Unfortunately, I have to let him out to read. "Man, this is heavy shit," he said as he turned a page.

"Cooterman! How you doin'?" Leo stuck out his hand and Cootie shook it. Cootie and Hester are the Company hand-shakers.

"Okay, lawman. Doin' okay! The chicks have got themselves into some shit, here, huh? The howlin' earlier. Shee-it! You shoulda heard it!"

"I did hear it once. I'll never forget it."

"I told Ray, but she says she's got faith. Gotta keep the faith, huh, lawman?"

"Right, Cootie. How about I go get my coffee cup filled and let you read that. You want something?"

"A Coke would be excellent! I don't get enough Coke. The chicks say it ruins their figure. Well, it don't hurt mine none."

"Coke it is."

"And you wouldn't have any Sunny Doodles back there, would you?"

"I'll check."

Leo is unfazed by our changes—now. I remember him as a fresh detective, all swagger and smirk, eyeing me and Ray for the first time with naked skepticism. After introducing me to the small group of officers, Ray said, "Before you think of her as mentally ill or a freak (Leo flushed at that), consider this: she survived abuse that would have destroyed most children, or adults, for that matter. It is her genius that she survived. Her genius. Multiplicity is not an illness. It is an adaptation. Remember it." I didn't feel like a genius then and I still don't.

But Ray is the one who showed me I am not crazy. That day, Ray explained she was going to take one of my personalities through regression. Leo smirked at that too. He thought he was going to see a show. But, the tough guy burst into tears when he heard the terrified screams of a three-year-old coming out of the mouth of a teenager. The second session, he almost fainted, but he kept coming back. Now, child cases are his specialty; he's good at it, and we are happy to take some of the credit. When I told the priest how I knew Lieutenant Gianetti, he was shocked ("You allowed people to sit in on your therapy?"), equating that with, I suppose, playing to an audience during confessions. But inviting the task force to sit in on a few of my sessions with Ray was my idea, not hers. I wanted the world to know. I wanted to educate people, because if there had just once been one person—just one—who had come to my rescue when I was one or four or eleven, maybe I wouldn't have lost so much of my life.

Cootie let his eyes travel each page, top to bottom. He read all the notes made by Gianetti and the transcripts of all the interviews. He did it rapidly. He doesn't know how he does it, he just does it. God knows he's not that bright. He doesn't understand what he reads, he's simply a camera. A very annoying camera. The rest of us interpret what he logs into his memory. By the time Leo returned, Cootie was done. He took the Coke greedily and chugged it.

"No Sunny Doodles or anything else today. The vending machine is bare. Cops eat a lot of crap. Sorry, Cooter."

"S'all right." Cootie shrugged and settled into a slouch. He gulped the dregs of his soda. "Man, I love this stuff. Great seein' you man. I gotta go."

Leo leaned back in his chair, coffee cup in hand, and waited the beat it took for me to come back.

"Why do you give him that stuff?" I straightened my back.

"Aw, it's just a Coke. He likes it. You should keep it around for him."

"He drinks it. I get the gas. We do let him have it occasionally, but only as a reward for doing something for us. If you just give him what he wants all the time, our bribes won't work."

He laughed. "You lead a complicated life, Shiloh."

We get that a lot.

"You want coffee?"

I declined.

He nodded toward the file. "So what do you make of it?"

Until I hacked into Cootie's memory, I wouldn't know all the details, but I had the gist of what he read. Don't ask me how this works. I can't explain it. "I didn't know that the children went missing at different times. I assumed they'd been taken together."

"That is just one of the weird things in this case." He took a sip of his coffee and scowled. Then he opened a drawer and rummaged till he came up with two packs of sugar. He ripped them open together and dumped their contents into his cup.

"Not much here," I said.

"That's the problem." He rummaged again and came up with a spoon. He examined it and rubbed the back of it against his shirt and then stirred his coffee with it. "The family is all accounted for except the uncle."

"Michael Keating."

He threw the wet spoon back into his desk drawer and tried the coffee again.

"Do you really like him for this?"

He raised his eyebrows and pursed his lips. "He's what's left over when you check out everybody else. You have a kid that disappears from a playground two blocks from her own building. The next day, an infant disappears from the same apartment where the first kid lives. The baby's in the nursery, in her bassinette. The mother is in her room, also taking a nap. The boys are at a ball game in the park. The nanny is under sedation in her room, which is up the hall. Everybody is accounted for except the uncle who says that on both days he was hearing confessions. I didn't think they did that anymore. So if he did know who he was talking to during the afternoon, the seal of confession prevents him from telling us so we can contact anybody to verify that he was sitting in that little box. Pretty damned convenient."

"But not necessarily untrue. Would somebody come forward on their own if they knew he was under suspicion? Just to help him out?"

"Father O'Hagan said he'd put the word out but there hasn't been a peep from anyone."

Leo is a practicing Catholic. He married a girl who had her heart set on being a nun till she met him. He used the priest's title without thinking. I had had to ask the priest, "What can I call you? I can't call you *Father*. It would confuse the children."

"What…oh…your…children, I mean…"

"Yes."

"Was it a priest who…hurt you?"

"No. It was my father. I can't address you as Father because it would frighten them if they overheard me."

"I see. Where is your father?" he asked softly.

"I trust he's in hell."

He turned his head away slightly so I couldn't see his eyes. I'm used to that, too. The men who have feelings are the ones who give me hope that there is a reason not to commit suicide, although Hawk remains skeptical. Not about the suicide part. She'd never let one of us do it. She has protected me from the knives, the pills and the razor blades, the lengths of clothesline that the others have kept hidden around and under mattresses and in the back of closets and even in the bottoms of our shoes. She remains skeptical that there is anything good in the nature of men. But that's her job.

"My name is Ryan," he had said, and stopped asking me questions. Now I asked Leo, "Does Michael Keating have a motive?"

"Other than the obvious?"

I didn't say anything and he continued.

"He is close to the kids. Spends a lot of time with the boys. Takes them to games and that sort of thing."

"But not the games in the park on the days the girls went missing?"

"No. They were at a school soccer game. The coach says both boys played both days. Anyway, sometimes they stay overnight at the rectory. Father O'Hagan has his own apartment, so Father Keating and an old housekeeper rattle around in the rectory by themselves. Since his brother died, Father Keating has devoted a lot of time to the widow and her children. This could be brotherly love, or he's got other motives. Used to be, that would have been a good thing. Now it's suspect. What a world, huh? The boys seem to think a lot of their uncle. They were shocked at any suggestions that he was fooling around with them. And they're city kids—eight and ten—old enough and savvy enough to know what *fooling around* means." He drank some more coffee, though he was clearly not enjoying it.

I nodded. All that was in the file, but it was good to hear Leo go over it.

"So Claudia Keating discovers she's pregnant about the same time as her husband is diagnosed with cancer. Pancreatic, so he goes—" Leo snapped his fingers. "About that time, she takes in this woman and her little girl to help with the boys and with the new baby when it arrives. They seem to be getting along. So Claudia is just home from the hospital, resting while the nanny takes her own daughter to the playground. Miriam is keeping watch on Anna who is playing by herself in the sandbox. She swears that she never took her eyes off the sandbox, but that some mothers or nannies were walking past and for a few seconds they were between her and the box and the sun was in her eyes. She squints and holds her hand up to shade her eyes and her kid is gone. She runs over and asks everyone, and within a minute or two, one of the mothers is on her cell calling 911. We've interviewed everyone we could find at the playground. Nobody remembers any strange people around. Just women with children. Then the next day, she is out of commission. They've given her something to knock her out, so Mrs. Keating takes her baby out in the buggy. She isn't gone long, because she doesn't want to leave Miriam alone too long, even though she is out cold. She takes her cell with her so she won't miss a call. The housekeeper has the day off but had volunteered to come back at six to cook them supper. Mrs. Keating gets what she needs, goes home. The doorman confirms that was at two. She puts her baby in the bassinette, checks on Miriam who is still out cold, and she goes to her own room and lies down. At three thirty or so, she wakes up and goes to the nursery. No baby. No obvious break-in. Nothing is disturbed. The apartment door is still locked. She calls everybody she knows, including the doorman. She calls 911. I'm telling you, this is the weirdest case I've ever been on and we've got nothing. Absolutely nothing. Nobody knows anything. No ransom note. No fucking anything."

Leo never got used to these cases in which he specialized. I wondered when he would burn out. I belched. *Damn it Cootie!* I heard the kid laugh.

I nodded. "So you don't mind if we put our nose in it?"

He shook his head. "Just tell me anything you come up with." Leo isn't territorial. He orders his team to just skip the pissing contests when it comes to kids.

"It says here the baby was a newborn. I don't know much about this stuff, but Mrs. Keating was strong enough to go out so soon after giving birth?"

"Strong or not, she did it. The drugstore isn't far. They get 'em in and out and up on their feet in no time these days. My Tina walked out of the delivery room. I felt worse than she did after Tony was born. I was a wreck." He rubbed the back of his neck.

"Are you going to arrest Michael Keating?"

"I'll let you know. You know him?"

"No. O'Hagan hired me. Well, actually, Claudia Keating hired me and the senior padre delivered her check. He came to see me this morning. Have you checked him out? He told me he had spent a lot of time with the family during and since the husband's illness. He paints himself a model of virtue. Expensive clothes and all."

Leo snorted. "He and his virtue were playing tennis the day Anna went missing."

"Chilly for tennis, isn't it?"

"Indoor court. One of those pricey deals on the pier. And he was at a benefit lunch for Catholic Medical Missions when Charlotte disappeared. He was the keynote speaker and sat at a table on a raised platform in front of four hundred people."

"O'Hagan told me that Mrs. Keating was afraid you were going to arrest the nanny."

"He did, did he?"

"He said it was the way you questioned her."

"We have a situation where a woman and her kid are in a fenced playground. I can't think how you get a kid out of there without someone noticing. So it occurred to me that she didn't have her daughter when she went in. She could have slipped in and people who recognized her assumed that Anna was running around somewhere. Then she sounds the alarm. 'My kid is gone!' Everybody goes nuts. She has an excuse to go nuts. And then the real kidnapping takes place the next day. Charlotte."

"Why? There has been no ransom request. And where is Anna?"

"Maybe she has friends taking care of her. Maybe that was to throw us off the scent of the real kidnapper, the one who took Charlotte. Maybe she gave Charlotte to someone. Just walked her over to the door and handed her out."

"It says here you took a blood sample from her that day, and she had taken almost enough pills to kill herself. It would have been impossible for her to have gotten up and taken Charlotte, even as far as the apartment door."

"I know. That's the one kink in our theory. But maybe she has a tolerance for the stuff, or maybe she took the pills after she took the kid."

"If there's no ransom demand—"

"They could get their money on the other end. Selling the baby on the black market. And in a week or two or three, when it all dies down and leads are cold, she'll say she is overwrought and wants to go back to Russia, and she'll take the train to Little Odessa in Brooklyn where her Uncle Boris and Aunt Natasha are taking care of Anna and they'll live happily ever after on all the money they got for selling Charlotte to a baby broker. Do you know how much a rich couple will pay for a white baby, no questions asked?"

Leo's cell phone rang. "Gianetti. Yeah, I'm here, Feeney, where the hell are you? You left half an hour ago to pick up a couple of burgers. What'd you have to do, kill the goddamn cow?" He slapped his hand over his phone and said to me, "You'll be talking to her. Tell me what you think and about the priest too."

"Which one?"

"Both of them." Back into his phone he barked, "No I don't want any goddamned mayonnaise! Who puts mayonnaise on a hamburger?"

The padre showed up at four o'clock with a cab to take us to the Keating apartment building. I couldn't get in the cab, so I gestured for him to go first. He hesitated, then I saw him decide to drop the chivalry and just get in. The woman who climbed in after him surprised him with one of her iridescent smiles and an extended hand. "Hi! I'm Hester!"

Every family needs a prom queen and Hester is ours.

Chapter 4

Ray Martinez owes me her career. I owe her my life. We both made a good bargain. She was an intern doing her time on the worst ward in a state asylum when she found me locked in a maximum security cell. I was fourteen. I was thirteen when they locked me up, but they didn't have anything secure enough in the children's ward, so I landed the corner suite in the women's wing, forgotten by just about everybody except the orderlies who brought me my food and meds and escorted me to the showers twice a week. Dr. Martinez asked that I be assigned to her. The head shrink was overworked and under-interested and waved her off with a *Fine, waste your time if you want to*. I was lucky that Ray wasn't a sadist, because she'd had free rein. She could have done almost anything.

The first thing she did was slowly dry out my drug-soaked brain. Then she introduced some life and color into my space. She brought me books, plants, paper and crayons (pens, pencils or anything pointy were against house rules), even a small battery-powered radio that got reception only intermittently, and a blue lava lamp, which fascinated me and which I still have.

Then she observed, listened and kept me company. Gradually, she figured out that I was not schizophrenic, brain-damaged, retarded or possessed by demons—all diagnoses that had been made by various people since my arrival. She first gained the trust of Hester and then Cootie. After several weeks she met Bethy and June and Sula and then everyone. She thought. Hawk was the last to show, and Ray said she was the only one who scared her. She still does. It was Hawk, she realized, who had landed us and kept us in lockup, drugged to our eyelashes. She also soon learned that Hawk did us a favor. I was safer in my cell than I would have been in the asylum's general population. As soon as Ray had a clearer picture of what she was dealing with, she explained it to us and asked if we would be her PROJECT. "This place wasn't my first choice. Yours either. If you will trust me and forgive me when I make mistakes...I promise I will not abandon you. We'll figure this thing out and then both of us can get out of this hellhole."

I didn't know at the time how hard it had been for Ray, a lesbian, Mexican-American med student, older than all her classmates, to find her way into psychiatry. She had to work her way through college and medical school, and the six more years to become a shrink. She was not physically imposing. On the short side, a little plump, but that look was deceiving. She was strong as granite. When we got to know each other, she told me she worked out and took martial arts classes. "So I can defend myself with you crazy people in here." She wasn't kidding and we took no offense. She didn't mean just the Company. The asylum was a dangerous place for the weak and unwary. Ray was neither. Her glossy black hair she kept short. She had large, warm brown eyes, still does, and a smile she still shows rarely, but that can light a room. I marveled at her stamina. I still do.

I agreed to be her study subject and she said she would get us out of the asylum as soon as she could and treat us free of charge for as long as we wanted. It took three years, but she was as good as her word. When she began to publish articles about her work with us, her reputation soared. She now has a lucrative private practice; she sits on the boards of numerous hospitals and clinics; she's written two books and is in demand world-wide for lectures and seminars as well as the occasional talk show. And she is still on call for us twenty-four/seven, though we don't need to call her much anymore.

Only recently did it dawn on me that she would have treated us for free anyhow, but by striking this deal, she made me feel like a partner instead of a charity case. Ray is a good human being. That was really the beginning of our therapy and being able to function: meeting one good human being.

I wondered how much Ray knew about this particular case. Since Cootie had read the police file, I presumed that now I knew more than she did—still precious little. The file was thick enough. Statements by a gaggle of people with varying degrees of involvement with the family. But something was missing, or wrong, and we'd have to sit for a while ruminating on Cootie's memory, and I'd have to ask the questions myself to gauge the answers before I could figure it out.

Back in my office, while I waited for O'Hagan, I chewed on the tough slice of pizza I'd picked up on the way back from the station and started a fresh notebook. Even when the case is only a surveillance to determine who is sleeping with whom, I keep a notebook. Usually, I am holding the pen, but if we switch and somebody else makes an entry, it doesn't matter because I know everyone's handwriting and we always note the time.

My first note was about O'Hagan. Before I even met the family, he was my first suspect. Why? Seen the news lately? I didn't trust this priest to tell me anything that would shed any light on the situation other than the halo-like glimmer around his own, expensively barbered head. His coming to me oozing concern, Irish charm and ready money only made me suspect him more. *We want you to find this monster,* he had said.

I will. Even if the monster is you.

I hadn't met the other priest yet: suspect number two. My third note: *Maybe they are covering for each other.*

But, as Leo had taken pains to point out, this case was complicated. When a child is missing and there is no ransom note, you can bet it's a sex crime and that the child will not survive. He or she will either die in the attack, or, if they are old enough to talk, be killed to be kept quiet. A missing infant is different. That could be anything from sex, to a woman with baby hunger, to, as Leo suspected, supplying the black market in babies.

Ray thought we could handle this case, but I knew I had to be careful. I felt Hawk lurking just behind my eyeballs, to the point where my head hurt. In the course of therapy, while the Company did not integrate, the filters between us began to disintegrate. We began more and more to be aware of, and even to "feel" each other's feelings. At least, the others do. I don't feel much, even though I now share many of their memories. I know about their feelings like you would know about them from seeing them on a movie or TV screen, or reading about them in a book. All except Hawk. She remains separate. I do not have her feelings or her memories. Really, I don't want them. Ray assures us that if we fused, all of these feelings would be mine and none of us would be dying any more than the Missouri and the Ohio rivers die when they flow into the Mississippi. This is her metaphor. So far no one is buying it. Anyway, if a situation calls for feelings to be expressed, one of the others takes over. Hester is the best one for that, really. She is just chuck full of warm fuzzy feelings. Usually, when she's around I take a nap. She's too damn perky for me.

Ryan O'Hagan was now reminding himself to breathe, as Hester, her hand still in mid-air, said, "We haven't met."

He offered her a limp handshake.

"Nice shoes." She pointed at his feet. "Armani?"

"Eh...yes."

"Lovely." She sighed with appreciation and longing, looking down at our unadorned black blazer, navy blue turtleneck and black slacks. "These clothes! They are *hideous*, but it's what we have to wear unless one of us gets the night out alone. Dressing like this—it's in our contracts, you see, because Lance and Cootie hate coming out in drag. And Isadora has absolutely no taste whatsoever so she doesn't care *what* we wear. But Olive and I, we *suffer*. I have some lovely dresses. And a Louis Vuitton handbag that is to *expire* for. So where are we going?" She beamed and beamed and didn't seem to notice that O'Hagan twice had to remind himself to inhale.

"Uh...it's right up there. That building on the corner."

"Oh, yes. I'm glad it's not a new high-rise. In my humble opinion, the high-rises have grown up just like termite colonies on the Upper West Side since the Eighties, and they have just *ruined* the neighborhoods. Ray says, 'Hester, you don't even *remember* the neighborhood in the Eighties because you weren't *here* then.' And Sugartime says, 'Honey people need places to live same as you do.' But Olive agrees with me." The cab slowed down and Hester batted her lashes and juiced up the wattage of her smile. "It was so nice to meet you. I hope we meet again soon. I'm sure you're *wasted* in the priesthood."

O'Hagan cleared his throat as if he had a cat stuck back there, and when the cab came to a stop he bolted out of it. By the time he had paid the driver I was standing next to him. "I should have warned you about Hester. She's...friendlier than I am."

"Among other things," he said, actually looking relieved to see me.

The doorman gave O'Hagan a familiar nod. The priest introduced us. "This is Victor."

Victor Pasqual. Off duty the day Charlotte disappeared. On duty the day before, when Miriam returned— "Hysterical, with a police officer and another mother for moral support, I guess. They were all pretty upset and it's no wonder. Cute little girl, that Anna. Shy. But she always said, 'Hi, Victor.' A terrible thing. Real terrible."

"Victor, this is the detective I told you about. She's to have access at all times."

"Right, Father." To me he said, his eyes focusing on something just above my right shoulder, "Nice to meet ya." His dark green uniform coat was unbuttoned. The gold trim around the collar and sleeves gave it a military flair, as did the gold braid on his cap. He reached for the house phone just inside the door. "I'll let 'em know you're coming up."

The walls of the cavernous lobby alternated between yellow-beige paint in need of a brush-up and old crackled mirrors hazily reflecting the shabby elegance of worn red velvet chairs and loveseats. The ceiling was ornate with scrolled plaster, and the border of tiled floor around the almost threadbare oriental carpet boasted a high polish.

In contrast to the spaciousness of the lobby, the elevator was surprisingly cramped and dark. Cootie didn't need an invitation. As he stepped in, I told him to keep his mouth shut. He slumped against the wall with his hands in our jacket pockets and gave the priest a goofy grin. O'Hagan pressed the button several times with unmistakable urgency, and we rose to the tenth floor. I followed him down a carpeted hallway whose walls were dark with blue flocked paper.

O'Hagan tried the door of 10C. It was open. As we stepped into the foyer, we were greeted by several things at once: raucous barking, a rhythmic thumping that came from down the hall to our left, a frisson in the atmosphere that was a palpable mix of fear, grief and confusion, and a big, love-worn, purple dinosaur smiling at us from the corner. On the wall to the right of the door, a red pegboard was festooned with children's jackets, sweaters and hats and a couple leashes. Beneath our feet was a multicolored braided rug. A Jack Russell terrier was charging up the steps, and Hester was awestruck. *What a place! What do you call it? What do you call this place?*

A duplex, Hester. It's a duplex.

Right. A duplex. Oh, I wish we had a duplex.

Shut up.

The dog hurled himself at the priest, who laughed, picked him up, holding him at arm's length to escape a snaking tongue, and then set him back on the floor. "Bungee," he said. "He is psychically connected to the doorknob." The animal sniffed my trouser legs and gave me a look of warning, *I'm watching you.* I thought, *That's fair.* Satisfied, he trotted away, and we followed him down into the sunken living room, which, like the foyer, gave the general impression of being lived in and child-friendly. Bungee took a direct route to the sofa, leapt up and curled quietly beside a small woman. He lowered his head onto her lap, but his ears were pricked, and his bright eyes never left me. She rested her hand on his back. *Claudia.*

The woman who sat next to her had to be Miriam.

Don't hurt the doggy. Please don't hurt him.

Bethy-June's whimpering was soothed by Sugartime: *Shhh, the doggy is fine. No one is going to hurt the doggy.*

The thumping continued unabated above us, like a distant heartbeat.

Claudia was petite with wavy light brown hair that didn't quite touch her shoulders. Given the shine, I assumed the wave and the color were natural. I saw, behind small glasses, blue, intelligent eyes. Her thin lips and nose gave her an elfin quality. Next to her, Miriam seemed lumpish, her dark hair sagging in a slept-in ponytail. Her sallow skin was smudged with fatigue. From experience, I knew that a drug-induced sleep can be as bad as no sleep at all and only prolongs the inevitable. She would have to experience the full onslaught of her grief sometime. Later was not usually better than sooner. Perhaps they had kept her drugged hoping that Anna would be found. But everyone knew the odds. If a child wasn't found within twenty-four hours, the chances were slim she'd be found at all. It had been three days. The nanny was just waking up and finding herself in hell.

"Thank you for helping us," Claudia said in a thin, breathy voice. Except for some fine lines around her eyes that showed her to be in her thirties, she had a childlike air.

My alters clamored in sympathy. Sugartime did her job. *Quiet! They don't need sympathy, they need their children.*

If there are any children left to be found, said Olive.

Shut up, said Hester.

All of you shut up and let me work. "Let me work," I said out loud. The priest stopped breathing again, but recovered faster this time. He was learning that he'd have to get either a grip or an oxygen tank.

The man in the chair across from the two women rose. He had been leaning toward them with his elbows on his knees, engaged in an earnest conversation. *Michael Keating.* I knew that from the dog collar and black suit, though the rest of his appearance surprised me. He was not cut from the same pattern as O'Hagan. He took a step toward me with his hand extended. I couldn't take it and didn't want to switch right now. Glances passed between him and O'Hagan. He withdrew his hand subtly and quickly clasped it in front of him in a priestly, but not fussy, gesture. He appeared to be anything but fussy.

I wouldn't say Michael Keating had a sad face. Rather, his was the face of a man who had known sadness. In fact, he had probably hit rock bottom and crawled up out of the pits hand over hand. His skin was rough and ruddy, like he had spent more time in the outback than church. He was small and stocky with dark hair brushed back without a part from a rather low forehead which gave him kind of an Old World aspect, or that of an earlier era, say the thirties or forties. Nothing like the fashion forward appearance of the youthful, well-kept O'Hagan.

Michael Keating's priestly garb, unlike the dapper clerical threads of his superior, was definitely off the rack, yanked off in a hurry and a long time ago. "Thank you for coming." He did not lower his gaze or turn away when he met my eyes. This almost never happens, even among those who have been forewarned of my…what Ray refers to as…*lack of affect.* She means that my face, my eyes in particular, lack the sort of expression that most people take for granted when they look at a human face. That expression changes and varies from happy to sad, anguished to ecstatic, or even bored or spaced out. Almost every human face has some recognizable expression on it, even in sleep. She says, with no disrespect, that I have a somewhat reptilian gaze that is off-putting. That's because, like I said, I, Isadora, don't have the feelings that are the possession of the other people that share this body. I get only their echo. I've seen the grief and the tragedies that come to people because of feelings, their own and other people's. I am better off without them.

I heard voices from above and several people appeared on the landing. An older couple, a man around thirty and a boy who was munching a cookie. They all paused to stare down at me.

Apparently, the priest had done some good prep work with these people. They were curious and they studied me a bit, but no one ran screaming from the room. So far, so good.

I could sense a general nervousness wash over the pool of feelings that had already collected in this place. I make people nervous. And not just because of my face. I don't do the things that primates, and *Homo sapiens* in particular, do to put their fellows at ease. The smile, the handshake—Ray says that the point of these things is not to express how you feel, necessarily, but to signal *I'm not going to hurt you.* Small talk is to humans, she says, what grooming is for howler monkeys. She says if we were howler monkeys, I'd be scratched and bitten and driven from the troop. I guess it's a good thing we're not, then, because I can no more make small talk with a stranger than I could pick fleas out of his hair.

Chapter 5

Manfred Burke had staged his entrance, of that I was sure. Descending the stairs, he said expansively, "We welcome you— to lead us out of our despair."

He spoke with moderately accented English. More pronounced than his accent was the note of mockery that permeated his tone. Perhaps it was habit and by now unconscious. *Born in Russia. Family moved to Paris when he was three or four. They came to America when he was about twelve, changing their name from Berkowitz to Burke. They did not enter the country as poor immigrants but with jewels sewn into their clothing and money tucked up in a Swiss bank. Manfred attained early acclaim as a designer and, with the business acumen of his younger brother Spencer, grew Manfred Designs into an enterprise that drew royalties from manufacturers of everything from dry goods to furniture, housewares to the high-end ice buckets and trays bearing the gold Manfred signature found in luxury hotels the world over. Manfred Burke was King of the Coordinates. He was Martha Stewart before she was a gleam in her daddy's eye and without the public persona. His was not a household name, but any buyer in the gift and housewares industries knew a Manfred design, whether his signature was on it or not.*

Hester piped, *He's got money he doesn't even know he has. House on Montauk, apartment in Gramercy Park, not to mention that villa in Umbria.*

I know, Hester, be quiet.

At the time of Anna's disappearance, he had been in his office, approving designs for his new spring line and browbeating his staff. I was surprised Leo even counted that as an alibi. This wasn't the sort of man to get his hands dirty. He gave orders.

He apparently hadn't noticed or had just ignored my momentary loss of focus on him. "...lead us out of our despair. Can you do that? My niece—you see she is suffering." No sympathy for the nanny. No feeling wasted on the peasantry. A sea change swept through the room when he entered. I sensed immediately that things would be different if he were not here. He was used to controlling and dominating any situation. He wouldn't have intimidated Leo, and he didn't intimidate me, but I was quite sure he did intimidate the other people here that I wanted to talk to. Then I wondered why he, the uncle, was here, and Spencer Burke, Claudia's father, was not.

The housekeeper, for that is whom I assumed the thirty-something man to be, said, "I'll make some more coffee," and disappeared into the kitchen.

Manfred Burke was poised on the middle step. He had big teeth and watery blue eyes that were magnified behind his brown-rimmed glasses. His overtanned and spotted skin was stretched over his face and bald skull. A pinkish gray fringe of hair brushed his collar. Cuffed and creased slacks perfectly matched his beige silk shirt and picked up the lighter threads in his tweed jacket. His wattled neck emerged from the folds of a russet paisley silk scarf.

"My beloved, my beauty." He addressed the little woman who stood to the side and just behind him. "This is Ms. Shiloh. Father O'Hagan was kind enough to bring her. She is helping the police."

His beloved stepped forward like a little hen who'd just found herself in the wrong coop, and the two of them, hand in hand, continued their descent into the living room.

Bungee raised his head and yipped twice to announce their approach. The boy slipped by the older couple and past me and went to sling his leg over the arm of the sofa next to his mother. He finished his cookie and Bungee readjusted himself to lick the crumbs off the boy's pant leg. Seeing there would be no more, the Jack Russell turned around again to lay his head on Claudia's lap, alert to the movements of everyone in the room.

"Danny?" I took a guess that this was the oldest son, the ten-year-old.

"Yes."

"I'd like you to show me the apartment."

He appeared reluctant but not nervous, and he didn't check with his mother. "Sure," he said, dismounting the sofa arm. Claudia patted his back, a gesture of *Go ahead* and *you're a good boy*. A loving gesture. The boy hardly noticed. He was used to being touched so by his mother.

"But we are all here." Burke made a dramatic gesture that encompassed everyone. "We were told you needed to speak to the family. You see, we have gathered."

"Mrs. Keating's father is missing," I said.

"He called," said Michael Keating. "He got caught in cross-town traffic. He is on his way."

"I will speak to you," I said to Manfred Burke. "But first I'd like Danny to show me the apartment. Wait here. Please." I looked down on the boy who was standing in front of me.

"Well, uh, this is the living room. What do you want to see next?"

"How about the other rooms on this floor."

He led me through a narrow archway off the living room into a dark hall, not bothering to switch on a light. The first room was a laundry room that housed a washer, dryer and a tall, narrow, metal cabinet. I opened it to find detergents and bleach, rinses, stain-removers and fabric softener sheets. An ironing board and iron were set up in the corner. On a table was a small television and a stack of folded clothes. On the floor was a plastic basket full of dirty clothes. The next room was just a tiny storage room piled high with old clothes, toys and winter gear. Everything was in boxes and bags and plastic modular bins, like you can buy in city closet stores. The last room was larger than the first two.

"This is Vin's room," said Danny. *Vin Parrish. The housekeeper.*

This is a man who knows how to Feng Shui! exclaimed Hester.

The room had dove-gray walls and a darker shade of plush wall-to-wall carpet, vertical silver-gray blinds over a window that seemed to open out to just a shaftway; a futon with a brilliant red cover; a comfortable looking, ergonomically correct, black leather chair under a halogen floor lamp; a sleek black metal desk with a small notebook computer on it. Books, CDs, a CD player and some black-framed photographs were neatly arranged on the metallic gray, matte finish shelves on the wall above the desk. Decent-sized speakers were attached to the walls on either side. A full-length mirror was affixed to the outside of his closet door adding the illusion of space and reflecting what little light there was coming through the window. A poster on the wall from a production of *Kiss Me Kate* added a kaleidoscope of colors and attested to the fact that in Shakopee, Minnesota, Vin Parrish had strutted his stuff as Petruchio. On the opposite wall next to a black speaker box was a wall hanging of the theatre masks, one smiling, one crying, done in pink and turquoise sequins. The masks gazed at themselves in the mirror. Looking back and forth between them I got dizzy and sat in the desk chair. The room was perfectly tidy and spotless, contemporary and comfortable, stamped with a completely different personality than the rest of the apartment I'd seen so far. I got up again and checked the bathroom—tiny, with sink and a shower stall, but no tub. The tiles were black and white and the towels and the rug on the floor were red.

"That's all that's down here."

"Okay, let's go upstairs." The thumping sound was louder in Vin's room than it had been in the living room.

He led me past a confused Beauty and an annoyed Manfred, back up the stairs, through the foyer and down the hallway. Family pictures, including several of Bungee, were hung asymmetrically all along the pale green walls. The thumping got louder. "What *is* that?"

"It's just Joey. He does that all the time...now." I wondered if *now* meant since his father's death or since his sister's disappearance.

The first room was light pink with a white daybed and a trundle. I assumed this was for Miriam and her daughter, and Danny confirmed this was so. Though very small, it was nicely furnished and cozy. I opened the closet. A few clothes hung there, mother's and daughter's. A suitcase was in the back. I opened it and found it empty. A couple pairs of child's shoes were lined up neatly on the floor beside an inexpensive pair of women's low-heeled black pumps. As I closed the closet door, I noticed three curly-headed dolls propped up on the upholstered window seat, which looked out to a view of Riverside Park and the Hudson River. Two of the dolls looked new and pricier than the clothes and shoes in the closet.

The next room was a bathroom. Blue walls, unmatched colored towels, a white shower curtain with cartoon characters scattered over it. "This is our bathroom—Joey and me. Miriam and Anna use it, too."

In the next room we found Joey, the eight-year-old, sitting on the edge of the lower bunk bed, bouncing a soccer ball with both hands. The bunk beds were against the wall to the right. Straight ahead were two desks, each bearing a modest computer. A host of things were assembled rather haphazardly on shelves, and attached to the walls were posters, photos and memorabilia from sporting events that they had either attended or participated in. I supposed that it was the younger boy who was in his dinosaur phase. The largest poster was of Tyrannosaurus rex, and various other extinct reptiles randomly grazed or hunted around the room. A few of the flying variety were suspended from the ceiling. There were also miniature cars, motorcycles and, in the corner, what looked like an instrument case. Perhaps the size for a clarinet. A fair number of books seemed to litter the place. Some were even on the shelves, including a hard-cover set of Harry Potters. The room was messy but not filthy. Claudia was not a control freak. When I opened the closet door, I felt Sugartime smile. On the floor was a pile of stuff that included papers and dirty clothes crammed in, no doubt at the last minute, because they were told somebody was coming over and would probably look in their room.

I sat down on the bunk bed next to Joey. "Hi. I'm Shiloh."

The boy acknowledged my presence with a nod but did not break his Zen-like concentration to keep the ball bouncing.

"Do you like Harry Potter?"

"He's not real." Bounce. Bounce. Bounce. "You can't like someone who's not real."

I rephrased. "Do you like reading the Harry Potter books?"

"I like the movies better."

"Are you a good soccer player?"

"Not yet."

Joey was a mini version of Danny. Both boys seemed small for their ages, both had sandy hair, dark blue eyes and freckles across their noses.

"Granduncle tells him to stop doing that." Danny nodded toward the bouncing ball and flopped into one of the desk chairs.

"Does your mother tell you to stop?" I asked Joey.

"No. She says it's okay. As long as I don't do it after six. She says the downstairs neighbors might get bothered, but I don't think they can hear it. Danny was downstairs once in Christopher's apartment and I bounced as hard as I could up here in my room and he said they didn't hear anything, so I think it's okay."

"I think it would be very satisfying to bounce a ball for as long as I wanted to," I said.

"Yeah."

"He drives everybody nuts." Danny picked up a puzzle cube and began to fiddle with it.

"Can I have a try at it?" I asked Joey.

"Sure." Somewhat reluctantly, Joey handed me the ball.

I bounced the ball a few times. "Tell me about your granduncle."

"Well, he's just granduncle. And there's Phoebe."

"You don't think of her as grandaunt?"

He shrugged.

Danny offered, "She doesn't like to be called anything but

Phoebe. Except for the things granduncle calls her."

"What does your mother call her?"

"Phoebe."

"Do you like your granduncle?"

"He's okay. He bought me my computer. And Danny's. Danny got one first, because he's older but mine is better because it's newer."

I looked at Danny, and he just rolled his eyes.

"What about your grandfather?" I stopped bouncing the ball but held on to it.

Danny answered, "He's okay. He paid for our camp. And he's paying for riding lessons for Joey."

"How about you. Don't you like horses?"

"They're okay. I'd rather ride a bike. When I'm old enough he said he'd get me one."

"Aren't you old enough for a bicycle?"

"Not a bicycle. A motorcycle. A red one. Like this." He held up a model of a red motorcycle.

"You like your uncle?"

Both boys smiled. Danny said, "Uncle Mike? He's cool."

"Does he buy you stuff?"

"No. He doesn't have any money."

"He bought us hot dogs at the game," Joey corrected his brother.

"Oh yeah. Mom doesn't let us eat hot dogs. She says it's junk food. Uncle Mike said we shouldn't tell her. You won't tell her, will you?"

"No."

Joey asked me, "What's wrong with your eyes?"

"My eyes are fine."

Danny reprimanded him, "Shut up! Father Ryan told us not to."

"Well, he didn't say she would look so weird."

"I do have a weird look. I can't help it." I bounced the ball again. "It's just how I look."

"Oh. That's cool." Joey was still eyeing me with great interest. "Can you do somebody else? Father Ryan said you sometimes turn into somebody else. Let's see you do it."

"I'm not a party game, boys. If it happens you'll know it. Can I talk to you again if I need to?"

"Sure. Will you turn into somebody else then?"

"Maybe."

"Cool."

"Wow."

"I'm very sorry about your father."

Joey lowered his gaze and reached for the soccer ball.

"Do you like Miriam?" I bounced the ball to him and he caught it.

"She's okay. Well, she used to be. Now all she does is cry."

"She was teaching us some Russian," Danny said.

Joey stopped bouncing and announced, "I can say, *Dos vee don ya.* You know what that is? That's goodbye. And I can say, My name is Joey. *Min ya zah voot Joey.*"

"Yeah, like you'll ever go to Russia." Danny went back to fiddling with his puzzle cube.

"I might. Granduncle said he'd take me."

"Granduncle escaped from there, he's not going to go back, moron."

"Well, perhaps if he has a reason to go back, after all these years, to show off his grandnephews, he might go," I said. I didn't want to start a sibling squabble.

"Yeah, right." Danny rolled his eyes again.

I got up and Danny put down his puzzle cube and led me to the next room. The nursery door was wide open, revealing a crib, monitor, stuffed toys, a bassinette, a rocking chair. Everything a baby or a new mother could possibly want. I stepped into this catalog shot for Bellini Baby. The room had pale yellow walls and white curtains sprinkled with tiny rainbows in primary colors. A chenille rug in multicolored checks warmed the highly polished wood floor. A mobile of jungle animals floated over the crib.

My eyes were beginning to hurt. On one wall was a huge laminated poster of the alphabet illustrated with the appropriate birds and beasts. Bethy-June was crying again. Lance crooned, *Kookaburra sits in the old gum tree-ee, merry merry king of the bush is he-ee.*

A lifelike baby doll and an oversized Raggedy Ann rested forlornly in the rocking chair. Barbie in many of her incarnations populated a high shelf, out of reach until Charlotte would be old enough to prefer them to the stuffed bears and pink fluffy pigs and green plush frogs that were scattered about and piled in the corner of the crib. Everywhere was color and whimsy and comfort. A loved child. A wanted child. Sula whimpered in raw longing. *Laugh kook-a-berry, laugh kook-a-berry.* I felt my people teetering at the edge of a yawning mouth of misery from which they were never far removed. *Gay your life must be.* If this is the feeling that Ray wants me to experience—no, thank you very much.

We had to get out of this room before they started howling. Danny ran after me. There was only one room left at the end of the hall. The master bedroom.

Its walls were pale blue-green with sheer panels of beige and brown over the windows. Next to the king-size bed was a nightstand with a lamp, an alarm clock and the baby monitor. The dresser was covered in family photographs. A La-Z-Boy chair, television, a small writing desk and another bedside table completed the furnishings. Walk-in closets. Spacious master bath and gleaming white tiles, white towels and rugs. Wooden shelves laden with plants were in place in front of the opaque glass windows.

I stepped back into the bedroom considering what I had seen so far: the doors, closets, windows—all possible entrances, exits or hiding places. All the windows had child guards. The place was safe, large and homey. I could see a very happy family here before the death of Mr. Keating. I saw a widow picking up the pieces with her sons and her new daughter, and then, this terrible thing happened. If we didn't get the children back, I couldn't envision happiness ever dwelling in this place again. I wanted very much that it should.

I heard Bungee go off almost simultaneously with the doorbell. I stepped into the hall and watched the housekeeper scoop up the dog and open the door to a man who resembled Manfred Burke but who was younger and slighter in build. His dark blue suit, white shirt and blue bow tie were crisp, perfectly tailored, conservative. He had more hair than his older brother and it was allowed to be its own steel-gray color. He carried a briefcase and smiled a toothy smile. As I approached, he hesitated only a second before offering me his hand in a businesslike way. The housekeeper distracted Spencer with an agile "How about a glass of iced tea, Mr. Burke? Or, I just made fresh coffee if you'd ruther." His southern accent poured over Burke like warm syrup. "Ms. Shiloh has asked everyone to congregate in the living room."

Vin didn't actually touch Spencer Burke, but he seemed to turn him around and herd him to the steps, reminding me of a collie I'd seen once on TV dancing a ram into a corral. With Spencer Burke headed downstairs, Vin put Bungee down, arched an eyebrow at me, and then queried the congregants below, "Who wants tea?" He took a mental count of nods, spun on the balls of his feet, and sallied back to the kitchen.

Bungee was in Claudia's lap before I reached the bottom step. Spencer Burke was apologizing. "I'm sorry I'm late. The meeting ran over." Michael Keating rose to offer him his chair close to Claudia. He declined with a wave of his hand and Michael resumed his seat. "And then there was a holdup on Eighty-sixth Street right in the park so we couldn't go back, we couldn't go forward. We couldn't go around."

He had no accent. Spencer had been born after the family arrived in the United States. He did not wear glasses and his faded blue eyes were more searching, less confrontational than Manfred's. He looked at me with curiosity and, I thought, a little hope.

"Spencer, sit down." Manfred motioned his brother to a chair although he himself was standing, and it occurred to me that he had been pacing back and forth since he came downstairs. He threw a loose gesture in my direction. "She took a tour of the premises. Now that she has intruded herself into every corner of my niece's home, perhaps we can get to business."

We heard a muffled ringing and Spencer took a small cell phone out of his suit pocket, looked at it, pressed a button, and put the phone back in his pocket. Manfred continued to twitch.

Spencer's eyes rested on his daughter for a moment, then he

said, "Manfred, why don't *you* sit down. Pour yourself a drink."

"I don't want a drink. Do you want a drink?" he challenged his brother.

"No."

"Why do you think I want one then? You will give her," he pointed at me, "the impression we are alcoholics—we sit around drinking at four thirty in the afternoon."

Spencer found a chair. Manfred seemed about to throw a tantrum when Vin cakewalked down the stairs balancing a tray heavy with frosty glasses of iced tea and made the rounds offering everyone a glass. Even Manfred took one, though he did not sit down with it.

Vin left the tray with its sugar bowl, spoons and plate of lemon slices on the coffee table. "Help yourselves," he said. He paused to say a few more words that were audible only to Claudia. She nodded and he murmured something to Miriam who gave him the same glazed expression she had shown me. He patted her knee and went back up the stairs to his kitchen.

Phoebe left her overstuffed chair to spoon sugar into her glass with plump little hands. She seemed shaped and confined only by the panty hose and shoes, the bra, and waist and neck bands, the wrist bands at the end of her blousy sleeves, the bracelets. Without them she'd have been just a dollop of yesterday's vanilla pudding. Her white skin untouched by sun or weather, hair the color of a baby chick, blue eye shadow—bluer than her faded, slightly protruding eyes—red pouty lips, matching red nails with old-fashioned round, almost pointed tips reminded me of a kewpie doll, old, carefully-kept, grotesque, since the paint on her lips seeped into the creases around her mouth, and mascara was smeared around her eyes. All she needed to complete the picture were a few dusty feathers stuck in her hair.

Claudia wore no makeup at all. Not even in the wedding picture that I'd seen on her dresser in which she and her husband looked like two happy children, playing at getting married.

Manfred Burke came to Phoebe's side and took some sugar. His liver spots were even more pronounced next to her white skin. They seemed—not an unlikely couple, but an unnatural one. He, some desert dweller, sun-dried and parched, and she an

inhabitant of a damp, sunless cave. She clearly did not join him
in his outdoor activities. Both the pink tint in his hair and the
yellow in hers looked like the results of color jobs from bottles
purchased by the case from their local discount drugstore.

*I'll bet he gets his rings and watches wholesale. People like him
always do.*

Hester, how would you know anything about people like that?

*People who have money buy wholesale. That's how they keep their
money. Everybody knows that. Look at his eyebrows. I'll bet he colors
them with the same stuff he uses on his hair. They need waxing.*

"My petal, would you like anything else?"

The ends of her cupid's bow lips rose almost imperceptibly
as she shook her yellow curls.

*They are an absolutely horrible couple. Dracula marries Baby
Jane!*

Hester giggled in spite of the fact that she hated giving
Olive credit for anything, even a good line. She said, *But there
are a lot of horrible people in the world who do not kidnap and murder
children.*

And a lot who do.

"I'm going to speak with your housekeeper," I told Claudia.
She nodded. "Then I'll speak to each of you."

As I mounted the stairs to the landing I heard Manfred say
in a lower voice, but one still audible, "Aghh! She is a freak!"

O'Hagan tried to soothe him. "Mr. Burke, she is highly
recommended by a good friend of mine."

"Who? Who is this good friend of yours who recommends
a freak?"

"Uncle, *I* hired her. Please."

"Freddy."

This was a new voice. I turned around.

"Yes, my darling?"

"Sit down, dear." Phoebe had taken a place on another small
sofa at an angle to the larger one inhabited by Claudia, Miriam
and Bungee. Manfred took his sweet drink and sat beside her,
muttering to the room at large, "What is this? A cruel joke? I
thought she wanted to talk to us?"

"I do. And I will," I said from the top of the stairs. "Wait your turn."

Smiles ghosted across the faces of the two priests. Spencer grinned outright. Claudia turned her head and looked at me squarely for the first time. She seemed oddly composed.

The short passageway leading from the foyer to the kitchen was lined with built-in closets. Opening doors, I found rows of canned goods, boxes of cereal, spices, packaged foods of every kind, enough to last this family through a siege of several months, plus cans of an expensive brand of dog food that would keep Bungee well fed for months as well; cleaning supplies, including mops and brooms, dusters and a top-of-the-line vacuum cleaner. I pushed on the shelves. They were solid and did not move.

The eat-in kitchen was modern: the white-tile-and-stainless-steel look softened by a vase of pink carnations on the table, white café curtains and a multitude of children's drawings stuck to almost every vertical surface. A grinning orange and yellow papier-mâché creature squatted on top of the refrigerator.

On the shining floor was an assortment of blue scatter rugs and a red, white and blue plastic placemat set with food and water bowls emblazoned with the name: BUNGEE. The kitchen was longer than it was wide, and at the far end, taking up almost the whole wall, was a free-standing mahogany china hutch filled with blue-and-white porcelain.

Oooooooooooooo! Look at that! It's Delft! It's blue Delft!

Yes, I know Delft when I see it, Hester. We're not here to admire the china.

Do you know how much that stuff costs? That platter, on the top there. That is over a thousand dollars.

Yes, seems extravagant just for a chicken carcass.

You are so crass. No sense of style. Food should be served beautifully. Not eaten out of cartons like we....

Vin Parrish was sitting at the small table by the window, sipping tea. He greeted me with a nod and returned to watching something across the street.

I pulled out a chair and sat across from him, issuing a silent warning to Hester and Olive to knock it off about the Delft.

"See that overhang?" He pointed to the building across the courtyard. "I think there's a pigeon nest up under there somewhere. We're hoping to see a chick take its first flight. The boys and I have spent hours here this spring watching. I don't know if we're too early or too late. Not too late, I don't think. But, I don't know nuthin' 'bout pigeons." He was trim, well-muscled but not bulked up. He had on black slacks and a form-fitting black T-shirt under a red square-hemmed shirt that he wore loose and unbuttoned. His head was shaved and a silver stud gleamed in his left earlobe.

"You get on well with Danny and Joey?"

"They're the lights of my life." He took a good sip of his iced tea, tucked in his lips and licked them, looking down at his glass. He noticed a smudge on the table and buffed it with his sleeve.

"How long have you worked for the Keatings?"

"Eight years."

"How did you meet Mrs. Keating?"

"I've known Claudy my whole adult life, if you assume I became an adult when I was eighteen. We were both at NYU. Saw her at a coffee shop on Fourth Street staring at a copy of *Twelfth Night* lookin' like a fawn in the headlights. So I sat down and said I could prob'ly 'splain it to her as I had just played Malvolio to stirring reviews in the Jackson, Mississippi Players-in-the-Round production the summer before. In spite of my keen insights into the comedies of Shakespeare, neither of us finished college, but we stayed friends. When Joey was born I was especially down on my luck—one of New York's b'zillion out-of-work triple-threats."

"What is that?"

"Triple-threat? Showbiz speak. Actor/singer/dancer."

I knew that. Hester knows everything, or at least, she thinks she does.

"She offered me a job. Said I could still go to auditions and she'd have a clean house without having to supervise anybody. Claudy was born to money, but she doesn't have any rich-bitch ways. Her cleaning ladies always ran roughshod over her. So, I took the job and she pays me a lot more than I'm worth. She says it's daddy's money so I might as well have it." He took a pull on his glass of tea. "Well, I don't go to auditions anymore, but Claudy has the cleanest apartment in Gotham." I had already noted the shiny kitchen and the perfectly organized pantry shelves. I suspected he earned his wage. "I also do some laundry and ironing. Honey, you could slice a turkey with the creases in those kids' pants! I even do the floors and windows...except for those two-story monsters in the living room. I get the vapors on a ladder. But I do just about everything else. Make up the beds and clean the bathrooms and cook. I'm a mean cook. And I can bake your buns off."

He turned his head toward the window again and wiped his eyes with a soggy tissue. He had recited his domestic talents with great sadness, as if none of his abilities had helped Claudia save her husband or child. He had put on a cheerful enough show in front of the family, but what I was seeing now was no show. He was the only one in the house so far who was acting normally under the circumstances.

Joey came tearing in, his soccer ball under his arm. "Danny got a cookie and I didn't!"

"You weren't here when they were being passed out, buddy. There's plenty left. In the bear." The boy went toward the counter and Vin pointed at him. "Hands! Hands! Give me the ball."

Joey surrendered his soccer ball and dragged a stepstool over to the sink where he climbed up, washed his hands, not very thoroughly. After a cursory blotting with a towel, he pushed the stool over a couple of feet in front of a fat bear-shaped cookie jar. He clambered up again and dipped his hand in, drawing out a good-sized cookie. He took a bite and was about to dip in again. Vin commanded, "*One* cookie, Miss Thing! I ain't been slavin' over a hot stove all day for you to have no appetite for suppah."

"Okay." Joey looked around the kitchen and gave a little sniff. "What are you cooking?"

"Nuthin'. Yet."

Joey smiled and ran out with his cookie.

His face deadpan, Vin extended his arm with the soccer ball poised on his fingertips and waited. In a moment, the boy ran back in, snatched it and streaked out again.

"Do the uncle and the father mind that you are a

homosexual?"

"I swannee! You get to the point, don't 'cha? No, not so I've noticed. In the design business, folks like me are coming out of the woodwork, so to speak."

"What does Vin stand for?"

"Alvin. I was named after my mother whose name is Alvinia. I go by Alvin back home but *nowhere else*."

"Did Anna spend any time with you and the boys?"

"A little. She is..." His eyes filled with tears again and he stopped talking and rattled the ice in his tea. He collected himself quickly. "She's only three, and they're older so it's not like they played much together."

"Do the boys seem to like her?"

"Joey is kind of indifferent, but I think Danny does. Danny has a strong sense of responsibility for his age. I think he took her on as a little sister. He's nicer to her than he is to his brother."

"Is Claudia affectionate with Anna?"

"Absolutely. She is an affectionate mother and she treated Anna like one of her own."

"How did the boys react to the baby?"

"I would say with curiosity." He looked at me shrewdly. "Are you wondering if the boys could have done something to the girls out of jealousy or something like that?"

"Could they?"

"Not in this universe."

"Why are you so sure?"

"Because I've known them since the day they were born into this vale of tears, and neither one of them has a mean bone. They can be wise asses, but I've never seen them do anything mean."

"Children can be savages." I ought to know.

"Some kids can. Little boys can be capable of all kinds of mayhem. But not these boys. You met them. What did you think?"

"I agree with you."

"You're makin' them stew down there, ain't cha?" He nodded backward, toward the living room, where I could hear some voices raised in agitation. Manfred's, and then Ryan O'Hagan's trying to soothe.

I didn't answer Vin Parrish.

He emitted a high-pitched, ticklish chuckle. "Do you want some tea? I'm going to have some more. There's plenty. That's about all I can do—keep the beverages flowing."

"Thank you."

He got up, happy for something to do.

"Tell me about Manfred Burke."

He brought out a large pitcher from the refrigerator and took out another glass and the ice tray from the freezer. "Oh, he's an old drama queen." He poured the clear amber liquid into our glasses and brought them to the table.

"Do you mean he's—"

"No, he's not queer that I know of, but who knows anymore? I don't." He returned the pitcher and the tray to the refrigerator and then wiped up a wet spot off the counter. "I like him. He's full of hot air mostly, artistic temperament, but I'm used to artistic temperament. Hell, honey, I've *got* artistic temperament. He and Spencer bought this place for Claudy and Dan when they got married. And he's been good to her since Dan died." He returned to his chair.

"Does she have her own money or does it all come from them?"

"She had a good chunk of her own from a trust fund that came to her when she was twenty-one. But that went to pay for Dan's education. College and law school took it all. Her dad pays for most of the big stuff like private school for the boys and now all the household expenses, which includes me and Miriam. Manfred buys the kids a lot. Tricycles and then bicycles. All their sporting gear. The most expensive sneakers and stuff like that."

"Of the two Burkes, who has the most money?"

"Well, now *that* I don't really know. Spencer's quieter. Not such a loud mouth. So he might have more money than anybody knows about. He's the bean counter. Manfred is the artsy fart. And he seems to spend more money on showy things. He takes vacations in exotic places and buys art to fill up his houses. Come to think of it...I would say Manfred, because there's a whole big pile of money that Claudia mentioned to me once, that to get it, they both have to sign something. So, they both have that whenever they need something big, but as far as personal money…Manfred probably has more. You'd have to ask them."

"Who bought all that?" I turned in my chair and nodded to the china hutch.

"Spencer. Claudia's been collecting it since she was little. He brings her a piece every once in awhile when he travels. She never uses it though."

I tasted the tea. It was delicious with a hint of fresh mint. "How well do you know the doorman—Victor?"

He shrugged. "On speaking terms."

"How about the other doormen and the super?"

"The same."

"Where do you live?"

"I inhabit an overpriced, squalid fourth floor walk-up *dump* in the Village. I'm staying here now. After Dan got sick, Claudy asked if I could bunk in and of course, I can. Where's the hardship? I mean *look* at this place! I'm in the guest room, down there."

"I saw it."

He made a quick mental adjustment as he realized that I had examined his room like everyone else's. "Well, it's been my room for a while. Claudy has asked me to stay before. Right after each of the boys were born, I stayed for a few weeks and once when she had the flu. So I sort of did the room. It used to be the maid's room. Guess it still is." He didn't smile.

"So what happened here? Do you have any ideas?"

He shook his head and lifted his glass to his lips again.

"Do you think the same person took Anna and Charlotte?"

"Well, it would have to be. It's really too much of a coincidence, isn't it? Maybe they took Anna by mistake. Maybe they thought they were getting a Keating kid and then realized it was a mistake and came back for the baby." He shrugged helplessly. "I'm just a dumb boy from Jackson. I can't figure it out."

I didn't think Vin Parrish was dumb at all. "I might like to speak with you again. Somewhere else. Outside the apartment."

"Sure. Call my cell." He reached into his pocket and pulled

out a black card with red raised lettering: VIN PARRISH and a phone number. "I used to entertain at parties and stuff. I still have these. Trying to use 'em up. Can't bring m'self to throw them away."

I put the card in my pocket. "Is there another room where I can talk to people alone?"

He jumped up. All of his movements seemed spring-loaded. "The den. Used to be Dan's home-office, but now it's the family room. TV and such-like."

I trailed him back to the landing. Instead of going down the stairs we turned right into a dark room. He switched on the light. "This do?"

A sofa and a wingback chair shared space with some oversized beanbag chairs and a game table. A large television set was ensconced in a shelf system that took up an entire wall and also housed, none too tidily, games, books, DVDs, CDs and videos. On a low table in one corner was a jumble of Legos. Pale sage carpet looked spanking new. The even paler sea-green paint looked fresh, the shelves and drapes new. Everything had been done to make over this room. The colors were subtle and exquisite, with upholstery in the right accents of darker blue and brown and green patterns and stripes. On the walls were fantastical pictures in vibrant colors to appeal to children's whimsy. I saw Manfred Burke's hand here, a light, sure hand that created a welcoming family space. I realized that he had probably made a lot of money because he was a good designer.

"This is fine," I said.

"It's not *too* comfortable is it? I know you want to keep people on *edge*." He sliced the air with the side of his hand in a quick, precise horizontal motion.

"I keep them on edge enough. I don't need help from the furniture."

He laughed his high-pitched cackle. "I'll leave you to it then, Cruella."

Ryan O'Hagan was the only one who welcomed my return. Living room conversation had ceased as soon as Vin and I appeared on the landing. I wanted to speak to Miriam, but it was obvious she was not going to be lucid any time today.

Mrs. Keating asked to take her back upstairs, and I turned my attention to Spencer Burke. He watched his daughter lead the nanny up to her room.

When his eyes met mine, I said, "Come with me. Please." He scrambled to get out of the overstuffed chair he had sunk into. "I'll do anything to help. I told the police, I'd do anything."

Anything but leave a meeting early enough to be here on time, Olive commented dryly. Less energy was required to ignore Olive and Hester than to force them back to the gyre. And Sugartime didn't interfere unless the little ones were involved or things got hopelessly weird. We weren't there yet. But the gals were seriously trying my patience.

Manfred Burke sighed loudly and sucked at his teeth. "If you wanted to speak to us all separately, why did we have to gather here? Are you enjoying torturing us?"

"*This* is not torture, Mr. Burke. This is simply waiting."

I allowed Spencer Burke to step into the den first. He picked the wingback, sliding the footstool to the side and sitting forward. I pulled out a straight-back chair from the game table and faced him from a few feet away.

"My brother overreacts. He'll forget all about this in a few hours. He doesn't hold on to things."

Like we care.

"I'll do anything to help. You can ask me anything."

As if we wouldn't, Olive snorted.

"Do you know what happened to Anna?"

"Of course not!"

"Charlotte?"

"No...I..." He shook his head in perplexity. "I don't understand it. I can't imagine what happened to Charlotte."

"I want you to look at some names." I leaned forward and handed him the list that Ryan O'Hagan had given me. "Is there anybody who is not on this list that should be? People that know your daughter, even indirectly—through you or your brother—an enemy either of you has made over the years? Someone who would want to hurt you through your family?"

He shook his head as his eyes went down the list. "I told the police...we make designs for towels and ice buckets. Not the sort of business where one makes enemies. It's just fluff."

"Expensive fluff."

He handed the paper back to me. "We have made a good living, but compared to an oil company or a retail chain, it doesn't amount to much. Certainly nothing to warrant a kidnapping. We had money from our father and uncles who were merchants in Russia. We've invested well. But we're not Rockefellers or involved in shady deals. We're audited regularly. You can check with—"

"The police already have. I just wondered if they missed anything." We stared at each other in silence for six thumps of Joey's soccer ball. "Call me if you think of anything you haven't told them. If there is something you don't want the police to know, something that will help me find the children, the police won't hear about it from me. I don't care about your business dealings, good or bad. My loyalty is to my client. Your daughter. I care about finding the children."

His face took on an even more confused and wondering aspect before it flushed red and the veins in his forehead bulged. "Do you think I would put any business interest ahead of finding my granddaughter?"

"I don't know you, Mr. Burke. I don't know what you would do."

He deflated as quickly as he had puffed up. "Of course, there is nothing. Nothing I can think of. Do you think we'll find her?"

"Chances are not good." He put his head in his hands. "Not for her or for Anna." The Burkes kept forgetting about Anna. "Are you married?"

He dropped his hands but kept his head down, looking at the floor. "You must know that I'm not."

"I ask you the questions because the answers lie in the person who answers, not in the facts. If the facts were all I needed, I would rely only on the police file."

He stared at his hands for a long moment.

I repeated the question. "Are you married?"

"I am a widower."

"How did your wife die?"

"She committed suicide."

This was news. The police file said his wife had passed away. Heart failure.

"When."

"Nineteen eighty." That matched the file.

"How?"

"She took pills."

"Do you know why?"

"She was depressed. The pharmaceuticals weren't as sophisticated then as they are now."

"How did that affect Claudia?"

He raised his head. "What in the name of God does this have to do with my granddaughter?"

"I don't know."

"Well, it didn't make her a happy sunny child as you can imagine. We had some difficult times. We got through it. She doesn't need this now on top of that, does she?" He was careening back and forth between subtle but clear states of anger, frustration and real concern. He was now almost plaintive. "Can you help find her child?"

"I am trying."

He ran his hand over his head and stared at the floor.

"You can go," I said. "I might want to talk to you again."

"By again, do you mean today? Should I stay?"

Oh, meet Mr. Compliance.

"No. You can leave."

He pushed on his knees to leverage himself out of the chair and walked slightly stoop-shouldered to the door. "Thank you. I didn't mean...I know you are trying to help. Anything that will help...I just don't understand all this."

"Will you ask your daughter to come up?"

He nodded.

I kept my seat, thinking about Spencer Burke. Though more controlled than Manfred, he produced as much static as his brother. I was getting tired.

Claudia entered quietly, Bungee slipping by her feet just before she closed the door. She sat on the sofa with one leg curled under her, as I had seen her on the sofa downstairs. The dog jumped up beside her. In her eyes, when she looked at me, was a realm of sadness into which I did not dare journey far. Especially not with my fatigue growing with every breath I took, with every bounce of Joey's ball.

"I want to speak with Miriam. I need her mind free of drugs."

"Without her medication, she just sobs and sobs."

"You have to let her."

Claudia sighed deeply and nodded.

"Who pays for your apartment?"

She said evenly, "My father and uncle have been taking care of it since Dan died. Maintenance and utilities and that sort of thing. When I got married, the apartment itself was a gift—from my father mostly, but my uncle contributed."

I did not ask another question so she continued. "Uncle Manfred said to me, 'Darling, if you're going to settle down with a gold digger you should be comfortable.'" She did a good imitation of her uncle's accent and a bad imitation of a smile.

"Do you have any money of your own?"

"My husband's insurance policy. I'm trying not to use it. Vin is helping me put it away for the boys' education. I'm not good with money."

"Won't your father and your uncle see to their education?"

"Probably," she sighed.

"Your family thought your husband married you for your money?"

"They were certain of it." Her thin lips curved up slightly. "It wasn't till after the boys were born that they finally accepted him."

"How do you know he didn't marry you for your money?"

"You are very direct, aren't you?"

"I'd be wasting your time and money if I weren't."

"Dan told me after we got to know each other a little that he was only going out with me for my money. If you knew him, you'd know why that was funny. He wasn't capable of using anyone, or manipulating anyone. Or lying. He was...clear. And he was strong. Michael is like that, too." She ran her hand lightly over Bungee's head.

We heard the front door open, some lowered voices. Spencer was leaving. A small but resonant *urrgh* issued from the back of Bungee's throat.

"I saw your wedding picture in your bedroom. Dan was slight in build. Not like Michael."

"My husband had juvenile rheumatoid arthritis when he was a child. He almost died. He never grew normally. He was just a little taller than me. His health was always fragile. When I said he was strong, I meant—"

"I know. The day Charlotte went missing...you went out that day?"

"Yes."

"Why didn't you call the drugstore and have them deliver?"

"I had to get out—I just felt like moving, you know? Getting a little sun and air. I wanted to maybe walk around the block, but once I got what I needed at the drugstore, I got tired very fast so I didn't get far. I just turned around and came home again. I put Charlotte in her bassinette and lay down for a nap."

"What drugstore did you go to?"

"Riverside Apothecary. On the corner."

"How long were you out, exactly?"

She paused. "The police asked me that. I think it was about twenty minutes. I can't be really exact. I wasn't wearing my watch, and I don't remember looking at any clocks."

"Where's the buggy?"

"Oh—it's in there." She pointed to a door behind her. I got up and opened it. The closet was just big enough for the buggy to fit. Some old boxed games and toys took up the shelves.

"Why is it in here?"

"I don't need it now, do I? It hurts me to look at it."

I closed the door and went back to my chair. "Why was the bassinette in the nursery? It had been in the bedroom. I saw the marks on the carpet. It stood there long before the baby was born—and then you moved it?"

"Because I didn't want...I cry at night. Since Dan died. I can't help it. I manage all right during the day, but I end up crying myself to sleep. I didn't think that would be good for an infant to hear. They absorb everything, you know. I had the monitor up loud. I know, if I had kept the bassinette in my room, this couldn't have happened."

"How do you think someone got in?"

She shook her head. "I'm sure I locked the door behind me. It's habit, you know. Living in New York. You close the door and you flip the lock."

"Were you on any medication?"

"Tylenol." Claudia didn't seem to mind my asking the same questions she had already answered for the police.

"Do you think Miriam might have gotten up while you were gone?"

"No. It looked like she hadn't even moved. She was like a log in there."

"Can you be sure?"

"No, but...they gave her a blood test. They said she had taken too many pills, actually. So now I keep them and give them to her."

"Do you know any of her friends?"

"No."

"Does she get a day off?"

She nodded.

"What does she do?"

"She goes to the park with Anna. They have gone to movies and to the zoo."

"Can you think of any motive for taking Charlotte?"

"There are many motives for taking children, aren't there?" She slumped down lower into the sofa. Bungee shoved his nose under her hand and she gave his head a stroke.

"No one has asked you for money. Is that correct?"

"Yes."

"If they had, would you have told the police?"

"Yes, why?"

"Some people are afraid to. They think—they're wrong—but they think that if they just pay the money and keep quiet their children will be returned."

"We were never contacted by anybody. I think..." She paused for a ragged deep breath. "Have you ever read anything about the Lindbergh baby?"

"Yes."

"They thought the baby was killed early. By accident. If Charlotte is dead, they maybe changed their minds about asking for ransom."

"That's what you think?"

"Yes."

"Have you told anyone else?"

"No. They all want to hope. But there isn't any hope. For anybody." She sat there, dry-eyed, as bleak a figure as I had ever seen. "I have two other children to get through this. Father Ryan says you'll help us get the girls back. I don't think they are coming back. But it won't do any good to arrest an innocent person. I know that Michael would never hurt anybody. He's too much like his brother. And I know Miriam couldn't have done it either." She had rearranged her hands into a tight fist, one hand clamped over the other. "I've seen how the police ask them questions, over and over." Claudia Keating carried a weight so heavy she was nearly crushed. But, not quite.

I asked, "How do you know?"

"Some things you just know, that's all."

I wasn't sure if she was composed or just numb. *Mothers know. Mothers know Mothers know and then they go. Swing the chariot sweet and low.* Bethy-June's voice carried high, sweet and hollow from the gyre. "Call me when I can talk to Miriam. Not a single pill till she gets lucid. And send up your uncle. Please."

It had occurred to me to not speak to him. I was so tired, and the thought of leaving him red-faced and sputtering with indignation was pleasing, but I let the thought go.

If you're too tired, I can finish.

"You know better than that Olive. That's not the agreement."

Oh, you'd like that, wouldn't you, Hester snarled. *Your little minute in the sun.*

This is too much for Isadora. Let me handle it, Olive replied in her most annoyingly patient voice.

Why you?

Because you, Hester, are a nincompoop.

While Hester and Olive bickered, the little ones began to whimper. Bethy-June stopped singing and began to cry.

Hush little baby don't say a word. Mama's gonna get you a mockingbird. And if that mockingbird don't sing. Sugartime's dusky alto calmed her, and as Manfred Burke entered, I reasserted my control over the two hissing divas. Their voices receded. Sugartime's song became pleasant ambiance.

Manfred chose the same chair as his brother. The wingback. He, too, balanced himself on the edge so as not to sink.

"You are an infuriating person. My time is valuable."

"What price do you put on your niece's child and Miriam's daughter?"

"Any price. I said we'd pay. I said we'd pay the ransom, for the nanny's child, too. For both of them. But there is no ransom. The police are useless. They have…"

If that looking glass gets broke,
Mama's gonna buy you a Billy goat.

As he talked on I felt a nearly overwhelming urge to sleep. I was exhausted from keeping my head above the heavy soup of emotions and brain waves in this apartment. I wondered how Bungee stood it. Dogs are naturally sensitive to such things. Of course, no matter how besieged Bungee felt, he didn't have a poodle, a spaniel and big-toothed German shepherd ready to come out at the drop of an eyelid. No, I had to stay with it. Manfred was winding down: "Did you see? I went on the television myself. The police didn't like it, but they are not helping, are they? They have nothing. So I went on the TV and I said, we'll pay. No questions asked. We'll give you money to just bring them back. But nothing happened and…"

I let him come to the end in his own time. When he did, I asked, "What do you think happened to the children?"

He slumped in his chair looking his age, which I remembered from the file was seventy. "I don't know. Nobody knows. Nobody knows. What could have happened? They didn't get abducted by aliens! What could have happened?" He seethed frustration. Accustomed to controlling everyone and everything, he was perhaps for the first time in a predicament for which he could neither buy nor intimidate a solution.

Or he's a good actor. The Russians, you know, invented acting.
You are an expert on Russians and theatre now?
I read.
When you're sober.
Below the belt, Hester.

Hester's and Olive's voices were so loud, I wondered that he couldn't hear them. "Thank you, Mr. Burke."

"That's all? You don't want to know where I was?"

"I know where you were. It doesn't matter. If you had anything to do with the kidnappings, you wouldn't have done it yourself. Would you?"

"No. You are right there. I don't even paint my own designs anymore. Others paint. Others draw. I say yes to this, no to that. But I don't design or paint or draw. But I didn't." The notion came to him suddenly and out of the blue that I might be accusing him of masterminding the kidnappings. "I didn't! And you are a monster to suggest it!"

If that cart and bull turn over,
Mama's gonna buy you a dog named Rover.

"You can go now."

"Monster! You are a monster." He had no idea. Still, I had the impression that his pilot light had gone out and his exclamations were just gas.

He stalked out and I heard him announce, "She is a monster! Phoebe, my darling, we must go. I will not stay here in the same place with such a creature."

"But..." Phoebe didn't finish her sentence. I came out of the family room as she was gathering her purse, white gloves and white straw hat with the red silk rose on the hatband. She passed me on the stairs, careful to avoid physical or eye contact. Her husband waited for her at the door.

"What set him off?" Ryan O'Hagan watched the couple leave, Manfred in a huff big enough to carry them both. "Did you accuse him?"

"I am accusing everyone. I suspect every one of you."

Out of the corner of my eye, I thought I saw Michael Keating smile.

In the absence of the elder Burkes, I felt the atmosphere

lighten. Sugartime's lullaby faded.

Ryan O'Hagan looked at his watch. "Do you need me to stay?"

I said no.

He stood up, smoothing his trousers and pulling at his shirt cuffs. "I have to get back to the church and prepare for Vespers."

"Goodbye, Father," said Michael Keating. "If I can," he glanced in my direction, "I'll get back in time to assist." Michael Keating displayed none of the nervousness of the senior priest. He regarded me calmly.

I sat on the sofa across from him as Ryan saw himself out. "Where's Mrs. Keating?"

"Checking on the boys."

I realized that the sound of the bouncing ball, which had become almost subliminal, was no more.

"You are at the top of the police's suspect list. Do you know why?"

He nodded to the side. "I can't prove where I was. At least a dozen people know where I was, but..." he shrugged and smiled with real humor. "I can't call upon them to vouch for me."

"No one in the parish has come forward?"

"I didn't expect anyone to. It was kind of a desperate request from Father Ryan. We get a lot of walk-ins. You know, lapsed Catholics, after fifteen or twenty years of not setting foot in a church, decide that this is the day they need to talk to a priest. It'll be another twenty years before they come back. The rest are parishioners who might not want to come forward and admit they came in. Their families might find out and wonder why they felt the need for an old-style confession." He lifted his eyes for a moment as if catching a stray thought. Then he mused, "For a long time priests could do no wrong. They were above suspicion. Now, we're like the butler. Everyone assumes we must have done it."

"Does that make you angry?"

"Of course not. It's the swing of the pendulum, that's all. This too shall pass. Besides, the church brought this on herself. I don't agree with the way they have handled pedophile priests."

"You don't look like a priest."

"I don't look like the average New York City priest," he admitted. "There are lots of priests in lots of places who look like me. Even worse." He smiled. "Anyway, what do you think I look like?" He leaned back and stretched his legs.

"A boxing coach."

He smiled again with genuine enjoyment. "I've heard I look like a sanitation worker, even a cop. My favorite was dog catcher. Nobody has ever said I look like a doctor or a lawyer. But boxing coach is good. I am a boxing coach, as a matter of fact, for some kids on the Lower East Side. I know that's not my beat. I'm helping out. Doing a little moonlighting for a buddy of mine down there."

"How did you end up here, in the city?"

"My health. I got a bug and the doctors said I needed a gig where I could get rest. Where I wouldn't have to dig wells and drainage ditches, build my own church and grow my own food."

"Where were you?"

"Brazil. Anyway, the church shipped me here. You go where you're sent."

I noticed he used the word 'sent,' not 'called.' "You're not happy with this posting."

"I'm happy to be close to my family. I got here just a few months before my brother was diagnosed with cancer. I was grateful to be here during the last year of his life. God and His mysterious ways." He made a little gesture of resignation.

"You don't seem as wrought up over this as the rest of the family."

"Wrought up?"

"Depressed, stressed, anxious…"

"Claudia and Miriam are in a pit right now. I can't help them out of it if I'm in the pit with them. Sorry for the cliché, but that's what it amounts to. What I can't do anything about, I leave to God."

"You think everything that happens is God's will?"

"Trick question." He sat up again, and leaned forward. "If you give God the credit for all the good stuff, then you have to blame him for the bad stuff. So if I say yes, I'm saying God wanted all the terrible things that happened to you, for example, to have happened, and if I say no, what am I doing as a priest?" He smiled at me, not apologetically, but with humility, as if, perhaps, he had wondered the same thing.

"Good questions. But what is the answer?"

"*My* answer is, 'I don't know.' I can't account for what is God's will and what isn't. It's a mystery. I leave it at that. I don't trivialize human suffering by shrugging and saying it's God's will. It may be, but it's not for me to say so." He gave a rather impish smile and said, "Father O'Hagan would have a better answer."

"Do you have any idea what happened to these children?"

The lines in his face deepened, his cheeks sagged with the weight of his next utterance. "I fear something very bad has happened to them."

"You don't seem worried about whether or not you are arrested."

"My arrest…or not…" From upstairs we heard the television come on. "…is irrelevant. Find Anna and Charlotte."

I wanted to ask him more questions, but I was once again fighting an oppressive drowsiness and couldn't trust my responses anymore. He could tell me that he had invented the Internet now and I would think, *Okay, cool.* I had to have some time without anyone else around. I needed to sleep and let Aurora paint.

Claudia came downstairs and fell into a chair. Bungee curled at her feet. The television was still going and the thumping of the soccer ball had not resumed. "Thank goodness for *Shrek*," she sighed.

Michael asked her, "How is Miriam?"

"I have her pills here." She patted her pocket. "I didn't give her any. When she asked for one, I gave her an aspirin. I don't think she even noticed. By tomorrow…tomorrow, she'll cry."

Vin made an entrance, bent over Claudia and took her hand in his. "Sweetheart, I'm going out for a smoke and do a little food shopping. You need anything?" She shook her head. "Are y'all staying for dinner?" He looked at me and at Michael Keating.

"Why don't y'all stay? I'll just pick up a few extra tomatoes. It's Tuesday, it's tacos."

"It's Wednesday."

"Oh."

"Tacos are fine."

"I'll walk Bungee when I get back."

She nodded and gave his hand a return squeeze.

"I have to leave now," I said, getting to my feet. "I'll be speaking to everyone again. If there is anything you want to tell me in the meantime, call me." I handed Claudia my card.

Vin went ahead of me, taking the stairs like a dancer taking stage levels. "If you wait a second, I'll walk out with ya." He went to Miriam's room.

I followed him but stayed at the door and watched him sit beside her in the window seat. She had Anna's dolls folded in to her breast and was staring out.

Vin patted her knee. "Darlin', I'm goin' out. You want anything?"

She focused on him, but her eyes were dull. Her skin, while too young for lines, still seemed old, without the luminosity of a woman under thirty. She didn't seem to have the energy to even shake her head.

He stood up and brushed the side of her face with his palm and left.

Looking down into the living room, I saw Michael and Claudia now seated side by side on the sofa. The priest was speaking—I couldn't hear what he was saying—and she was nodding her head gently.

Chapter 6

The lethargy I had felt inside the Keating apartment lifted as soon as I closed the door behind me. Vin pushed the button for the elevator. "I'll take the stairs," I said, and headed toward the Exit sign at the end of the hall. I didn't need Cootie or anybody else coming out now.

"That's a good idea. My legs are like Jell-O sittin' in that kitchen all day." He trotted after me. "That is—if you don't mind the comp'ny."

"I don't mind."

"I should use the stairs every day. Up and down." He got to the fire door at the end of the hall ahead of me and held it open for me.

As we descended the gray-walled stairwell, Vin asked, "Well, whaddya think?" He shook out a cigarette from the pack in his shirt pocket.

"About what?"

"About *whu-ut*?" He cackled. "You came here to scope us all out. Sort truth from *li-iiies*," he drawled. "Fact from fiction.

Father Ryan says you got some kind of mojo. So what's your mojo tellin' you?"

"I couldn't get a clear impression on individuals. Too much in the atmosphere."

"Why did you want us all together, then?" The question was more reasonable coming from Vin than it had been coming from Manfred Burke.

"I wanted to observe you all together. See how you are as a family."

"And how are we, then?"

"Peculiar."

He twiddled his cigarette between his fingers. "I don't know much about normal families," I said. "But I know this isn't one."

"They've had a lot of tragedy. You know what they say— every family is happy in the same way and miserable in its own way. I paraphrase."

"*Anna Karenina.*"

"You're a reader?"

"One of us is. Did you know Claudia's mother was a suicide?"

"She mentioned it."

"Just *mentioned* it? No details?"

"No." He patted himself down for his lighter and found it in the back pocket of his pants.

"You're such friends."

"I never pressed her." He tapped his cigarette against the side of the lighter. "She'll tell me when she's ready—or not."

"She has photographs all over the apartment. Of her and her husband and the boys. There's you and Miriam and Anna. There's a dozen or so pictures of the dog. Not one of her uncle and his wife or of her father or her mother. Why is that?"

"Well, I got pictures of my dog Fred and my friends and Claudy and the boys all over my hovel and none of my mother and none of my brother or my father. My family pictures are in an album somewhere, but I don't have them out. I left Jackson to get away from all that."

"But she hasn't gotten away, has she?"

"All the more reason not to have to look at their pictures."

"If she feels that way, why didn't she move away?"

We kept going down and right, down and right. Vin paused a moment on the landing we had just reached, and looked at me thoughtfully. "Frankly?" he said. "I don't know. But, I think... it's complicated." We started moving again. "Claudy is fragile, in a way. She lucked out when she met Dan. He took care of her, and because the Burkes didn't like him, they kind of kept their distance. There was no actual estrangement. Nobody ever had words or anything like that...they just didn't see much of each other. And Dan was practical. The Burke money...he could have taken it or left it. He wasn't hung up about it one way or the other. But it gave his boys a standard of living they wouldn't have had otherwise and there didn't seem to be strings attached, so he took the gifts that were sent and was happy to have the apartment. He paid all the expenses while he was working. When he got sick, the Burkes slipped in and picked them up."

"Strange," I said.

"What especially?"

"O'Hagan, when he hired me, described Mrs. Keating as strong...no, the word he used was tough."

"Well, maybe he doesn't know everything."

We came to the ground floor and finally emerged in the back of the lobby. I saw a different doorman on duty. "Who's that?"

"Arturo."

Arturo Cole: on duty the day Charlotte was taken.

Vin hailed him from across the lobby. "Hey, Arturo! *Qué pasa!*"

The doorman wore the same style of uniform as his predecessor, but this one had sharper creases and all the buttons buttoned, even though the air drifting through the open lobby doors felt warmer than when I first arrived. He had short-cropped hair, dark, acne-scarred skin.

"Vin! How is everybody today?"

Vin shrugged. "Emm, you know."

Arturo Cole nodded gravely, with a military air.

Vin pointed his unlit cigarette at me. "This is Shiloh. She's helping the police."

The doorman faced me squarely.

I said, "You were here the day Mrs. Keating came back with the baby. She called you to tell you Charlotte was missing?"

"Yes."

"How long was it—from when she came in to when she called you?"

"Forty-five minutes, give or take."

"And no one strange to you went in or out during that time?"

He took a deep breath and lifted his eyes past me to some private horizon. "I'm here most of the time during my shift, but I carry bags and do things for people. Help them in and out of cars, call cabs, get packages out of the mailroom—my face isn't always pointed the right way. I take a whiz, get a cup of coffee. I can't stay in one place for two hours. I don't really remember every move I make at every minute, so I'm pretty sure, but I can't be positive. There's no security camera."

"What do you think of Claudia Keating?"

He raised his eyebrows slightly before answering. "She's quiet. She's a nice woman, but quiet. And sad. Kind of sad, I always thought, even before all this happened."

"Has she ever asked you to walk her dog?"

"Bungee? That little rat-on-a-rope? He hates me." He grinned and shook his head.

"I may want to talk to you again."

"Sure."

"One more thing. Mrs. Keating came back around two o'clock. Not on your shift."

"I pulled a double that day. Victor needed to do something and I covered. He's done it for me. Management doesn't care as long as shifts are covered and it doesn't cost them overtime."

"Thank you," I said.

"Later, man," said Vin.

As soon as we stepped outside, Vin lit his cigarette and took a deep drag. The sun glazed the sides of buildings like butter, and the breeze that had fluttered and flapped around the city for two days was at rest. These are the rare moments when New

York seems at peace with herself, resting in her own quiet glow. A bird twittered in the single tree in front of the building. Then a couple of cars passed, and the moment was over.

"You want a cab?" Vin asked.

"No." My energy had returned in full. I wanted to walk Claudia Keating's route the day Charlotte went missing. "I'm going around the block. Which corner is Riverside Apothecary on?"

"Thattaway."

He fell into step beside me. Riverside Apothecary was privately owned, featured expensive products with fancy wrappings in the windows, and was less than a minute's walk east from the apartment building.

As I stood contemplating the display of Crabtree and Evelyn creams, perfumes and soaps, Swedish loofas and small wooden implements, the use of which I couldn't imagine, Vin asked, "So what's this mojo like? What do you do exactly?"

"I listen to people. I watch them. I can usually tell if they are lying or not. I pick up things...Arturo feels guilty."

"About what?"

"That he *didn't* see anything. He feels like he should have been at that door every second. Even though that would be impossible, as he took pains to make clear—mostly to himself."

"You picked that up. You a radio receiver or something?" That was as good a metaphor as any. "Well, Father Ryan said you were good."

"We'll see how good I am. Leo and his team are good too. They follow evidence. What I do is different."

"Well, with respect to the detective and his team, what they been doin' hasn't come up with jack. So we definitely need somebody doin' something different."

"Mrs. Keating told me that she started around the block when she left the drugstore. She didn't say she crossed the street. So, she...went north on Broadway."

"I guess."

Vin kept up with me as I turned north. "Do you know how far she walked that day, before she turned back?"

"Uh-uh."

"She said she was out for about twenty minutes so I'll see how far I get in the next ten."

A homeless man, bundled under shabby sweaters, a coat tied around the middle with twine, wearing a muffler, gloves and a knit hat pulled down to his eyebrows, approached us pushing a grocery cart full of junk—probably all his worldly goods, items painstakingly collected for as long as he had lived on the streets. Other people passing him gave him a wide berth.

Give him some money, pleaded Hester.

If we give money to every street person, we will be *a street person.*

Olive, you're a cold bitch.

And you're a stupid, sentimental one.

While Hester and Olive sniped at each other, I saw Vin dig into his pocket, and as the man rattled past, drop some coins into the Styrofoam cup wired to the side of his cart.

"God bless you," the man muttered to Vin, who replied with a nod and kept pace with me.

We passed a small restaurant with outside tables.

Aren't we hungry? When did we last eat?

Shut up, Cootie, all you think about is food. Go back to the gyre. You won't feel your stomach.

Cootie chattered through Olive's reprimand. *Look there's a falafel place. Fast food but not junk. We could get that. You're always saying—*

Cootie, Olive is right. We're working. We'll eat later.

"What's the matter?" Vin eyed me. We had slowed down. "You look like you got a headache."

"A little one…just a little buzzing in my ears. It comes and goes."

"Migraines?"

"Not exactly."

"Take something for it?"

"Usually, just a nap. It goes away."

Ooooo, there's a nail salon. When we're done, I need a manicure. My hands are an embarrassment. Why, I hardly wanted to shake hands with the reverend today, they were so awful.

A detective's hands don't need a forty-dollar manicure.

Well, what do you care, Olive, you have man hands.

They're the same hands you have, Hester.

It's how I use them. With expressive grace and femininity. On you, they're hams.

I picked up the pace again so the Company wouldn't have time to comment on every shoe store, Korean vegetable market or bodega we passed. And my head was beginning to hurt.

Hey! A Gap! I wanna get me one of those jean jackets in the window. Man they are so cool.

I'm not going around in a jean jacket!

I stopped and held my head in my hands. *All of you. Shut up! When we get home, I'm calling Ray.*

Oooooh, she's calling Ray.

We'll renegotiate. You won't be allowed out of the gyre when I'm working.

You need us when we're working.

I don't need this! I'd rather do it without you.

That shut them up. For awhile.

"Hey, you want to stop and get something for that headache?" We were standing in the middle of the sidewalk. Vin was peering at me with concern. "There's a *Duane Reade* across the street. You want me to get you something?"

"No. It's better now. I have a technique. I can sort of will it away. They're gone now, for awhile. The *pains*."

We get it.

People passed us without paying attention to us the way New Yorkers do to preserve psychological space in a city with so little physical space. We started moving again. A heavyset, older woman walked toward us, her orange frizzed hair sprouted from the edges of a green bandanna. She was apparently unaware of the psychic space rule, because without slowing down, she looked me right in the eye and said, "I'm going to try to shit one more time." She kept on walking past us.

Vin looked at me, his mouth slightly open. I said, "She must be having issues with regularity."

He doubled over and squealed with laughter. He hadn't finished his cigarette but dropped it and ground it and kept laughing.

We came to the end of the block. Only a few minutes had passed. I turned left again onto the street, headed west, away from Broadway. The street was residential, quiet and shaded with tall trees whose new leaves filtered the sky like lace.

Vin stopped laughing, coughed, and said, "What are we doin' exactly?"

"I just want to check out the neighborhood."

On our side of the street we passed a couple of brownstones and then a twelve- or fifteen-story apartment building. Just beyond it, we came to a brick building set back from the sidewalk. Flush with the walk was a wrought iron fence and gate festooned with signs, artistically rendered in bright colors.

From the gate, a sidewalk curved in to steps going up to a narrow portico. From the portico, two doors gave entrance to the building. The one straight ahead of me was large, wood and ornate, and the second at the western end was an ordinary door with a small glass window and another sign. The patch of ground in front of the building was planted with grass, small bushes and flowers. A small, gated oasis of serenity just off busy Broadway. I perused the signs. Heartwood Buddhist Center taught everything from Buddhist studies, yoga and meditation to flower arranging and calligraphy. They offered, among many things, silent retreats that lasted from ten hours to nine days, a vegetarian cooking class on Wednesday nights, senior citizen activities on Tuesdays and Thursdays, and childcare for people attending classes.

Vin said, "It's a monastery or ashram or somethin'. You see them in their orange robes at the market over there sometimes." He pointed toward Broadway. "They're nice and friendly and don't proselytize. Except for the shaved heads, these women seem pretty normal." He ran his hand over his own shaved head.

"Women?"

"Yeah. They're all women. Nuns. Or…I guess you call 'em nuns. I don't know much about them, but they don't cause any trouble, and the neighborhood is no worse for their being here. Prob'ly better."

I pushed the gate. It was not locked.

If Claudia came this far, she would have been out about twenty minutes.

Vin and I walked back to Broadway and joined the congested bustle of the five o'clock street. We were close to Columbia University. Everyone was a bit glazed and private with relief from classes or a workday over, determined to get home and close their doors behind them. Vin was still with me as we walked south. "Aren't you going shopping or something?" I asked.

"Or something. I need the air. How far you goin'?"

"Eighty-first."

"Well, I ain't goin' that far. I just need a stretch, stoke up on some nicotine, and then I'll be goin' back."

I try to tune out as much as I can in crowds. For me, it is like negotiating a whitewater of humanity in a little raft of private psychic space. To notice everything would drive the dullest wit stark mad. In my case, I didn't have that far to go. But someone stood out in the crowd ahead. A brown-skinned man, shirtless. The fact that he was shirtless and carried something draped around his shoulders, like a long piece of yellow tubing, was why I noticed him in the river of pedestrian traffic. At this time of day, people were in working clothes or school duds. This was the wrong neighborhood and the wrong season for shirtless men.

Vin shook out another cigarette, and I watched him perform his ritual of tapping it against his lighter before igniting it.

When I looked away from Vin the shirtless man was near, and just as he passed me close on my right, I saw what he had around his neck. Not yellow tubing.

Chapter 7

"Welcome back."

The aroma of coffee was strong in my nostrils. I was seated at a small round table across from...oh, yes, Claudia Keating's housekeeper and friend, Vin Parrish. There was half a cup of frothy coffee in front of me. Another in front of him. I looked around. Starbucks.

"Welcome back," he said again.

"What happened?"

"You bailed, honey! You were there one minute, then that guy with the big ole yella snake walked by and you looked like death on a cracker and went to Vegas. Where *did* you go, anyway?"

I blinked. I remembered seeing the tubing and then the small head with its black little eyes.

"Who...."

"I met somebody very interesting."

"Who?"

"A gal named Sugartime. We hit it off. I got the feeling she was kinda southern." He played with an unlit cigarette.

"You met Sugartime?"

"She said you were under too much stress back at the apartment and then the snake…we had a nice chat but she had to go. Said she could only be out for about twenty minutes or so. What happens—she turns back into a pumpkin, or what? Anyway, she left. And now here you are again."

"She doesn't usually come out at all. She takes care of things *inside*."

"Well, I guess there was a mutiny on the Shiloh or something. Honey, your body is like a timeshare! You blew my mind more than the first time I saw the Macy's Day Parade! You must give your friends a thrill ride." He wasn't disturbed at all.

"I don't have any friends." I decided to try the coffee. As I suspected, it was sweet. I took a swallow anyway.

"You don't have any *friends*?" His voice slid up an octave.

"No." I took another swallow. I needed the sugar and the caffeine.

"Honey, why not?"

"Most people can't stand what you just went through. Though I haven't blacked out like that in a long time."

"Well, honey, *I* didn't go through nothin'. *You're* the one went through it!"

Nobody had ever taken this attitude. "And they don't deal well with…it wasn't a headache I had on the street before. I just had to quiet the voices."

He took a sip of his coffee and wiped milk foam from his upper lip and said, "Well, I figured that after I talked to Sugartime. Anyway, you got one now."

"I've got what?" I really wanted to get home.

"A friend."

"You can't be my friend."

"Why not?"

"Because you are a suspect."

He laughed out loud. "Well, if you're any good at all at what you do, you will soon find out that's *crazy*! I love those kids more than I've ever loved anybody except my dog Fred. I love them as much as I loved that beagle, and that's saying *something*."

He was telling the truth. And Sugartime had talked to him.

The only other person she had ever talked to was Ray. Even Leo had never met Sugartime.

Chapter 8

The light on my answering machine blinked furiously. One message would be from Ray, the others from Leo. I hit the play button and sat on the edge of my bed to pull off my boots.

"Shiloh, it's Leo. Call me."

"Hi, gang." That was Ray. "Somebody give me a call when you get in."

"Shiloh." Leo again. His voice taut. "Call me on my cell."

"Shiloh! Where the hell are you? Call me at home." Full-blown annoyance with a trace of worry.

I didn't want to talk to anyone, but if I didn't call Leo back he'd send over a blue-and-white, and I didn't need Hester trying to play with a couple of beat cops this evening, so I pressed his speed dial number and took the receiver back to the bed.

He answered with a bark, "Shiloh!"

"Hello, Leo." I pulled off my socks and flexed my toes.

"You just getting home *now*?"

"I had a glitch."

"What kind of glitch? What do you mean *glitch*?"

"Nothing serious."

"Are you all right?"

"Yes."

"Well, what did—Keep it down! I'm on the phone!"

I heard in the background a rising swell of laughing children and yapping dogs. "Sorry," he said. "What did—Take it outside! I can't hear myself think. Teeeeee Naaaaah!"

I heard more background chaos and then Tina's voice over it and then quiet. She must have herded everybody into their backyard. Leo has four children, two dogs and at least three or four neighbor kids in his house at any given time.

Not confident that the peace would last in the Gianetti house, I got right to it. "Forget Charlotte," I said.

"What?"

"Forget Charlotte. Find Anna."

"You know she's dead? Charlotte?"

"I know you can't help her. Don't waste your time trying. Concentrate on Anna. She might still be alive. What else have you got since I looked at the file?"

"We don't have a clue. That's not just an expression. We really do not have a fucking clue. We've just about exhausted the Russian mafia angle. But we'll leave that end open for now. We have interviewed everyone in the building again, and in the neighborhood, and still come up with squat."

"Anything come back from the Amber Alert?"

"A few lame-ass leads and we followed them, but nada." He paused. "No one we talked to that afternoon said there was a man in the playground that day, so we figured we were looking for a woman."

"Or someone who could convincingly play a woman," I said.

"Yeah, we thought of that, which is why we are back to looking for anybody at all."

"Miriam said that Anna was in the sandbox with another child. Have you found that child?"

"No. Nobody could remember which kid it was. None of the kids we talked to played with Anna that day."

"So, two children might be missing and only one reported?"

"Right. Except, who wouldn't report a missing kid?"

"Maybe the other child was a plant. Brought by the kidnapper."

"Shit."

I couldn't believe he really hadn't thought of that, but it sounded like he hadn't. I also knew that this was not Leo's only case, and he might be relying on Feeney to do a little thinking. Guess that wasn't working out.

"So, can you at least tell me who wasn't telling us the truth?"

"Nobody was lying that I could tell. I didn't get to talk to Miriam. She was still drugged up. I didn't get the whole truth either. There were too many people there."

"Couldn't you get them alone and—"

"I will." It didn't help to interview them one at a time in the family room. It's like when you are allergic to cats. It doesn't matter if all the cats in the house are locked in the bedroom and you're in the living room. You'll still get sick. I knew that going over there. "I just wanted to see them all together. This is a strange family, Leo. I intend to speak to each of them alone, away from the others. You checked their bank accounts, the two Burkes?"

"Yeah. No large withdrawals. We don't think they got a ransom note."

"I don't think so either. I don't mean withdrawals. Did you check for large deposits?"

"Deposits?" There was some dead air. I knew Leo had clapped his hand over the receiver, and he was mentally kicking himself and cursing Feeney, who, in his defense was his junior detective, a newbie I had yet to meet. Newbie Feeney would be in for a tongue-lashing and a butt-kicking. In a second, Leo was back. "We'll check it."

Poor Feeney. "And don't just check under Burke. Check under Berkowitz."

"What are you thinking?"

"Just check."

"All right. How much money are we looking for?"

"How much is a little girl worth these days?"

"Is that all you're going to tell me?"

"I don't have anything else. I have to think, Leo."

He muttered a curse as he hung up.

I didn't undress, just stretched out on my bed and closed my eyes. I saw dolls. Dolls make me uncomfortable. The more realistic the doll, the more queasy it makes me. So many dolls in that apartment. So many doll faces. The Barbies, the baby doll, the Raggedy Ann, the curly-headed dolls in Miriam's room. And when I thought of them, I saw Phoebe Burke among them, with her ancient, painted doll face. Then the people all gathered before me, looking at me with hope, despair, challenge. And the faces of the children, who I had only seen in pictures, along with the doll faces came alive and gazed at me. Their little mouths formed *O*s in silent cries, and the little *O*s became snake eyes, and all against the sound of barking dogs. Dolls, dolls, baby dolls, barking dogs, bouncing balls. The silence of the mothers. Miriam paralyzed with grief and drugs. Snakes walking on the streets of New York. The king cobra who curled around the Buddha, rising up behind him and over him, flaring his neck to shelter him from the rain through the night of his enlightenment. "Lance."

Yes, Isadora.

"Tell me a story."

Once, a long time ago, in the land of Egypt, there was a Pharaoh. A paranoid Pharaoh. A bad man, all powerful. He sent out a decree over all the land...

Thursday

Chapter 9

I woke up the next morning under the covers, in pajamas, hair still damp, reeking of Hester's various herbal soaps, rinses, creams and powders, and with the usual taste of blood in my mouth. I did the finger check, and as usual, came up clean. When I turned on the coffeepot I found a yellow sticky note above the switch.

I called Ray.

    Olive.

I don't know why she bothers to sign her name. Even with only three words I can recognize Olive's back slant. She is the only one of us who is left-handed. I was glad she called. It meant that I didn't have to for a while. I didn't feel like talking to Ray about the blackout, even though I knew that Olive would have put the worst possible construction on it. *Isadora is not holding up well, Ray. I fear she is becoming unhinged.* I also knew that Ray wouldn't take Olive too seriously. She has learned to listen between the lines. She says the people who demonstrate no self-interest at all are Lance, Sugartime and Hawk. The rest of them, in spite of our contracts, still have personal agendas that have to be factored into any conversation.

I didn't feel hungry. Hester, no doubt, had had one of her healthful breakfasts of organic something or other in soy milk. So I updated my notebook while I waited for my coffee to brew. I had a lot to think about. Vin Parrish for one. He was the only one, besides Miriam, who seemed to be expressing any normal signs of grief over the two missing children. And, he was the only person I'd ever met who was more fascinated than disturbed the first time he'd seen me switch. I bet, when it happened, he hadn't even stopped breathing.

Usually, the least that people do when they see a switch for the first time is stop breathing. Not because our manner of speaking or our behavior changes, ordinary people do that all the time. They speak as someone else in order to be funny or to make a point or just to show off. Actors do it to make a living. No, what stops people's breaths is not that I speak in a different manner, but that I speak in another voice; not that my face suddenly looks different, but that they are suddenly looking at a different face. There are resemblances of course, like there would be in a family. But unless you are dealing with identical twins, there is never any mistaking that family members are different people. Even Ray hasn't been able to get us all in photographs or videos. The only reason I know what everyone else looks like is because Aurora has painted each of us.

The coffee was done. I poured a cup, topped it with milk and strolled over to Aurora's corner of the flat. Our portraits hung on one wall, with mine in the center, a bit larger than the others; her homage, I suppose to my being the firstborn. One of the few considerations I got. Aurora's self-portrait was very small, in the outer orbit. The first time Ray saw our gallery wall, she was stopped in her tracks and voiced her astonishment in Spanish, then in English. "Holy smoke! She's got all of you! My God! They are perfect! Who is she?" It was the first time we told her about Aurora. Being deaf and mute, she couldn't come out to the psychiatrist herself, and if she did, what would she do? "Paint, of course," Ray said. "Tell her she can come to me in my office. I will have paints for her. She can paint for me." But to Ray's continuing disappointment, Aurora has never appeared to anyone. We only know of her existence because of her paintings.

I could see my own face in the mirror, and she had captured me as well, or better than, any camera. It was from this portrait that I first understood what Ray described as my reptilian gaze. Aurora had rendered me full face, from a slightly upward angle. Even knowing that it was my own face I was looking at, I had no feeling of me in it, any more than I had with any of the other portraits.

The first ring of portraits included Hester. Some things remain constant in most of them. The hair stays black and straight, with a shoulder-length blunt cut and bangs. The eyes remain dark, but nothing else is really the same. Hester's lips are fuller than mine. Her cheeks are more flushed and fleshed out and she has deeper laugh lines around her eyes and smile lines around her mouth. She is just generally rounder all over. Lance is also in the first ring. He seems smaller than me. When he inhabits this body he takes up less space, and he has a dreamy, wise expression, with a heavier brow and thinner lips. He has none of the rosiness that is Hester's (none of us have that). His skin goes flatter, though he cannot grow a beard. He knows what he is and that he cannot live life fully as a man. He has channeled his energies into being a poet and a storyteller. His voice is low and mellifluous. I have tried, but I cannot produce his sound. He sometimes goes to a small Village coffeehouse for open mike sessions. His poetry is very depressing, but well received on those few nights he has gotten up to recite it.

I am food for my guilt,
the feeding ground
for the lions of my rage.

He has not tried to publish anything. His poems are not that good, he says. He makes them for himself and whoever might want to listen, but never puts anything down on paper. I hear his voice in my head, but it is not quite the same as hearing it played back on Ray's tape recorder, just as seeing the faces of the Company in my mind's eye is different from seeing them in photos, or Aurora's portraits.

I don't understand how Aurora sees us all so much more

clearly than we see each other, but she does. Olive's face is longer, horsier, with a deep crease between her eyebrows and a downturned mouth. Her voice is lower than mine, but not into Lance's register and just a little pinched sounding.

Hester's voice is high, chirpy. No mistaking her soprano, which can go from breathy to shrill in the same sentence.

Hawk has never been photographed, but there she is, in the corona of portraits around my own. Ray says it's a good likeness. Her bones are bonier. Her cheekbones are prominent, and her eyes almost black. There is something wolfy about her face. The first time Ray met her, all she heard was a snarl. Back in the state hospital while I was being weaned from all the drugs they had been giving me, I was in withdrawal and unsteady. I reached for something on the floor and Ray thought I was going to fall and hurt myself. All the intern intended to do was steady me or at least slow down my fall off the bed. She grabbed my arm and heard that snarl for the first time. Hawk whirled on her and literally bared her teeth. "I felt like a Little Latina Riding Hood with the big bad wolf," she told me.

"What did you say?"

"I didn't say anything. I squeaked. She almost broke my wrist and I almost wet my pants." Ray laughed, but she had been scared. Hawk realized she meant no harm and growled her first words to Ray, "Till we know you better, no sudden moves."

She agreed.

I've never heard Hawk speak. We do not share the body. Ray says, "Well, if a wolf could talk—a really pissed off—you know, cornered and dangerous wolf—that's what she'd sound like." Hawk has never allowed herself to be recorded.

Before forming the Company we were a small anarchy ruled by confusion and self-interest, like a team of dogs all tangled up in their traces biting and snarling at each other and trying to move in different directions with nobody getting anywhere.

I had a headache. I knew it would pass in about half an hour. At least it wasn't a hangover headache. Our Olive, you see, drinks a little.

I passed the other portraits...Cootie looking like his name— disheveled, cocky, a little goofy; Aurora with blond hair and blue eyes...that's how she sees herself. Ray said if the others could paint themselves, they would look quite different from the way she and Aurora see them. Hester, for example, in her own mind, has bright red hair. In Aurora's portrait, Sugartime looks a little like an ancient, but ageless Queen Latifah. Ray thinks that is because, since Sugartime is outside so seldom, Aurora has had to paint her portrait from the inside only.

I finished my coffee in front of Aurora's easel. Ray had taken special pains to set up this studio for her. She paints mostly at night, so strong overhead lamps that simulate natural light flood her corner of the apartment, and for those rare times she is out during the day, the corner windows give her light from the east and the north.

Ray installed shelves and bought a used artist's cabinet with drawers for canvases and paints and brushes. Aurora's other paintings are lined up against the walls all around the apartment. Some mysterious communication passes between Aurora and Olive, and when Aurora is ready to let a painting go, Olive wraps it up, calls a cab, and takes it down to a Soho gallery run by Robin Bartholome, who loves to trace himself back to some English duke or other. Aurora's paintings are selling for more and more money. Robin is always leaving messages asking for more paintings. *At this point in time,* he is fond of saying, *I could sell at least ten more of those flower dealios you do so well. Think pink. Call me.*

This morning I saw that Aurora had finished one of her grimmer streetscapes. They don't sell as well as her florals and lighter street pieces, but Robin keeps a few on hand for the odd fan of all things dark and drear. I was thankful there were no snakes in it.

Aurora paints the city as a battered queen whose beauty is not in her surface glitter—the shop windows, the galleries and museums or gilded skyscrapers—but in the freedom she grants to the different, to the strange and the estranged; in the volunteers who serve people they don't know for no other reason than the oxygen they get for doing good, which makes the flame inside them burn brighter; in her window boxes and courtyard gardens and in the care people have for their dogs and cats and parakeets; in her block parties and festivals; in the hearts of the workers who remain with their colleagues while a building falls and crushes them to dust. All this sings on Aurora's canvases, and that is why she pays our rent.

I went back for my second cup of coffee. My headache was gone. Now I could think. I had a gauzy sense of what had happened in the Keating household. I couldn't grasp the details. But what I knew was only a part of it, and I couldn't tell Leo till I had the rest, because, in its parts, it didn't make sense, even to me. Yet.

I also had to deal with the pressure this case was putting on the Company. Of course, the unexpected sight of the snake had driven all of us, except Sugartime, back to the gyre. But that might have happened even without our involvement in a child-abuse case.

Why do people keep snakes? Multitudes are terrified of snakes, so there must be some kind of rush in walking the streets with one of these animals draped around your neck. The cruelty is also to the snake, keeping it in a small apartment or aquarium, so far removed from its natural home. But mostly, the cruelty is to its food. A living creature is placed in a container with the snake. This is not natural selection with a predator culling the weak or the old, the sick or the slow. Just a poor creature with no chance, forced to wait in absolute terror—

The phone rang.

Chapter 10

The answering machine kicked in. "This is Shiloh and Company. Please leave a message. One of us will call you back."

Then I heard a thin, tentative, "Ehhm...hello. This is Claudia Keating."

I picked up the phone. "I'm here, Mrs. Keating."

"Oh... I think if you want to talk to Miriam, it should probably be...now. She's having a few good minutes. I don't know...how long..."

"I'll grab a cab and be right there." I abandoned my last cup of coffee, pulled on some clean clothes, slipped into loafers and ran out. Cootie hailed a cab.

Victor was expecting me and sent us up without seeming to notice Cootie's adolescent rasp, or what Olive calls his ever-present, shit-eating grin.

Claudia was waiting for me in the doorway. Bungee barreled out and gave me a raucous but amiable escort down the hall. He shut up as soon as we were both inside with the door closed.

I said, "Thank you for calling." I smelled coffee, and heard the arrhythmic bouncing of the soccer ball and what sounded like television cartoons coming from the family room.

Claudia, looking even more exhausted and hollow-eyed than she had yesterday, pointed me to the kitchen but did not come with me. Miriam was finishing a bowl of cereal. Vin was filling her cup with coffee. He greeted me with, "Hey, there. Want a cup?"

I shook my head and he paused, for a moment uncertain as he looked at Miriam, then back at me. "Well, give a holler if you need anything." He replaced the pot to the coffeemaker and left the kitchen.

I pulled out the chair opposite her and sat down. "Do you know who I am?"

She nodded.

"Did they tell you I was coming over to talk to you?"

She nodded again. Hair that had never known a shine was pulled back tight in a rubber band with bobby pins holding the sides. Her gray sweatpants and white cotton blouse didn't do anything to streamline her chunky physique. She'd probably always been heavy, from a poor family who had lived mostly on starch, and fat when they could get it.

"Do you think you can answer a few questions? The police might have already asked you, but I need to ask again."

She glanced up at me but her eyes dropped again as if the pull of gravity was more than she had the strength to resist.

"How do you like living here?"

Her shoulders unhunched a little. "I like it very much. We are happy here, Anna and me. I expected to be treated like a servant, you know. But this is America. Claudia…Mrs. Keating, she has treated me well. Like a friend. I felt, you know, at home here."

"Does everyone treat you that way?"

"Everyone? You mean, Vin? He is quite wonderful. I had never known anyone…you know, like him in Russia. But he is quite wonderful. Anna loves him very much."

"How about the Burkes. Do they treat you well?"

"Oh, yes. It was Mr. Spencer who paid for my way over here. He said that it was worth it to have someone trustworthy to stay with his daughter and help her. She lost her husband you know. She was so sad when I arrived. So sad." She stared at her coffee cup and empty bowl. She was not drugged, and she was not sobbing. But I felt this was only a temporary condition, as Claudia Keating had advised, so I pressed on.

"According to the police file, the day Anna disappeared she was wearing purple overalls, a purple shirt and a purple corduroy jacket. When I looked in your closet yesterday, I saw an outfit like that. Not the jacket, but the overalls and the shirt."

"Her playsuit. She has two. Purple is her favorite color."

"The purple clothes looked brand-new. Her other clothes didn't."

"She got them for her birthday last week. Mr. Spencer gave them to her. One to wash and one to wear, he said."

Miriam's English was good but careful. She had come here to study and was probably a diligent student.

Roses are red, violets are blue…

"Maybe I will have a cup of coffee. I'll get it." I got up from the table and took a clean cup out of the dish drainer and filled it up. "Do you think they have any cream?"

"No cream. They have the skimmed milk."

I decided to drink it black and sat back down. "Did you have a party for Anna's birthday?"

"Yes. Claudia had cake with many candles, and ice cream. The Burkes were here. And Vin. She asked if I wanted to invite anyone else. But there is no one else."

"Did Anna get lots of presents?"

"Yes."

"What did she get? Besides the purple clothes."

"Vin gave her a book. Mr. Manfred gave her a paint set. You know, finger paints for a small child. Victor even came up with a big doll for her. Danny and Joey gave her a puzzle. She was so happy."

I was afraid she was going to break down any moment so I kept the questions coming. "What did Mrs. Keating give her, besides the cake and ice cream and the candles?"

"It was quite wonderful. She made up a little book of tickets. They were to the Children's Museum, and one for the Natural

History Museum, and to movies and to a play. And a coupon for a dancing class to see if she liked it."

"Yes. That is a wonderful gift for both you and Anna. What did you give your daughter?"

"I gave her a doll. She loves dolls, my Anna. Victor asked me what she would like. I said she likes dolls. That is why he brought her the big doll. She was so excited. So happy. Two brand-new big dolls on one birthday."

"What time were you at the playground?"

"About eleven."

"How do you know the time?"

"We always go at the same time every day. I get home from my class at ten o'clock. We have something to eat, and we go to the park. Just the two of us. Every day. Except Saturday and Sunday."

"And the sun was in your eyes for a moment and you couldn't see her. What did you do then? Put your hand up to shield your eyes from the sun or change your position so the sun wasn't in your eyes anymore?"

She hesitated only a second. "I moved over on my bench. And I put my hand up. I did both."

"Do you know who she was playing with in the sandbox?"

"She was by herself."

"The police wrote down that she was with another child."

"I...I...no...I don't think so."

"Where is Anna's father?"

"I don't know. He is in Russia."

"Are you sure?"

"But he wouldn't take her."

"Why not?"

"I never told him. He never knew that I was with child."

"Could he have found out?"

"How?"

"People you knew in common. Your friends in Russia."

"I have no friends in Russia."

I knew that Leo was checking that angle as well as the Russian mafia to see if there was a connection of any kind to Miriam. The police hadn't found anything yet, but I had to ask,

"Miriam, do you know anyone in the Russian mafia, either here, or in Russia?"

"Mah fee ya?"

That was a word she hadn't learned in her English class.

She's never heard of Estee Lauder either, Hester cracked.

What?

Well look at her! She's positively scaly!!

She's not scaly. Olive always objected to Hester's forays into hyperbole.

She will be if she doesn't moisturize, and soon.

You are, as usual, Hester, inappropriate.

Well, our face would look like hell if it weren't for me. There's lip gloss in your pocket, Isadora, why don't you put some on?

"Russian criminals," I said, rubbing my forehead hard. "They are organized and make money and do very bad things, including kidnapping."

"I don't know anyone like that. I don't know anyone…except Claudia and Vin. And the little boys."

"Do you have friends from school?"

"No. I go to my class and come right home to study and take care of the children."

"How about other nannies or mothers at the park. Are any of them your friends?"

She just shrugged and kept her eyes down. "Will you find my Anna?"

"I am trying. And the detectives are trying. Lieutenant Gianetti is very good at his job. If anyone can find her, he can."

"Thank you. Miss…"

"Just Shiloh."

I left the kitchen and made my way to the door, pausing to listen. The TV was still on. The soccer ball was quiet. Claudia and Vin were in the living room. Bungee barked and Claudia held on to his collar.

Roses are red, Violets are blue.

I ducked into Miriam's room and closed the door.

Why do they say violets are blue when violets are more of a light purple? Olive, the queen of verisimilitude, rode over the voices of Bethy-June and Sula.

"I don't know," I snapped. "It's a mystery of etymology or botany. When I have time, I'll look it up."

I moved the dolls over, sat on the window seat and looked out. Across the street was Riverside Park. Through the trees that were beginning to show their leaves, I glimpsed sparks of sun reflected off the metal swings and monkey bars. I checked the clock on Miriam's dresser. It was passing ten thirty.

Roses are red, Lavender's blue. If you will have me, I will have you.

"Can we not do old English poetry now? Thank you. I get it."

I remembered something from yesterday. Maybe I wasn't getting it. I jumped up and opened Miriam's closet and shoved hangers to the side till I found the purple overalls. Across the bib was embroidered in darker purple thread, a perfect violet. "Well, I'll be damned."

You need to pay closer attention, Isadora. Olive. I hate her when she gets all Mother Superior on me. Especially when she's right.

There was a rap at the door. "Come in."

Vin Parrish stuck his head in. "You all right? I heard some—"

"Tell me about Miriam."

He took a deep breath and said on the exhale, "She was starting to get happy. Then all this happened. I don't think she had what you'd call a wonderful life in Russia. We're all afraid she isn't going to survive this if they don't find Anna."

"Do you ever wear women's clothes?"

His nostrils flared slightly, and his face flushed in anger. "Do you?"

I didn't respond.

"Not unless I'm getting paid for it. I can be pretty convincing—especially if I shave before I put on my blush."

"So you have performed as a woman?"

"Well, I'm not a female impersonator. I've just donned the occasional caftan on stage as a goof."

"Do you own women's clothing?"

I saw him sag, sadness replacing anger. He knew why I was asking.

"No. I don't do my cabaret act anymore, and I didn't keep any of the costumes except some of my Elton John glasses. I used to do a wicked Elton."

The resemblance was there even though Elton John now had more hair and quite a few more pounds.

"Sorry I got hissy," he said.

He let me pass him going out. Claudia was sitting on the sofa. Miriam was in the chair across from her, still clutching her coffee cup. They weren't talking, but I sensed no awkwardness. Claudia was in a pair of blue slacks with a striped blue and white top.

Mary Mary quite contrary how does your garden grow?

I walked down the hall to Claudia's room. Vin didn't follow me. He just leaned against the balustrades and watched me. *With silver bells, and cockle shells, and pretty maids all in a row.*

I looked in Claudia's closet. She had clothes in black, white, gray, brown, greens and a variety of blues. There was nothing red, or pink or yellow…or purple.

I checked the clock on her nightstand. I had to go.

When I came out of Claudia's room, Vin was still leaning against the balustrade. "I have to run out and check something. Ask them not to go anywhere for a while."

Chapter 11

Behind their bars, the parents and nannies were nervous as chickens with a fox sniffing around the henhouse. By the time they were discreetly dialing their cell phones, I had seen what I'd come to see. I didn't blame them. I do look suspicious. Even when I'm not prowling around a playground. I decided to wait.

Can we go in and play on the jungle gym? Sula's shy little voice hurt. She was used to getting "no" for an answer, but none of us took any pleasure in it.

No, baby. We can't. We can do something else, later. I promise... Sugartime would have to think of something. I was out of ideas.

I really would like to play on the jungle gym, though.

In about four minutes a blue-and-white came cruising quietly, brushed on either side by the bushes that flanked the down-sloping lane, which was just wide enough to accommodate a four-wheel vehicle.

I don't know all the officers in the Upper West Side precincts, but I know quite a few. I knew this one. Her name is Nicole and she has more of the ingénue about her than Warrior Princess, but she's a very good cop. She grinned when she recognized me—a rosy, Irish girl grin that didn't go with the badge, gun and nightstick. "Hey, Shiloh, we got a call about a suspicious character. Guess that's you." Her voice was as sweet as her face.

"Guilty," I said.

She had put two and two together as soon as she saw me. "You assisting Gianetti on this one?"

"Not officially. I was hired by the mother of one of the kids. But if I come up with anything, Gianetti gets it. You responded to the calls when Anna Stern was taken?" I already knew she had.

"Uh-huh."

As with everyone else I had questioned so far, I knew what she had already told the police, but people remember different things at different tellings, and I was a different sort of listener. "Did anything strike you that day?"

"Well, everything struck me. It was impossible, for one thing." She gestured toward the high bars and sturdy chain-link fencing that enclosed the playground. "There are no gaps, no weak points. Anyone forcing his way through there would have needed wire cutters or a tank. He would have attracted attention. There's only one entrance." She pointed to it. "With a sign that clearly states no adults admitted unless accompanied by a child. And the parents here are pretty observant." She was thinking out loud more than talking to me.

I said, "Not everybody is a parent. There are a lot of hired nannies. I imagine some of them are less vigilant than a parent."

"Mm hm."

"What else?"

"It doesn't make sense. How did someone get out of here with a kid? It's not likely they drugged her and threw her over the fence, though we considered it. They'd probably have thrown her to land in the bushes over there. Might have been hurt, but probably not killed. And wouldn't somebody notice a kid being tossed?"

"Anna is a small child."

"Yes, very small for her age. Still."

"Can you swing me by the station? I want to talk to Leo."

"Aren't you afraid people will think we're arresting you?"

"Does it matter?"

"Guess not."

"Do you mind calling and seeing if he's there?"

Nicole dialed the station as we walked to the car. Leo was there and advised I was coming in.

To my chagrin, Hester climbed into the backseat. I had wanted Cootie. He was easier to get rid of.

"You're Nicole, aren't you?" Hester leaned forward, eager for a chat.

Quick glances were exchanged between Nicole and her partner in the front seat. Nicole's said, *I told you about this. Just keep driving.* Her partner's look had the words *freak show* in it somewhere. Nicole smiled over her shoulder and said, "Yeah. Who are you?"

"I'm Hester. I don't think we've met. And you are?" She flashed a smile at the male officer at the wheel.

"That's Officer Faylo," Nicole volunteered.

Hester purred, "Hello, Officer Faaay-loh."

"Hi, Hester," he said, keeping his eyes on the street ahead and stepping on the gas.

I should have taken the subway.

Chapter 12

Both officers looked immensely relieved as Officer Faylo stopped the car in front of the station house and let Hester out.

She made her entrance, murmuring, "I wish I weren't in this nasty black blazer. Why can't we wear the blue one sometimes? Black does nothing for my complexion. Why didn't you let me get my nails done?"

Come on Hester, we're working. I need to be out.

"Chill, Isadora. I just want to say hi. It won't kill you. Rudy! It's me, Hester. Long time no see!"

Rudy didn't approve of Hester. But he gave her a nod and dialed Gianetti's number and said pointedly, "It's *Hester.*"

"Go on up," he said around his wad of gum.

Hester sashayed up the stairs and through the clutter of desks and chairs, beaming at everyone. Fortunately, the place was pretty empty. The few officers in house that day didn't pay much attention to her, and she was soon flinging herself into a chair next to Leo's desk.

"Hi, Hester. How's it going?"

"My *God*, Leo, why don't you *paint* this place?!"

"I'm a little busy."

"Not you *personally. Have* someone do it. Get some convicts. Bring in a *contingent* of the *condemned* from Rikers to slap paint on all the stationhouse walls. This vile, dingy, *putrescent* green is so *offputting*. It needs a *makeover* like on TV."

"A trip to the police station isn't necessarily supposed to feel like a day at the spa. Let me talk to Isadora."

"Don't be rude. Leo, you've put on more weight. We've talked about that."

"Tina tells me the same thing."

"Are you sleeping, Leo? You're not sleeping. Am I right? Look at you. Your eyes would shame a raccoon. Do you want a heart attack, Leo? Is that what you want? Because you are on the heart-attack path. Living on heart-attack row. Am I right?"

For God's sake, Hester. Shut up! That was all of us.

He sighed. "I don't mean to cut you short, Hester, but I really need to speak to Isadora."

Hester turned out her lower lip in a pout.

Leo was not blessed with patience. "Hester, scram!" He waited a moment then asked me, "What's with her?"

"She's restless. I've been working a lot. She hasn't been out much." Hester is never out as much as she'd like. She just seemed to be getting her way more.

"So, what have you got?"

"I just came from the playground. You know Miriam's lying."

"I know, Shiloh. We have made some contacts in Russia to find out if there's a connection between the Berkowitz family and Miriam's family."

"Is there?"

"Nothing shows up, but a lot of paperwork over there seems to get lost. Is it a coincidence that Claudia Keating is of Russian descent and hires a Russian *au pair*? But Father O'Hagan actually brokered the deal through church contacts. Miriam is Catholic."

"Stern? That's a Jewish name, isn't it?"

"A couple of generations ago her family converted to avoid

a pogrom or something. She is a second-generation, bona fide, practicing Catholic as far as we can tell. So is Claudia. Not second generation, just practicing. The Berkowitzes were Jewish, and as Burkes they remained Jewish but not observant. When Claudia converted to marry Dan Keating, the Burkes apparently didn't bat a lash over it. There are a lot of coincidences here. We are checking on them all. We haven't found any connections."

More officers had come in and taken their places at their desks. The phones started ringing and two more uniformed cops, one of whom I recognized as Jimmy Stokes, brought in a small, angry woman in cuffs. She was struggling and spitting obscenities. He pushed her down into a chair but couldn't make her shut up. Jimmy had come to only one of the task-force training sessions with Ray and me. He was the only attendee Ray ever reprimanded during a session and he never came back. He was still a beat cop.

Jimmy Stokes was a big guy, and too much beer and too many fast-food burgers had blown him up even bigger. I know there are a lot of big guys who can aptly be described as gentle giants. Jimmy Stokes wasn't one of them. He was the giant at the top of the bean stalk that everyone fears. No doubt he was an asset with crazed drug addicts and scrappy drunks, but with everyone else, he was overkill.

Leo raised his voice so he could be heard over the increasing volume of noise in the room. "Oh, we checked bank accounts again. Didn't find any large deposits or withdrawals that couldn't be accounted for. We didn't find anything under Berkowitz. We're still checking. Feeney! Good. Let's find a room so we can hear ourselves think. Bring the file."

Feeney, Leo's new partner, approached, trim and sleek in a perfectly tailored gray suit and blue tie. He was young and offered me a smile that was a bit too hearty. I knew Leo had tried to prepare him for me, and he seemed hell-bent on taking me in stride. He gathered up a file and some loose papers from Leo's desk, and we all headed to the interrogation rooms. As we passed Officer Stokes I said, "Hi, Jimmy," and he nodded back.

I looked down into the face of the still protesting woman. Thin and unhealthy looking, she appeared to be older than her voice, her heavy makeup caked into the lines around her mouth and eyes didn't help. Her hair, yellow straw, was held up with a couple of rhinestone barrettes. With both hands she clutched a small, square, lime-green plastic purse in her lap. She ignored us as we passed, still arguing vigorously with Jimmy and his partner about the injustice of picking her up while walking. "Yeah, street walking," said Jimmy.

"Well, where else is a person supposed to walk?" Her speech was Staten Island, straight up. "I was going to the sto-ah. I decided to let my limousine driver sleep in. So I walked." I admired her insolence.

The interview room was lit by one grubby overhead bulb. There were bars on two high, grime-encrusted windows. As we pulled up chairs around a small table and sat down, I asked, "Why do you guys arrest prostitutes, Leo?"

He shrugged in resignation. "Yeah. It's a waste of time. Write your congressman." Feeney looked shocked. Leo ignored him. "So here are the possibilities as I see them." He pulled his notebook out and referred to it occasionally, although I felt that he had this whole case in its every detail burned into his brain.

"One. There is no connection between the kidnapping of Anna from the park and Charlotte from the apartment. One child is three years old, one is an infant. They are totally different targets. Infants are usually stolen by crazy people who want a baby for themselves, usually women with baby-hunger, you know, or by people who sell them. The no-connection theory has only one flaw: it defies credibility."

"I agree," I said. Feeney nodded his concurrence enthusiastically. We ignored him.

"Two. They are connected but only because the second kidnapper saw an opportunity. He, or she, could take an infant, say to sell the day after Anna's kidnapping, and, they hoped, would throw us off the track by making the two events seem related. That one is actually more plausible the more I think about it. It means we have two kidnappers who are not related, who operate in completely different circles for completely different motives. The connection is simply one of timing and opportunity on the part of the second kidnapper."

He glanced at me for a response. I had none, so he continued. "Three. They are related. The same person or persons took both children. But again, *motive*. With no ransom note, I'm stymied. Maybe there's a ransom note I don't know about, but I don't think so. I think I'd have sniffed it out by now. Or you would have. Did you?"

"No."

"Okay then. I have the task force working all the angles, but I don't see anything here that resembles anything I've ever seen before." He paused, his eyes on me. "So, what do you think? You have powers of perception that flatfoots like me and Feeney here don't have."

"Did anybody notice the garbage cans on the playground?" I asked the question of both Leo and Detective Feeney.

Feeney replied. "Yes. They're all over the park."

"And they're mostly all lined with black plastic bags." I waited for the sun to rise on the NYPD. It didn't. "That's how he got her out. He walked out with a full garbage bag slung over his shoulder and nobody noticed. Dressed like a park custodian. They wear sort of green work pants and shirts. They don't have the spit and polish of a police officer, or the muscle of the sanitation workers. Anybody can look like a park custodian. Anybody at all. You know they're mostly down-on-their-luck people getting back on their feet, people working for their welfare check, that sort of thing. They're ubiquitous. They are all over the parks. You see them, but you don't see them."

"Shit." Leo threw his notebook on the table. "That would be the only way."

Feeney asked, "But wouldn't someone have seen him, or her, putting a kid in a bag?"

"Not necessarily. The playground isn't busy that time of day. Most people are where the swings are. I was just there. You have that big Jungle Gym thing in the middle. On the other side of that, if you aren't paying close attention, and if no one was actually sitting over there...and it's possible they weren't, somebody could be working and no one would pay attention to what they were doing."

"So, why would Miriam lie... You said she lied... Are you

saying she was part of—"

"No, I'm not saying that."

"Feeney!" Leo snapped. "Get a couple of our people to go back and talk to everyone who was in that playground that day and ask them if they remember seeing any park workers or trucks or anything. Then call the parks department and find out who was working that day in that area. Maybe we are looking for a real employee of the parks department, not just somebody posing as one."

Feeney scribbled notes in his own notebook earnestly and said, "Right."

Leo looked at me. "What else?"

"There is something strange about this family. I know that the husband just died. Well, within the year. They are all still reeling. But there's something else. I feel it. Have you ever been somewhere unfamiliar and you heard a sound and you can't tell what it is or where it's coming from?"

Both officers just looked at me, Leo, with his world-weary frustration, and Feeney with a curiosity and puzzlement that was, at the moment, more about me than about the case. I said, "The file said that Claudia's mother was deceased."

He quickly flipped a couple pages over in the file and said, "Yes, she died in nineteen eighty. Heart failure."

"Every death is heart failure, Feeney." Leo's voice had the effect of a soft crack of a small whip.

The detective blanched. "We didn't...I didn't follow up on that. I'll..." He was pushing away from the table but I stopped him.

"Never mind, Detective. She was a suicide. Don't you find that interesting, Leo?"

Leo rubbed his hand over his face roughly. "How did you find that out?"

"I asked."

Leo was angry. I knew he was as angry with himself as he was with his junior detective, but Feeney didn't know that, and he looked worried.

"Have you ever seen Claudia cry?" I directed this question to Leo.

"No. People don't always show their emotions in front of the cops."

"How many mothers of missing children have you interviewed?"

"Too goddam many."

"How many of them never shed a tear in your presence?"

He threw his pen down on the table. "She's the only one." It rolled and was stopped by his notebook.

He's always throwing things. Why is that?

Feeney jumped on the idea. "Are you saying Mrs. Keating—?"

"I'm just saying that there is something special about her. I'm going back this afternoon to speak to her and Miriam alone. The rest of the family won't be there."

Leo reached for his notebook and pen and wrote something. He asked me, "Did you talk to the doormen?"

"Briefly. Arturo Cole admits that he might not have been there every minute between the time Claudia came in with the baby and the time she reported her missing. Victor wasn't on duty that day. That doesn't mean he wasn't there, in or around the building somewhere."

Feeney referred to the file again. "So, let's say the off-duty doorman is lying. Victor Pasqual. He's married to his high school sweetheart. They live on the main floor of a house in Woodside. His mother lives in the basement apartment and they rent the upstairs to an elderly couple, no relation. He has a five-year-old son. His wife works three days a week at a beauty parlor in their neighborhood. She leaves the son with the grandmother. They go to church every Sunday. He doesn't gamble or have any expensive hobbies. He goes bowling every other Thursday night with some buddies. They've been doing that since high school. The man is stable."

"Salt of the earth we walk upon," added Leo, with grim sarcasm. "Doesn't mean he isn't also schtupping the doctor's wife up in Five-B on his lunch hour."

"I'm just saying—"

I interrupted them. "If the baby didn't go out the front door that day, maybe it was just taken to another apartment in the building and brought out later."

"We've interviewed everyone in the building and we searched every apartment several times. We had a team of officers do that the same night. We sealed the building till it was done and came up with nothing but a lot of folks embarrassed over their housekeeping, a lady with too many cats and a couple with four dogs—their lease only allows two. They are all bassets. Nobody knows they have four. They just think the same two dogs get a lot of walks. But basically nobody copped an attitude. Everybody was happy to help when they realized two children were missing. I did suggest to the cat lady that as the cats start dying of old age, she not replace them."

"How many did she have?"

"Seven. But they all looked healthy so I'm not calling animal control. A lot of older people who have lived there for years and years are more frightened than anything else. They remember when their kids were young and played outside in the street and in the halls. Those days are over. There's one old lady rents a room to a Columbia student. We checked them both out. The old lady can hardly get around anymore and the student is pre-law, from Wisconsin. She is seldom there and when she is, she has her nose deep in a book. Not much of a social life on or off campus. Couples, families, roommate situations. And everyone with children of their own are scared pissless. I don't blame them. Oh, and we found one place with handcuffs still attached to the bed."

Feeney grinned and blushed like a kid who had just stumbled across his first stash of condoms.

"We determined it was consensual shenanigans between the gal and her boyfriend. We also checked financial records to see who's in debt. They all are, except the lady with the cats, Claudia Keating and Victor Pasqual. Being in debt to your eyeballs is no longer a suspicious circumstance. It is the American way of life, or at least, a New Yorker's way of life. Pasqual and the cat lady, therefore, seemed suspicious for their solvency."

"Anybody have medical expenses, someone in a hospital bed, or a relative in a care facility?"

"Not that we discovered. We did check that, though." Feeney seemed anxious to prove they hadn't overlooked anything else obvious, like the cause of Claudia's mother's death.

Feeney went on. "We're still looking at the doormen, even the ones who weren't on duty that day. All the doormen have access to keys and are familiar with the building—the back stairways, the utility rooms and laundry rooms, that sort of thing. Any one of them could have hidden somewhere and probably gotten out without being seen. Someone, even the janitor, could have gone up to the apartment while Claudia was out. Hid there, or in a utility room on the floor or any other floor, waited for her to come home, snuck in, took the baby, and then hid out again in some room somewhere till the next doorman came on shift. A baby that small could be carried in a tote or something. New Yorkers are always loaded down with bags and backpacks—it's a security nightmare."

"Isadora, you want coffee? I need some coffee." Leo rarely called me Isadora. I nodded. I'd been warned about the station house brew, but I needed some.

Feeney offered, "I'll get it. How do you take it?"

"Light. No sugar."

Feeney left.

"You're very hard on him, Leo. He doesn't seem so bad."

"I never wanted him on the task force, let alone as my partner. But his old man has political connections so I couldn't say no. He came in cocked like a cheap pistol—and as full of himself as a bag of shit."

"More than you were when you started?"

He grinned at me, then he conceded, "He might make a good cop if I ride his ass hard enough."

I was certain that if ass-riding were a way to make a good cop, Feeney would end up the best.

Leo got serious. "Tell me why you said we shouldn't look for Charlotte." He had wanted Feeney out of the room for this.

"I have a feeling. That's all."

"Do you think she's still in the building?"

"No, not really. I just wanted to be sure you had covered that possibility."

"We did. I can't officially close the file on her without something more than your feeling. You know the statistics and so does everyone else. It's a cold trail. After this many days…"

Feeney returned with a mug of black coffee for Leo, light for me and a mug of tea for himself. We dropped my unhelpful intuition for the moment and let the junior detective launch his own theory. "This has been gone over before…What if the nanny's child isn't really missing?" Feeney eagerly proffered his own theory. "What if she's faking the whole thing? Let's say she sold the baby—she'll pick up her own kid, collect her money and join her boyfriend Pavel in Palm Springs."

"It's possible," Leo offered. "Find me Pavel."

"Leo, let's go back to the no-connection theory," I said. "Anna has no family but an immigrant mother. She's a perfect victim. Blond hair. Blue eyes. Pretty. The kidnapper thinks her case will not be pursued. It will in time just go away. From the first kidnapper's point of view, it might be just bad luck that the Keating baby was taken. Because now there *is* a connection. Now a child has been taken from a prominent family who have the resources, and now it won't go away."

"We investigate a missing child no matter who the parents are." Leo bristled a little.

"I know that, Leo, but I'm just saying that from a kidnapper's point of view—"

Feeney jumped in, "And, from the second kidnapper's point of view, it is just good luck Anna was taken because now the real motive for taking Charlotte is less clear."

"I don't think so," I said.

"You don't think what, that the second—"

Leo and I were running around a cul de sac.

"Out of the box, Leo! Out of the box! You are following leads in a specified order. Things aren't connected like this."

"Hey, Hester." Leo grinned in spite of himself. "Breathe, Feeney."

"Training a new puppy, Leo?"

Feeney blushed pink.

"And a cute little puppy he is, too. If you ever slip your collar, let's go for a walk sometime."

He was now purple.

"Feeney's married, Hester."

"Puppy lost his tongue?"

"I better go check on that...that thing." Feeney rose and left the room with even more speed than when he went to get us coffee.

"You nearly made puppy wet his papers, Hester. We're following all the angles. What have we missed?"

"Well, obviously, you missed something since you have nothing. Am I right?"

"I assume that you are...there...when Isadora does her interviews. Did you think anyone you talked to was lying?"

"No. But, that only means we've been asking the wrong questions."

"Give me some new questions then."

Hester thought for a minute. I hoped she might relax and I could slip back, but she didn't. Her thought patterns were hard and strong.

Just as she opened her mouth to speak, Feeney stuck his head in. "Lieutenant, they've found the body of a little girl."

"Where?"

"Central Park."

"Forensics there?"

"On their way."

"Okay. Shiloh, we'll have to continue this later."

Hester let me have the floor. "Leo, can you keep this out of the news for awhile? Let me talk to Miriam first. They shouldn't hear about this on TV before they hear it from you or me. Not even a report about an unidentified child."

"I'll do my best. But somebody probably already has it. You better get up there."

The junior detective scrambled madly to gather up the files and throw back his tea.

"Feeney, you don't have to bust a gasket. We can't do anything till forensics is done with the scene."

Jimmy Stokes was alone now with the straw-haired woman. His partner was nowhere in sight. As we crossed the room to the stairwell, she stood up and, Jimmy yelled, "I said *sit down!*" and shoved her back into her chair. She landed hard enough to snap her head back and force her to grab the side of the desk as her chair started tipping backward.

Oh no, I thought as I felt myself overpowered by Hawk, who came out and took a step sideways, placing her hand on the back of the woman's chair to stop it from going over. "You didn't have to be so rough."

All heads in the room looked up, and Jimmy, alone and on the spot, said, "She was told to sit down. You're interfering with..." he stared into Hawk's black eyes and didn't finish his sentence, but he was spoiling for a fight. With someone.

Hawk smiled. "Oooohh, Jimmy, take me on." It is never a good thing, Hawk smiling. Hers is the smile of a famished wolf gazing at a wounded deer. There is no malice in it, just pleasure at an opportunity.

The room was silent, then Leo said in a low voice, "Jimmy."

Jimmy stood fixed in Hawk's gaze and couldn't or wouldn't back down.

"Jimmy," Leo said, not louder, but with more intensity. "Stop messing around. Book her or let her go."

The tension ebbed slightly. "This is my collar!" Stokes spat in defiance.

Is she the mother? Is she the mother?

The mother is gone. She won't come back. Hush, baby.

The glass door to the captain's office opened and Captain Calafano, small in stature, thin and straight as a nail, strolled over to where Hawk stood facing Officer Stokes. "Is there a problem?"

"Nope," said Leo. "There a problem, Jimmy?"

"No sir. Just finishing the paperwork and then she can go." He sat.

I came back, feeling a little dizzy. I focused on the woman. "You all right?"

"Sure." Hearing that she was being let go, she took the wise course of saying no more.

When I looked back at Officer Stokes, he was an odd shade of pale and Leo, grinning, kicked the leg of his chair, "Breathe, Jimmy. Just breathe. We gotta go."

I turned to Captain Calafano. "Hello, Captain."

"Shiloh. Hear you're helping out on the Keating case."

"If I can," I said.

He nodded, turned, and strolled back to his office.

As we walked away, I heard Jimmy Stokes mutter, "Freak bitch."

Outside, Feeney headed around back to the parking lot, and Leo put his hands in his pockets. "Helping fallen women, now, Shiloh?"

"I doubt she fell. She was probably pushed. A long time ago."

Leo snorted his agreement. "Who was that?"

"Hawk."

"I thought it might be."

"Call me at Keating's," I said. "Leo."

"Yeah."

"Jimmy Stokes is a lawsuit waiting to happen."

"I know. The captain knows it. He's watching him." Feeney backed out of the lot and stopped to let Leo get in the front seat. Leo slammed the door, and the car squealed off.

The straw-haired woman stepped out of the station and blinked in the bright sun. When she saw me, she approached me, a little shyly. "Thanks," she said. "I just wanted to go for a pee. I been sitting there and told him I said nice, 'look, I have to go to the little girls' room.' He was being an asshole." She started to cry. Her cheap mascara formed muddy rivulets down her face.

Give her some money.

While Olive was raising her usual objections to Hester's compulsive philanthropy, I reached into my jacket pocket. I took three twenties and two tens out of my wallet and handed them to the woman, feeling light-headed and strange. Not sure if it was me or Hester speaking, "Look, I don't know how much you make, but—give yourself the night off."

She took the money quickly, slipped it into her purse and snapped it shut. "I have a place. I'm not homeless."

"I didn't mean to imply that you were. Just get some rest."

She cried harder. "Are you a cop?"

"No."

"I can't pay this back." She sniffed and wiped her eyes and smeared the mascara across her cheek, which was sunken in one place. One or two back teeth missing. I wondered how this wreck of a woman earned any money at all.

"Who would you pay it back to? You don't know me."

She nodded and turned and walked away from me, her ankles wobbling on spindly high heels, as fast as her precarious balance would allow, as if she were afraid I'd change my mind and want the money back.

Is she the mother? Why did we give her money? Isn't she the mother?

Isadora just wanted to help her. She is not the mother.

I headed in the opposite direction hoping that the first thing the woman did was buy herself a good meal, which reminded me that I was hungry. There was no time to eat.

On the way to the subway, I stopped to use a public telephone. I needed to talk to Ray, tell her about Hawk, but there was no time for that either. This was more important. I found Vin's card in the pocket of my jacket and dialed his number.

"Vin, are you at the Keatings? Do you have the televisions on?"

"Nope. Should we?"

"No. Don't turn them on. Is Miriam there?"

"Yep. What's going on?"

"I'll be there in a few minutes. I need to talk to her. Nothing's going on, but...just keep the televisions off till after I get there."

Chapter 13

Victor greeted me at the door with a two-finger salute to his cap. "Go on up. They're waiting for you."

A warm wind drifted in behind me as I made for the stairwell. I couldn't risk somebody coming out in the elevator and not leaving. I had no time for Hester's act or Cootie's attitude.

I sprinted up the stairs. On the tenth floor landing I paused a moment to let my breathing slow to normal and went to 10C.

Vin answered my light knock. Fear of the news I might be carrying lay silently in his eyes as he welcomed me with Southern friendliness, "Come on in. You want a glass of something?" I heard a couple staccato barks from behind the closed door of the family room.

"Miriam?"

He made a large, open-handed gesture toward the living room below, where Miriam sat, hunched, on the sofa.

I took the big chair across from her, the one occupied by Michael Keating during my first visit. I could see why people gravitated to this area of the living room. Green plants overflowed the well beneath the windows whose sheer curtains softened the sunlight that poured into the room.

Ray tells me I am too abrupt. I tried to soften what was to come by saying, "Hello, Miriam. I just have a few more questions, if you don't mind."

She shook her head, not meeting my eyes. She was in a plain white blouse and black capris, with only white socks on her feet. Her hair was in its limp ponytail, her skin still mottled with grief and fatigue.

"What classes are you taking?"

Once again, I surprised her by my question. She answered readily. "English. American history. And American literature."

"Three classes. That's a lot of work."

She nodded, rather innocently. Now she was looking right at me.

"Are your grades good?"

"Yes. They are very good."

I heard a rise of children's voices from the family room and some quick yelps from Bungee.

"You have a scholarship, don't you?"

"Yes."

"So you have to keep your grades very high to keep it."

"Yes, but I get As. Only As." She was earnest in telling me this. Her visa might depend as much on her keeping her scholarship as on her job with the Keatings.

"Do you stay up late to study?"

"No...not always. Anna goes to bed early, and the boys are in bed by nine o'clock, usually."

"Were you up late the night before Anna was taken?"

Her eyes widened. She said yes.

"Did you have an exam or a paper due that morning?"

"A paper, for my American literature class." Her voice got smaller.

"What was the paper on?"

"A book. *Moby Dick*."

"That is a difficult book. Even for someone who is not studying English at the same time. You must have worked very hard on it."

"Vin helped me. He explains many things to me."

"How long did you work on that paper?"

"Many weeks."

Ray says my habit of absolute stillness drives people nuts, so I shifted my weight in the chair and leaned forward. "Miriam, I went to the playground this morning. I saw the bench where you sat. At the time of the day that you were there, the sun doesn't hit that bench. Not directly. The sun couldn't have been in your eyes."

Miriam's face crumpled and she cried, silently, holding the sides of her head in her hands.

"You weren't watching your daughter."

She just shook her head, her face a rictus of grief.

"You were exhausted. You fell asleep. And you don't know for how long."

Her wail brought Claudia running out of the family room. I heard her tell the boys to stay put. Bungee yipped at her heels. Vin charged out of the kitchen. All three of them eyed me accusingly. Claudia sat beside Miriam and put an arm around her shoulders. The Company was silent, but I felt them all there, like an audience at a Greek tragedy on the edge of their stone seats.

When Miriam had quieted a little I continued. "There aren't many people in the park at that time of the day. You didn't make friends with other nannies or mothers because you used that time to study. While Anna played, you sometimes read, didn't you? And sometimes, you dozed off. This day, you were exhausted and you did more than doze. You fell asleep. The other people who were there were only watching their own kids."

Claudia gazed at her with maternal compassion. So did Vin. Miriam sat with lowered head. Vin pulled a wad of tissues from the box on the side table and handed it to her. She sobbed quietly into it.

The family room door banged open, Bungee barked afresh, and Joey hurtled himself down the stairs. "Mom. They found a dead kid in the park! I just heard it on TV. They found a dead kid!"

Danny was right behind him. "You stupid moron! I said shut up!"

Miriam started screaming. Claudia and Vin both tried to put their arms around her.

Danny kept shouting, "You moron! See what you did? I told you to shut up."

"Well they did! Find a dead kid. They did!" Joey yelled back and then started to bawl.

Claudia spoke a sharp word to Bungee and he stopped barking. Vin left Miriam to pick up Joey. "That's enough, boys. All right, buddy, it's all right. Nobody likes the messenger, that's all. Not your fault." Joey sniffled into Vin's black T-shirt and Danny flopped into a chair.

I caught Vin's eye. He said, "All the sets were off. I checked. I didn't hear the TV come on."

Neither had I. We had been absorbed in Miriam's crying.

The phone rang and Vin carried Joey to the phone set on the end table. "Keating residence. Yep." He handed the receiver to me.

"Leo?"

"It's not her," was all he said.

"Thanks." I hung up. "It's not Anna. That was Lieutenant Gianetti. He is there in the park and the child they found is not your daughter. I'm sorry. I got here as soon as I could. I didn't want you to hear the news till after we knew if the child they found was Anna or not."

Claudia acknowledged me with some gratitude and helped Miriam to stand. Together they went upstairs to the nanny's room. Vin, still carrying Joey, motioned Danny out of his chair to follow him. "I'll fix us all strawberry malts in a minute. And we'll watch the new video I just rented for y'all."

"What video?" Joey sniffled.

"Something about a basketball team. And Olympics and stuff. You little jocks'll just *luuuv* it. Now let me talk to Ms. Shiloh for a minute and then I'll be up. Now scoot."

He put Joey down and the boy followed his older brother back up to the family room. I heard Danny say, "Moron" and Vin heard it too. He said, "Daniel, knock it off."

He turned to me, "Well, that was a heap a fun. When I looked in on 'em they were playing a video game. I thought we were safe. It's not Anna. But it's somebody's little girl. I need a smoke." He sighed. "So how did you know Miriam fell asleep?"

"I knew she was lying, and that was the only logical explanation. I didn't believe she had anything to do with kidnappings. When I saw the park, I was sure. I think she was lying to herself as much as anything."

"So you know how they got Anna out of the playground?"

"We think it was a park worker or somebody dressed like one. They probably took her out in a garbage bag."

He shivered in revulsion at the idea of putting a child into a garbage bag. "How did they get her in the bag? Wouldn't she—"

"It wouldn't take much to put a little chloroform over her face and tuck her in the bag. It could be done in seconds."

"I better get at those strawberry malts before the howlin' starts again. What now?"

"I'm going to talk to the Burkes again."

"Good luck with that," he said.

I could still hear Miriam weeping in her bedroom, but it was no longer a gut-wrenching wail. Claudia was speaking in soothing tones. I went up the stairs and looked into the room. "Mrs. Keating. I need to ask you one more question."

"Yes?"

"Alone."

She patted Miriam on the shoulder and came to the door. We hovered in the hall a moment, and then I escorted her and Bungee down to her own bedroom. "Sit down. Please."

She sat on the edge of her bed. I stood by the dresser. Bungee sat, leaning against her leg, his ears pricked, every muscle ready to spring into action at the next sign of crisis. I picked up Claudia's wedding picture. She and Dan looked so young. Happy babes in the woods. I placed the picture back carefully. When I spoke to her I felt there was someone else present. A third person. Maybe it was Dan. Especially here in their bedroom. I didn't believe in ghosts. But, her feelings, her memories were so strong, he would be present in her mind so distinctly, that I would be able to feel it.

"Claudia." I hadn't called her by her first name before. "I

have to ask you this. I will know if you tell me anything but the truth. You understand?"

"Vin and I talked about that. He says you are like a radio receiver. You pick everything up. That's how you knew about Miriam, isn't it? That she never had sun in her eyes. I understand. What's your question?" The priest O'Hagan was right. And Vin was right. She was tough. She was fragile. Like porcelain.

"Did your uncle or your father ever molest you?"

She flashed me a bright hot look, like a mirror catching the sun. If I hadn't been watching her closely I'd have missed it. She didn't hesitate. "Neither one of them ever put a hand on me."

She met my scrutiny and I knew she wasn't lying. It would have explained so much about this family.

"Is that all?" she asked. Her voice had remained thin, as I'd always heard it, throughout our short conversations, but this question took me off guard. Her meaning wasn't clear. The Company was present. We would all mull over today's events separately and together and something would come of it later.

"I'm not giving up. Is that what you want to know?"

All she did was blink, as if we had established a code. One blink for yes. Two blinks for no. She gave me one blink. "I'm not giving up," I repeated and left her sitting there stroking the Jack Russell who had jumped up on the bed beside her.

I passed Miriam's room. She was quiet, lying on her side. I suspected that Claudia had this time given her one of the real sleeping pills. I heard movie music coming from the family room and the blender churning in the kitchen. I let myself out.

She's not lying, said Hester as I pushed the button for the elevator.

The doors opened, and Olive stepped through. "She's not telling the truth either."

Chapter 14

Cabs are just small dark spaces on wheels, and elevators, small spaces on cables—worse. But subway cars and buses are different. For one thing, they usually contain more people. Safety in numbers. More importantly, they are bigger. Size matters.

So I went back down into the subway and took the express. I stepped into the first car. The only passengers were five young men in taxicab-yellow T-shirts emblazoned with black letters proclaiming them *Jews for Jesus*. Each had a canvas shoulder bag full of taxicab-yellow pamphlets. As I passed by them to get to the rear of the car, one of them offered me a brochure. I declined. The Jewish purveyor of Christ just smiled and tucked the pamphlet back in his bag. They were a happy bunch, full of high purpose, camaraderie and relentless certitude.

At Times Square I had to change trains, which meant walking through the underground station. This doesn't prompt a shift because it's fairly wide open and brightly lit, but beneath Times Square it is hard for me to think in the din of a constantly moving human population, machinery, trains passing through from all directions, and commerce; for here are sellers of wares and gizmos that move and sparkle for late commuters realizing at the last moment they've forgotten a birthday or anniversary, and here they'll find a serious gift for a child or an amusing token for an adult. Here are shoe shiners, peddlers, tiny places to leave a silent watch and pick it up on your next pass through, ticking, and people asking for money—they're not supposed to. There's a law against panhandling in the subways. People give them money anyway—they're not supposed to, but they do. Get your shoes shined, your watches repaired and find entertainment. Usually it's a band or single musician with a violin, a guitar or battered marimba. Often it's an Ecuadorian combo with flutes, little drums, and yes, gourds. Today the crowd was watching a contortionist perform on a grubby plastic sheet spread over the cement floor. Rap music brayed from a boom box. He wore a skin tight, silver-and-black leotard that covered him like paint from neck to wrists to ankles. A skintight hood, like a diver's wet suit, blackened his head and neck. His white mask, its features merely sketched, suggested an Asian face. I thought Kabuki without really knowing why, since I don't think I've ever seen anything Kabuki. A couple people tossed coins onto the plastic sheet. His continuous movement was crab-like, spider-like, comprised of slow acrobatics and yoga postures. While his flexibility, strength and skill were impressive, his performance as a whole was disturbing. Nor were his movements in sync with any rhythm generated from the boom box.

Skirting the crowd, I made my way to the stairs leading down to the R train. The platform was nearly empty. The relative quiet enabled me to try to make sense of the little scene Claudia had played with me in the bedroom. So brief. So straightforward. She hadn't been offended by my question. Her answer was definite, without hesitation. What was wrong? I heard a small *creech creech* from below and saw a rat scuttle across the track and disappear into darkness on the other side. The animal was about a foot long, not counting the tail, and the same color as greasy cement.

I felt Olive shudder. *Why can't they get rid of those things?*
Poor thing, said Hester.
It needs a bullet in its brain.

You have no compassion. They can't help it if they live in filth and squalor. Who created filth and squalor? Not them. Am I right?

I'm in no mood for your bleeding heart. Rats! Snakes. That creepy spider person. Good God what next? Please don't say a giant cockroach. I want off this case, Isadora. Right now. We're headed for trouble. I feel it. This rat. That snake. They can't be good omens.

Very Kafka.

Lance?

I'm afraid I agree with Olive, Isadora.

Lance rarely participated in Company discussions, or arguments. *I think we should give the money back—*

Not all of it! We did put in two days!

All right. Give some of the money back and move on before something really bad happens.

"Something bad has already happened. Two kids are missing."

Before something bad happens to us, Hester wailed.

"That's already happened, too. I'm not quitting. End of this discussion."

Saved by the train. I boarded hoping that tomorrow morning I wouldn't find a painting of rats and spiders.

Ray had taught me, when things got too complicated inside my head, to concentrate on the outside. I sat down and observed my fellow midday travelers.

New Yorkers are readers. In any subway car, on any bus, you will find bestsellers and classics, and all the major genres including sci fi, romance, mystery and magazines ranging from the *New Yorker* to *People*. The riders who aren't reading usually have their eyes closed. I can't do either. I stay alert.

At Thirty-fourth Street, a heavyset African-American woman with no neck got on, squeezing in with a knot of people all trying to push into the car before the door closed. She was puffing like she had had to run to catch the train. "I feel like I been power bombed by Battista!" She panted to all those around her, "I'm so sorry. So very sorry," apologizing for squeezing her ample person into the crowd. "Yes, yes," she answered some query in her head. "Yes, yes, yes," she repeated. No one paid her any attention.

At Twenty-eighth Street, the doors opened and YesYes woman got off and three men got on and immediately began to sing gospel in perfect three-part harmony, *This little light of mine, I'm gonna let it shine* with a heavy beat, provided by one of them pounding the floor with his cane.

Well, the Jews and the Blacks are all coming out for Jesus.

Olive!

What?

I got out at Twenty-third Street, tuning out Hester and Olive's argument over political correctness and rat rights.

The Gift Building was full of showrooms displaying samples of high-end tsotchkes where buyers from department stores and mom-and-pop shops all over the country came to place orders for this year's fashion themes and colors as well as the centuries-old classics. There were no cheap souvenirs here. They were in the building across the street. Here were Waterford, Lennox and Lladró—all the best brands of things imported and domestic that no one needed but, if you had the money, you wanted.

The lobby was spacious, like a courtyard for the showrooms on the main floor, whose windows looked out to the street, and whose inside walls and double doors were glass, the better to display their wares to all who passed by or through the building.

I had no buyer's, vendor's or police badge. I had to trust the Burkes' promise to help in the investigation and that they would let me upstairs. The woman at the desk eyed me sharply. The likes of me didn't usually seek entrance to the holy halls of high-end wholesale. In her navy blue blazer and starched white blouse, her minimalist black ribbon tie, she might have been a prison matron. I stated my request and without taking her eyes off me, she picked up the phone, dialed a number. "This is the registration desk. A…" She looked at me again. I gave my name. "…Ms. Shiloh," she said into the receiver, "is here to see Mr. Burke." Spencer or Manfred? she asked me. I said either one, which she repeated into the receiver. After a moment, she said, "Thank you," and hung up. Without another look in my direction, she typed into a small machine that thrust out a label like a rude tongue. She tore it off and handed it to me. It said in big red letters: **Visitor** and today's date. I pulled off the waxed paper backing and stuck the label on my jacket. "Excuse me, what room are they in?"

She scrolled down her computer screen. "Fifth floor. Room five twenty-four. Elevators in the back."

"Thanks," I said.

She never cracked a smile. She didn't like anybody who wasn't here to spend money. Or maybe she didn't like anybody.

She thinks the same thing about you, kiddo, said Olive.

I know.

As we passed the windows of the main floor showrooms, Hester slipped into her acquisitive mode, greedy for everything she saw. A quivering mass of I WANT.

Olive, on the other hand, while a connoisseur of art, did not much care for *stuff,* even expensive stuff. *Probably made by slave labor in some third-world country to provide doodads for the maids of people with too much money to dust.*

"Thank you for your politically correct insights. Now pipe down."

Another matron in a matching blazer, blouse and bow tie, supervised the bank of elevators, making sure that nobody got on without a badge. She smiled at mine, revealing a mouth full of braces. I didn't come to again till I was walking down the halls of the fifth floor. Who had ridden the elevator? Silence from the Company. They were playing games now. Contract negotiations were in order. It had probably been Cootie, but how he had blocked me out completely, I didn't know. He was annoying and often whiney, but he was no saboteur. Hester? No answer. I felt a little nauseous and walked the halls looking for 524.

I was walking through what seemed like a warren of showrooms, some spacious, and some just overstuffed closets, but all spilling over with samples. Glass windows, glass shelves, glass everywhere. Shiny tiled floors.

Fashion, form, precious little function. Unlike Olive, I didn't think it was all bad. An object was endowed, first by the giver and then by the receiver, with meaning. On a night table, one of these things would be dusted with care by someone remembering the giver or the occasion, or the vacation where she found it in that quaint little cottage store by the sea where it smelled of fish and wild roses, and she would remember the morning she ate fruit and pancakes and watched seagulls glide over the kelp beds. I had a dust catcher that reminded me of Ray and Maria and my first Christmas out of the asylum. I spent Christmas Eve in their home. The gift they gave me was the first I ever got and one of the first things I could say I ever owned. A carousel horse, rich in detail, colorful, and very well made, surprisingly heavy for its size. It doesn't do anything, but I very much like looking at it and holding it. I even enjoy dusting it.

Chapter 15

The tableware, barware and textiles of the Manfred line were displayed festively on shelves and at set tables, with dishes and drinkware in everything from china and crystal to plastic and paper. Elegance to whimsy—Manfred was your man for formal dining, picnics, or pool and patio parties. The Burkes' showroom was filled with light and every halogen was focused on a shelf or a table as if each were a ministage. Spencer was at a small desk at the rear of the showroom, a phone tucked between his shoulder and his ear, talking and scribbling on a yellow pad. He smiled at me and gave me a short wave. He was wearing, if not the same blue suit I had first seen him in, one just like it. I imagined his closet full of blue suits, white shirts and black bow ties. The official uniform of the bean counter.

A twenty-something woman rose to meet me from behind a desk just inside the door. Her blond hair glistened under the lights, her toothsome, showgirl smile—practiced but genuine enough—remained, even as the welcome drained from her eyes when they met mine.

"Hi," she said, smiling. She would give Hester a run for her money. "You must be Ms. Shiloh."

"Just Shiloh."

"I'm Kim. Spencer is on the phone with our showroom in LA. He might be awhile, but he said to make you comfortable. Can I get you some coffee or tea or a soda?"

Her long nails were painted to match her lipstick, which matched the pink flowers splashed across her silk blouse. Her high heels were the same beige as her suit. Her makeup was heavy but expertly applied. She went with the décor. Mixed in with the merchandise were flowers. Cut flowers on the tables, flowering plants in large ornate pots strategically placed to complement color schemes while not getting in the way of a display.

I declined her offer of refreshment, though I could hear Cootie whining faintly for a Coke. "Can I ask you some questions?"

Her smile flickered, but she rallied. "Sure." She returned to her chair behind the desk and offered me a chair next to it. I declined that as well. "Do you like your job? He can't hear us and I'm standing in front of you, so he can't see what you're saying even if he's a lip reader, which I suspect he's not."

She had to rally again, but she managed. "I do like my job. I mean it's better here than in a gray office cubicle all day. I don't think I could do that."

"Do you like working for the Burkes?"

"Sure."

"Why?"

"They're nice. Interesting. I get to meet people from all over the country. All over the world sometimes. It's fun. Hectic during shows, but I don't mind."

"How many computers in the showroom?"

"Mine." She indicated the machine that occupied the corner of her desk. "And the one in the office back there. Spencer uses that one. The police took them both, you know."

I did know.

"For two days," she added.

I knew that too. They had found nothing even remotely unsavory. The few passwords required for some business and shopping sites, Spencer had given up freely. There seemed to be no attempt to hide anything or make anything inaccessible to the wrong people, and nothing of any consequence had been erased. All financial and sales data was stored on a large computer in the main business office in New Jersey. The police had printed out lists of the toys, clothes and books he had ordered, all of which Cootie had seen in the file. Spencer was fond of books about business, conservative politics and spy novels. Some of the toys I had seen in the bedroom of the Keating boys.

"It sure makes you stop and think—how much we depend on computers, doesn't it, when they're gone? The police had them for only a couple days and we could hardly do anything here."

"Does Manfred use them?" The only prints found on either computer belonged to Spencer, Kim and the cleaning lady, who came in after hours. They had interviewed her and come up with nothing except pleas not to tell the Burkes that she was Web surfing on their time.

Kim laughed. "He won't touch a computer. Not even a calculator. It's a point of pride with him. Never touched a computer and never will. The police looked at everything. They took all our cell phones, too, and I think they got calling records for all our phones. It's a good thing I only ever call my mother and my boyfriend." She laughed again, nervously this time.

I knew that the police had searched and didn't find any hidden phones or laptops. They found nothing at all. That did not mean there was nothing to find. In the same way I needed to see the playground for myself and ask the questions myself, I needed to see, at least, Spencer's computer. "I'll just be back there for awhile," I said.

"Okay, let me know if you need anything." The phone rang before she could make any further offers and she picked it up. "Manfred Designs. Kim speaking."

The office in the back of the showroom was not much more than a walk-in closet. The large window overlooking Madison Park made it bearable. Against one wall, a counter placed over two short filing cabinets served as the desk for the computer, a phone, a Rolodex, and some papers, pens and order forms. On the opposite wall, on a built-in shelf, rested a small fax machine and a printer. Between them were two office chairs. I rolled one directly in front of the monitor and sat down.

The computer was on to its screensaver, Manfred's ornate signature—the company logo. I checked the Burkes' e-mails first, knowing they had been scoured thoroughly. Nothing of interest had been found there. I didn't find anything either. I opened the Web browser and the list of Favorites. Spencer had bookmarked news sites and the online versions of trade publications, national directories of stores and buyers, again everything aboveboard just as documented in the police file. Still, I opened each one and printed out the home pages to study later. Among them I found a flower and garden site. Someone was apparently fond of flowers. I suspected Manfred. But he didn't touch the computer so why would he have an online flower site? And it was Spencer who had given Anna the playsuit with the embroidered violet.

"Kim? Whose idea is it to have the flower pots?"

She rolled her chair back so she had a sight line into the office. "Spencer. Flowers are kind of a hobby with him. Manfred approves as long as they don't clash with his colorways."

"Wouldn't think Spencer has time to take care of them."

"He doesn't. We have a plant service come in twice a week. They're pretty, aren't they?"

I started entering all the letters of the alphabet in the search box. Every site starting with the letter entered that had been accessed appeared in a drop-down box. They were mostly the same sites I had already opened from the bookmarked list. Other sites had to do with his travel—hotels, information and maps of the cities and vacation spots. I printed them all out. Spencer continued his phone conversation.

"Kim?"

She rolled her chair back again and smiled.

"Do you make their travel arrangements?"

"Only for Manfred. Spencer makes his own."

"Do you use the same travel sites that Spencer uses?"

"Yes. We have a travel agent that gives us special rates."

"Camden Travel?"

"That's them."

"Thanks."

I took the papers from the printer and as I folded them to stuff them into my pockets, Manfred walked through the door. The showroom lights spiked off his glasses and his face was lost for a moment in a mask of light. He was dapper in sage-colored trousers, matching shirt and tweedy jacket. Today, he wore a tie in a muted green. With one more step into the room the light was not directly on his face and I could see his skeletal features grinning down upon her. "So, Beauty, are you ready for your spanking?"

"Manfred, you are sooo bad!" Kim twittered.

"Ehhh," he sighed. "And you, Beauty, are so very good. Any messages?"

She handed him three pink message slips. He caught sight of me and scowled. "What is *she* doing here? She will scare away our customers."

"Spencer said…"

"All right, all right." He dismissed her explanation with an irritated wave of his hand and positioned himself in the doorway to the office. "I must return my calls. You tell me please when I may use my phone. Kimberly, my beauty, could you order me a cup of Sanka with skim milk and two slices of dry whole wheat toast, please. I missed lunch and I'm famished."

She nodded and reached for the phone.

"I'm finished," I told him. I felt a rising tide of nausea.

He turned back to Kim, and spoke as if he were introducing me to her for the first time. "Our interrogator. Our inquisitor." Turning back to me, he asked, "Are you still wasting my niece's money?"

Even though he stepped back, giving me ample room to pass him, I felt a prickling over the entire surface of my skin and the wave of nausea was replaced by dread, like I was tipping over the side of a cliff. *No! You aren't allowed…Gatekeeper!!*

Just before the gyre enveloped me, I heard Dora telling Kim, "You can sue that old fart for what he just said to you."

Chapter 16

"Doctor Ray?"

"Hola, Chiquita! How are you?"

A pause. "Doctor. Ray?"

"Yes, *Chiquita.*"

"Everybody's gone."

No, I'm here, Bethy-June!

"Did you look around? Are there any notes from the others?"

"There's stuff."

"What kind of stuff? Where?"

What stuff?

"On the bed. Papers. White papers and pretty, shiny things."

My printouts. What the hell is that other stuff?

"Bethy-June, if you get very quiet, you can't even hear Isadora? Let's get very quiet now. I'm right here. Close your eyes and breathe slowly. I'll wait. Are your eyes closed?"

"Uh-huh."

I'm here, Bethy-June!

"Now breathe calmly and slowly. I won't hang up."   She listened to the shallow breathing of a child on the verge of tears.

Then, just above a whisper, Bethy-June said, "I don't hear anybody. I'm scared, Doctor. Ray. I'm all alone. Are they all dead? Who's going to take care of me?" She started to cry.

Bethy-June! Sugartime! Where is everybody? Why can't she hear me? Gatekeeper! Let them up. What's happening?

"Okay, *Chiquita*. I'm coming over. It will be all right. Don't worry."

"Okay."

"Just play on your quilt or lie down and try to take a nap. I'm leaving my office right now."

When Ray hung up, Bethy-June stifled a sob and I screamed. But no one heard me.

Chapter 17

I struggled to surface from my murky dream. I knew Ray was wondering, *Are they all asleep? Trapped in the gyre? Where is the gatekeeper?* I heard the fear in my doctor's voice as she called to me again. Ray had, in a manner of speaking, trained the Company to respond like little dogs to her calls. "Isadora. This is Ray. Wake up now." Then more commandingly, "Isadora."

I knew she was afraid that she was looking at Stone Baby. The last time Stone Baby was out was back in the state hospital, when Ray was an intern and had moved too fast, pushed too hard exploring memories in too much depth with too little finesse. She brought out Stone Baby, and there was no reaching past her. She lay comatose, oblivious to her surroundings for eight days. Ray was frantic and even considered shock treatments. And then I just woke up. Well, Sugartime woke up first and told her, "Go a little easier, or you won't get anywhere at all. I think you can help this child, but go easy." And so she did.

Ray tried again. "Isadora!"

I jerked my thumb out of my mouth and sat up. "What are you doing here?"

"Bethy-June called me. She said she was alone."

"Oh. Right." I had to strain for the memory. "I've got to…" I scattered toys and dolls getting to my feet. "Where are my…" I took three strides to the bed to check my papers. "What's all this?" Bethy-June had mentioned papers and other things. I didn't know what she was talking about. The children babble.

Ray just shook her head.

I picked up a sheet of paper. "These are the homepages I printed off the Burkes' computer. But all this…Dora!" I remembered everything now and checked my pockets. I found a small scrap of paper. *If we can't keep the bad bitch down, what are we gonna do?* The blocky scrawl was Cootie's. "Damn it!" I wadded up the paper and threw it. Ray watched me calmly from her place on the stool.

I let my anger fly at her. "This shouldn't be happening. Where is the gatekeeper? She wasn't supposed to be let out. Everything is…" I realized I was waving my hand over the bed as if it were the replica of my disordered life. "I don't have time for this. We were past this!"

The expression on Ray's face didn't help. It was almost a smile. "You're angry."

I felt like throwing something at her.

"Isadora, you're feeling and expressing anger." I had heard her go on for hours over the years about how I could have feelings of my own if my personalities integrated. Whenever I exhibited anything resembling a feeling, she felt we were that much closer to fusion, her goal more than ours. "Olive said you were unraveling. Is she right this time?"

"No!"

"Sit and tell me. Who was the note from?"

"Cootie. Ray, I don't have time. I have to find a missing kid. It might already be too late."

"When did you last eat?"

"I don't know." I tried to put the papers in order. "I'm almost there. I just need a little more time and I can give something to Leo he can use, but they keep…and then that snake."

"What snake?" She swore softly in Spanish.

"Olive didn't tell you?"

"She left that detail out."

"Vin—Keating's housekeeper—and I were out on Broadway after my first meeting with the family, and this guy was out walking his snake, for God's sake, and I didn't see what it was till I was *this* close. The next thing I know I'm in Starbucks drinking sweet coffee with Vin who's just had a chat with Sugartime."

"That's interesting." She kept her voice calm, even though the apprehension was back and full-blown, and even though she knows it's no good trying to fool me. But I didn't care about her feelings or mine. Not today.

"And at the police station, Hawk came out."

This news startled her more than the snake. "Who threatened you?"

"Nobody! Someone else was being threatened. Or at least it looked that way. She's never come out before to rescue *somebody else*. And Hester is getting pushier, and Olive is getting pissier. I can't shut them up. When this is over we are going to radically renegotiate these contracts. And then Dora came out in the showroom just as I was going to talk with Spencer Burke and I couldn't stay. I tried but—where is the damned gatekeeper? What is he *doing?*" We referred to the gatekeeper as he, but who knew what it was? I imagined some little gremlin operating the sluices in my head, letting personalities flow in and back, and after years and years, when we could hear each other, when we were all out of the gyre, but not out, inhabiting the body fully... Only Dora was not allowed access because she had broken the contract that allowed us to function, to work. It took all our combined strength to keep her in the gyre, and if the gatekeeper was asleep or getting weak or sloppy we were in trouble. Well, I already knew that. I asked Ray once what would happen to the gatekeeper if we fused. "He is absorbed like stitches as a wound heals. He is a function of your brain, only for as long as you need it."

Sometimes I think Ray just makes things up as we go along.

"Isadora, wait...go back. You said you couldn't stay for Dora, but you stayed for Hawk?"

"Yeah. And what is all this *stuff?*" In my attempts at creating some order, I was really only making more of a mess.

"It looks like Dora is up to her old tricks."

"Oh, crap! I don't even know where all this is from to take it back. She must have stopped into a lot of showrooms on her way out to filch all this stuff." I picked through small silver items, a Fabergé egg, an expensive-looking fountain pen, miniature cloisonné boxes, tiny porcelain figurines, a crystal tea light candleholder and a gold-rimmed shot glass. I didn't care as much about the stealing as the time she wasted doing it. "The only thing from the Burkes' showroom, I think, is this cheese knife. I need to study these Web sites tonight. I don't have time for all this." I threw the knife on the bed. It bounced. "I *can't have* Dora out now. Where is the gatekeeper? I can understand Hawk, maybe, but Dora? What's he doing?"

"Maybe this is a warning that he can't keep things under control. Maybe he's already lost control. Maybe you should stop."

"Well, I can't stop. I just wish the little bastard would do his job. I can work around the others if I have to. But she's a menace."

"Let's talk about—"

"No. I have to work. Time is passing and I have nothing to show for it because of all these interruptions!" I sighed. "Ray, I'm fine."

"Isadora, you are not fine. Look at you. The system is in chaos. If we just take a little time here, chaos is sometimes a good opportunity… Look, you stayed present when Hawk came out."

"So what?"

"When has that happened before?"

"I don't know…"

"Never, Isadora. Never. This might be the time to—"

"No!" I stopped shuffling through papers and junk on the bed. I felt myself hyperventilating. "I know what you want. Not now." I thought *not ever*, but said again, "Not now."

"When, then?"

"There's a child who is getting closer to dead every minute!"

"You have already spent an hour on that play quilt with your thumb in your mouth as a five-year-old." Ray was seldom this harsh with me. "How much more time are you going to waste with your system in chaos? Dora taking over without your permission or consciousness, you lost an hour for a snake on the street. You can't spare an hour to talk to me?"

"Not about—"

"About what? Say it."

"Hawk."

"What about Hawk?"

I felt a panic rise in me that was familiar. "I can't. I can't. Not now. I will. Ray, I will. Not now."

Ray usually knows when to stop. "Did you wake up this morning with what you thought was a mouth full of blood?"

"I'm used to it. Doesn't bother me anymore. Look, I know what she did. Why do I have to remember it? What's the difference?"

"Until you remember it, you can't accept it. You'll never be whole. It's the last big thing standing in your way."

"Nothing is in our way. We're fine. Just back off."

This time she did take the hint. "Maria is probably waiting dinner for me. I tell her not to wait, but she always does." She cast those brown eyes at me, that went from warm to piercing in nanoseconds. "You don't have to get through this by yourself. Don't practice your independence when the stakes are so high. Call me...every few hours. Till this case is over. Isadora?"

"Right. I'll call you." All the second pages were mixed up with all the first pages. "I have to sort these out. Dora did this on purpose. The bitch shuffled them."

"Well, I'll just use your bathroom before I take off. Eat something. Low blood sugar never solved a case."

When Ray came out of the bathroom, Dora had removed my blazer and boots, shoved over the stolen showroom samples, tossed the papers to the floor, and was lying on her side, her head propped up on her hand. "Long time no see, Señora." She smiled.

Ray sighed. "Dora. How long have you been back?" She resumed her perch on the stool. Now, I was grateful she wasn't leaving.

"Hello, Dora, how are you, missed you, how've you been?" Ray didn't react. Dora shrugged the shoulder she wasn't leaning on and answered her own mock greeting. "I'm fine, thank you. Been back awhile. Since the snake. The gatekeeper was busy... everyone running like scared rabbits. Oooooh." She wiggled her fingers in a cartoon-scary fashion and breathed, "Then, I just slipped out."

"Is Isadora there now? Can she hear me?"

"Maybe."

You damn well know I can! I couldn't stop her from taking over, but at least this time I didn't black out. I was still *there*.

Ray said, casually, "Before you go..."

"I'm not going anywhere."

"Before you go, tell me something."

"Mmmmm?"

"Snakes. Why does Isadora and most of the Company black out when they are in proximity of a snake? I know of two other instances when this has happened."

"Did you miss the class on archetypes and symbols? I can lend you a book."

"If that's all it was, she'd faint when she sees a cigar. She doesn't."

"How should I know?"

"I don't know, but I think you do."

"You think many things. You are a thoughtful person. You've put on a little weight there, haven't you? Since last we met? Menopause not being kind? Your hair is almost all gray, too. Tsk tsk tsk. I imagine we are responsible." That was probably the most truthful thing I ever heard Dora say.

The fine lines around Ray's eyes crinkled slightly. She was used to Dora's taunts and always seemed merely curious about what Dora would throw at her next, about her age, her weight, her being Mexican, gay or whatever else Dora could dredge up. Ray kept to her train of inquiry. "Isadora doesn't know why she reacts so strongly to snakes. The others don't know. I think you may be the only one who does."

"Why don't you do one of those regression thingies you like to do. Go on Oprah. No, wait, you've been on Oprah, haven't you? Okay, Dr. Phil. They are so dramatic. 'Youuuu are getting sleeeee peeee...' ...'Daddy daddy no! Nooooo!!' Movie of the Week."

"People can't remember what they weren't there for. I want you to tell me."

"Whoa! I just heard you telling Isadora she had to..."

"Had to what?"

"I know you've been trying to get her to remember Hawk's little fit of pique with Daa-dee, but she can't remember it if she wasn't there..." Dora tossed Ray's words back at her in a kind of sing-song. "Besides, we all know what Hawk did. Who cares if we share the memory?"

"It's part of the process. Part of the therapy. You know that. As more memories are shared, the more—"

"Yeah, yeah. The *therapy*. Why are you still around? It's been years. Are we like Helen Keller? We're stuck with Teacher for life?"

"You know the deal."

"What deal?"

Ray considered her thoughtfully. "It's possible you don't know, but I doubt it. I made a promise to Isadora. I promised I would never abandon her. No matter what she says or does. She, however, is absolutely free to move on and never contact me again."

"Good. I'd like you to leave now and never come back. I am moving on."

"You, however, I will haunt until you are extinct. I made no promise to you. Now tell me about the snake. Is it a painful memory? Is that why you are stalling? Or do you just like wasting my time?"

Dora just snorted and flopped over on her back, for once tired of the game. "Oh, all right. It isn't such a big deal. If she were going to freak over something you'd think it'd be buckets. That damn bucket nearly crippled me. Anyway. I don't really know." She studied her nails. "I merely surmise."

Ray waited for her to continue.

"Once I woke up with my knees pushed against my chest, sort of folded up. It was cold, I remember, and dark except when

I looked up and there was a circle of light way up. Straight up. The sky. But it was getting dimmer. I reached out. The sides of the well were rough, mossy, and there were lots of holes and crevices where the rocks and bricks had fallen away. There was a snake draped over me. Must have come to me for warmth. I figured Daddy Dearest had put her down the well to punish her for something, and they all took off when the snake found her."

"How old were you?"

"I guess four."

"How long did he keep you in the well?" Ray asked softly. She's never gotten used to hearing these stories. She probably thought she'd heard them all.

"I was down there several hours. Till after dark. I don't know when Isadora was put in the bucket."

"Was that when you were born?"

"Oh, God no! I'd been around forever. I just stayed below everybody's radar."

"Why did you come out in the well?"

"Somebody had to hang on if he tried to shake her out of the bucket or start yelling if he never came back."

"You weren't terrified?"

"It's always been my job to not be terrified. Besides, it was a harmless little snake."

"Did you remove the snake?"

"No. It was sort of...company. It wasn't doing anything. Just trying to be warm. I talked to it. Named it Slimman. Not bad for a four-year-old, huh? I was always the precocious one. When he pulled us up, I was afraid when he saw it he'd kill it. But he just laughed and threw it in the grass along with me. I could hardly walk. While he was dragging me back to the house, I left. I knew nothing good was coming."

I remembered the drag back to the house and my legs and back hurting me. I thought he'd beaten me, even though I didn't have any bruises. I blacked out a lot during my childhood and never understood why till after Ray told me in the asylum. But I still didn't remember going into the bucket.

"Thank you, Dora. Now let Isadora come back, please."

"Make me." She stretched, languorously, and put her hands

behind her head. Gazing upward, she said, "Since El Snako, I've been watching everything—strangely…from above. Like an out-of-body experience, you know? Like Casper, the fucking ghost, stuck up on the ceiling. It feels good to be back, embodied, as it were. I'm not nearly ready to go yet."

Ray is always as fascinated as she is frustrated by Dora. The rest of us just find her aggravating, especially Hester. *I'm fascinating. Why doesn't she find ME fascinating?*

Oh, she does, Hester, she's just more used to you, that's all.

No she doesn't. Hester is so predictable.

Oh shut up.

Dora is my twin. The other alters look different, more like themselves, but Dora looks exactly like me, Ray says, except for the wicked cunning shining in her eyes and the almost exaggerated expressiveness of her face. Ray has also warned me, "She'll kill you and die laughing." Dora has power of her own. She is mercurial and beautiful and has landed us in trouble repeatedly since we were children. When the Company began to function together, we gained the strength to keep her in the background, like Mr. Rochester's wife. The gatekeeper is our Mrs. Poole and, occasionally, Dora slips out and starts fires.

"Isadora needs to work," Ray said, reasonably. "Lives are at stake."

"So?" She yawned and cuddled deeper into the pillows.

"Don't you care that she might be able to help?"

"Why should I? Who cared about us when we were living with the devil?"

"You always managed to duck out of the worst parts, from what I hear."

"You don't hear everything. Anyway, you're not that concerned about this case. You're not even sure she can solve it. I know what you're doing."

"You do."

"You think this will put enough pressure on the Company so they'll get all shook up, the status will get all un-quo'd, and *voila!* Fusion! Isn't that right? And *then*, you can write the last chapter of that book you just can't finish, because, without fusion, there's no cure—no big whup. No talk show tour, no movie option. No reclining on your lucrative laurels. But mostly you just want to get rid of me. You've never liked me."

Ray laughed. "As usual, Dora, you are the overweening egotist. You've made all this about you. *You*, I must remind you, are nothing."

Dora raised herself up on her elbows. "I am the only whole person here. *She's* a shell for all of us. That's all she is. She's a waste of your time, Signora Doctor. And the rest of them are just brain farts. I'm the real deal."

"Isadora is the firstborn. You are all come-latelies."

"We saved her."

"She saved herself. You're the by-product. Like ash from a coal fire. I think it's time to clean the furnace."

I sensed a tiny flicker of fear in Dora. She turned to her side again, assuming a sensuous curve. "I'm the one you should be talking to. We could do more than talk. I don't mind that you're a woman." She traced little circles with her index finger on the wine-colored brocade of the spread.

"I'm here to help Isadora. That's my job, that's my wish. That's all I'm ever going to do…is try to help Isadora."

"Isadora schmora! There is no 'I' in Isadora. She's nothing. A *big empty*." Her expression transformed like images on a screen without transition, from vicious to sympathetic understanding, and in honeyed tones, she said, "You're afraid I'll tell? I won't tell."

You won't have to tell, you know I'm here and if I know they'll all know.

"Yes you will. But that's not why I won't have sex with you."

"I *wouldn't* tell," she pouted. "Who would I tell? They don't talk to me. They won't talk to me. And I can't talk to them. They don't hear me." A note of quiet despair crept into her voice. "I'm really quite alone, you know."

Ray laughed out loud. "You remind me of Susan Hayward in those old movies that Maria likes to watch. You're very good, really."

"I walk alone," she muttered.

"Not entirely," she corrected her briskly. "Why do you think

I'm here? Bethy-June called me."

"That whining virus." Dora dropped her tragic air. "She's like a remora. You know, those weasely sucky little fish that attach themselves to the big fish."

"To sharks, actually."

Dora's eyes gleamed. "Yes, sharks, actually." And she smiled like one.

"Cootie has been out, too. He left a note for Isadora in her pocket, just in case you didn't wreak your usual havoc to get everybody's attention."

"Those fucking brats! Why don't they just die?" she said through a nearly clenched jaw. Then she started to giggle. "Why don't they grow up…" Her giggle escalated to laughter, "…and leave home!"

Ray smiled at the joke and at her.

Her laughter subsided and she let her head fall a little sideways as she studied the psychiatrist. "Oh, Ray, I've missed that smile of yours. Your pearly whites against that lovely dark skin…it's enough to oil the hinges on a lady's heels." I felt her pushing her tongue against the inside of upper teeth, revealing a glimpse of its underside through her relaxed and slightly open mouth.

"You wouldn't tell the Company. If you were successful in seducing me, you would call Maria."

"Oh! I would never do such a thing."

"Of course you would. Calling my partner of thirty years would give you more pleasure than the act itself."

"You're one clever little spic, aren't you?" She was through acting now. "How did you pay for medical school again? Cleaning other people's houses? And how many years did it take you? Let's see, you weren't that young when we first met, and you were still an intern. Doing the math—"

"And you, my dear, are as entertaining as ever. But, now you have to leave."

"Like I said. Make me." She stretched, this time without sensuous intent, merely to anchor herself more securely to the spot.

"You know how I can tell you aren't the real deal? Because

you can't stay out forever."

"Neither can she!"

"She can. Now, when she leaves, it is by choice and she doesn't go far. She stays out of the gyre."

That hadn't been true in the last couple of days.

"You don't know everything."

"Isadora has been in charge for four years now. The others come out when they are needed and by invitation only."

"Not lately."

"Seeing a snake is an unusual circumstance. You are an entity. An alter. Not real."

"I'm as real as you are."

"No. You are not. You will never be anything on your own. You will always be just a piece of her. If you die, Isadora lives on. If she dies, you're...dead."

"Play your psycho semantic games if you want to, Signora Doctor. You have no power over me. Neither does she. Nobody does."

"I'll have you arrested."

"For what?"

"Shoplifting."

Oh, Ray, good!

Dora picked up a silver bracelet and positioned its crystal charm to shoot a mini rainbow on the wall. "Hester is always whining about not having pretty things." She tossed it down with a flip of her wrist, sighing, "You try to be nice..."

"You never do anything nice and you don't care about Hester. You like the thrill of getting away with it. So here's your deal. You go away now—let Isadora finish this case—I'll let you get away with this. Don't go away, and I'll call the cops right now." Ray took her cell phone out of her pocket and flipped it open. "I have the number on speed dial."

"You wouldn't put Isadora in jail."

"I would put you in jail. I will not pay your bail. And you'll stay there with the drug addicts and puking drunks—"

"You've made your point." She flattened the pillows with a sweep of her hand and lay back once again, voluptuously. "Sure you wouldn't care to share this bed with me before I go?"

Ray pressed a button on the phone.

"All right! But when this case is over, if Isadora isn't locked up with the loonies again, I'll be back."

"Fine. See you then." Ray snapped the phone shut.

She sat up. "No, you aren't going to let Isadora stay in jail. As soon as I go back to the gyre, they'll all be back and you will bail them out."

"Go!" Ray displayed an unusual flash of anger.

"I have a right to be in the world!"

"Go now, Dora, and I won't send you to jail, and when this case is over, I'll give you more time out."

"You can't make promises for the Company."

"No, but I can persuade them."

"How do I know—"

"Dora, you have lied to me every time I have seen your face, but I have never lied to you."

"I'll get more time out?"

"Yes."

"And a trip?"

"Fine. A trip."

"I want to go to an island and lay on a beach and sip cold gin and fuck my brains out with the natives. She's got the money. She and Olive just won't let any of us spend any, the tightwad bitches. Besides, I *am* in control. The brats just came out when I took a little nap."

"You've been sleeping for two years. You're telling me you needed a nap? Give it up, Dora. I promise that when the case is over, I will tell the Company that you need more time out, you need a trip. Now go. I'm through with you."

Dora lay back again and closed her eyes. Her breathing became quiet.

Chapter 18

"Is she right? Do you want to finish your book?"

"Isadora?"

"Yeah." I reached for my boots, which Dora had tossed some distance from the bed.

"You were here?"

"It was like she said, only I was the ghost on the ceiling this time. I was sort of hearing it from outside instead of inside. Well, both, actually. What's that about?"

Ray was smiling at me in a way I didn't like.

"Stop smiling. Like that."

"Like what?"

"You have that proud parent look on your face. You know I hate it."

"It's been awhile since you've seen it."

"It's been nice."

"You going someplace?"

"I don't know, why?"

"You're putting your boots on. And you've rebuttoned the top two buttons on your blouse."

"Dora always leaves me feeling undressed. So what's the look for?"

"Dora."

"You're happy to see *her*?"

"That's not all that happened."

"What are you talking about?"

"She came back, but she shared space with you and the others. And you shared space with her. That's never happened before. And there's some…emotional integration."

"So what? We still aren't talking. I don't want to share space with that bitch. She just slows me down. Interrupts things. And emotions don't help me think. I need to think."

"But it's a new development. Like sharing space with Hawk."

"We can discuss the Return of Dora some other time. And the…Hawk thing…just has to wait. Right now I have a kid to find before she's just a body. If she isn't already. Make yourself useful. Read these." I handed her a bunch of papers I'd picked up at random.

"What are they?"

"Pay attention. I told you. They are the home pages of all the sites that the Burkes access from their office computer. And I'm told it's just Spencer—Manfred supposedly never touches them, but that might not be true. According to the police file, the sites were the same on Spencer's home computer."

"What am I looking for?"

"If I knew that I would tell you, or I wouldn't need you to read them, would I? And get that look off your face."

"Isadora, I will examine these papers, but you can work on this case and drop the resistance at the same time." She'd lost the smile and spoke almost softly.

"Not now, Ray. Just not now."

"All right." She spread the pages out on the counter and put on her reading glasses and concentrated. Without looking up she said, "And to answer your question, yes, of course I would like to finish my book. You are my cash cow."

"I'm also your biggest headache."

She eyed me over her reading glasses. "We're even, then?"

"Uh-huh. Hungry? I'm starved. I'm going to order Chinese."

Ray dialed her cell, and I heard her speak to Maria in Spanish. I always thought at least one of my alters could have bothered to learn Spanish, but none of them ever had.

She snapped the phone shut. "The neighbors dropped in while she was waiting. They have eaten up all my dinner. So I am ready for Chinese."

I ordered while she read, and then I went back to reading myself. When the food came, we sat at the counter and ate and read at the same time. When we were through with our respective batch of home pages, we exchanged them and read and ate some more. We finished eating and reading at about the same time.

"Well?"

She slid her empty carton of chow fun away from her and burped discreetly behind the back of her hand. "I'm not the detective. I don't see anything here at all. Pretty standard-looking Web sites, but I don't know anything about the wholesale business, or finance either, for that matter. Shopping sites...well, Maria does all the shopping. You need to show them to experts in the field. You said the police already examined all this stuff?"

"Yes. They didn't find anything out of the ordinary."

"Maybe there is nothing to find. Did you eat all the dumplings?"

"Sorry."

"Maybe what you're looking for isn't on a home page. But then, I don't see how you're going to find it. The possibilities are infinite. Almost." She shrugged and reached for a fortune cookie. Cracking it open, she pulled out the tiny banner and read, "Put no trust in cryptic comments."

"Well, that's mine, obviously," I said. "Now read yours."

She smiled good-naturedly and cracked open the second. Her smile broadened. "There has been an alarming increase in the number of things you know nothing about."

I smiled back. I can't say I ever felt this ticklish feeling go through me before that caused this smile. It wasn't entirely pleasant, and yet...Ray laughed. I like Ray's laughter. I prefer it to that proud parental smile she gets when I seem to make progress, even if the progress is more in her mind than in mine.

She gave her knee a little slap. "It's getting late. I've got to go." She slipped off the stool. "Remember what I said. Call me. Frequently. Dora promised to stay away while this case is open. I don't trust her, but she knows she can trust me to call the cops if she comes back early. Let me take the evidence."

We used the plastic bag from the Chinese food to contain Dora's loot. "I don't know how she does it. Anybody else would have gotten caught," I said.

"Dora has a way about her. If you could work together, she could be a great asset."

"In case I need something shoplifted or some other reason to be arrested."

"Like you said, she gets away with things. That's a good quality in a detective, don't you think? If you could harness that quality...she's devious, manipulative and quite beautiful."

"You think Dora is beautiful?"

Ray chuckled. "The children of Lucifer are often beautiful."

"Who said that, Freud?"

"No, Agatha Christie. Maria reads her aloud. It's how she learned English. You're beautiful, too, Chiquita. You just don't know it." She tied a knot in the top of the plastic bag. "I'll hang on to this stuff till the case is over. I'll need the evidence. Then I'll find a way to get it back to the Gift Building and they can sort out where it all goes. I don't know what else to do. In the meantime, I'm an accessory to shoplifting." She shook her head and said goodnight.

I shouldn't have bothered to put my boots back on because I just had to take them off again. I was dead tired. Staring at these pages any longer would do no good. I'd have to have a fresh look at them in the morning and find some experts to show them to—people who were not connected to the Burkes. I couldn't explain the feeling I had that there was something here, if only I had the eyes to see. Tomorrow I hoped I could find the right pair of eyes. Tonight, I hoped that Dora's fear of Ray calling the cops would keep her at bay. I had no illusions that she was really gone.

I sprawled on the bed in my clothes and murmured, "Lance, tell me a story."

How about a little Edgar Allen Poe?

"A bit creepy for our present situation, don't you think?"

No, I think you should hear this one. This is called The Purloined Letter.

"Have you told me this one before?"

No. It's about hiding something in plain sight.

"Oh?"

On a gusty autumn evening in Paris, begins the tale of something simple, and something odd…

Friday

Chapter 19

The first thing I noticed upon waking was the kitchen knife sticking out of my forehead, and the taste of blood in my mouth was particularly strong. I did my usual finger check...it came up clean. Focusing on the far wall, I could see that all of our portraits, except for Aurora's, had been slashed or gouged, but the knife was left in mine.

I eased myself out from under the covers, always curious about what garb I will wake up in. This morning, I was not surprised to find myself in a satin negligee that I had never worn. I'd seen it before. It was Dora's. So much for her staying gone till the investigation was over. At least I woke up in my own bed. Alone. I had wanted to get rid of this little number, but Olive, ever practical, said *why bother? She'll just steal another one.* So we kept it.

I wrapped myself in my flannel robe and headed for the coffeepot.

While I was trying to decide what to do—take the portraits down so Aurora wouldn't see them, or leave them—they were hers after all; she would have to know what happened to them sooner or later, and wondering where Olive was—she would know what I should do—a new painting on the easel caught my eye. I approached it, cautiously, fearing rats and spiders, or that it was something else nasty left by Dora.

All I saw in it were flowers. I was relieved. Aurora frequently painted flowers. This painting was different, however. It wasn't paint, for one thing. I touched it with my finger. It was dry. She had used crayons, not children's crayons, but those expensive things you get in art supply stores. And she hadn't used a canvas, just a square of poster board. She had obviously drawn this very quickly. Something else was different about the rendering from what she usually did. This was like a garden, but not a realistic garden. The flowers were floating in a dark space with no discernible light source. Robin Bartholome always said that Aurora performed magic with light on her canvases. Maybe it was supposed to be a night garden, or a garden in a solar eclipse.

I suppose somebody will buy it, I thought and turned to make my coffee and stepped on the home page of the garden site I'd printed out from Spencer's computer. It was lying unfolded on the floor by the easel. Only this one page. All the other pages were still on the counter where I had left them. I looked at the picture again.

Aurora was speaking to me, but what the hell was she saying? "Why can't she just write notes like everybody else, dammit?" She signed her name to her paintings. I knew she could write. "Why is everybody so damned peculiar?" I couldn't tell if Aurora had come out before Dora had done her damage, or after. But I couldn't worry about it now.

And since Aurora wasn't going to tell me more than what was in this picture, I needed someone who knew something about flowers and gardens. I threw on some clothes, took the poster board and the hard copy of the home page, grabbed my wallet and keys and went out. Ray would be angry that I didn't call her right away. Dora's symbolic murder of the lot of us, excepting Aurora, would compel Ray to take some sort of action. I didn't know what, but whatever it would be, it would take me off the investigation and I couldn't have that. I would tell her, but later, when I didn't feel I could be of any more help.

I walked over to Broadway and then two blocks south to Flower Power, a flower and plant store run by an aging hippie.

He wore his gray hair in a ponytail, had a grizzled unkempt beard, and favored India cotton shirts (*That is sooo forty years ago!* Hester moaned when we first met him) open at the neck, the better to show off a peace medallion suspended on a strip of well-worn leather. His blue jeans were always patched and his braided leather bracelet was nearing the end of its life. Soon it would just fall off. When it finally did, Hester bet that the spell would be broken and he would cut his hair, shave and put on a suit. He smiled at me when I came in. The smell in here was wonderful. Green plants, fresh soil, flowers. And a whiff of patchouli.

"Hey, Shy, got something for me?" When Aurora started painting, we brought small paintings of flowers to him and he sold them on consignment. We still brought him things, though not so often since her larger paintings were doing so well downtown. "I can give you a special price on tulips. Got a load of them. Lilacs will be in soon, I expect. They blow out. If you want some, put your name on the list and I'll give you a call. No peonies yet. Put your name on the list for those too. We don't get many."

His name was Chris Johansson. He was originally from somewhere in the Midwest. He'd come to New York by way of Southern California. He was one of the few people in my life who hadn't gone all glassy-eyed when he met me. I guess, considering the things he'd seen on many a drug trip gone bad, I didn't strike him as so weird.

"I don't know if you'll want this. I need to ask you about it. Look at it and tell me what you think." I handed him Aurora's painting.

"Whoh-ooh! What's that little sister of yours been smokin'?"

I had started to tell him my story once, but I think he didn't want any more stories in his head. He'd tuned me out. I never tried again. He had the idea that Aurora was my little deaf and dumb agoraphobic sister. I left it at that. It wasn't such a bad description of her.

"Nothing that I know of, but she picks up ideas and I was wondering what you could tell me about this."

He studied it and tugged a strand of his sparse and straggly beard. "Far freakin' out, man."

"Explain."

"Well, I know your sissy doesn't get out, but she knows her plants." He tortured his chin hair some more. "This is just wrong."

"Wrong how?"

"It's a garden, right? I mean, some sort of garden. It's not a bouquet. It's plants growing, not cut and arranged, and it looks like outside. You see a hint of a fence there maybe, or the edge of a wall." He turned the painting and cocked his head and brought the poster board back to right side up. "But you'd never find this stuff growing together in a garden. Not on this planet."

"What do you mean?"

"Plants have seasons and climates. Some plants grow in hot weather, some in temperate. Some plants grow, like, in the freakin' rainforest, man, and some burst their little blooms on the lone prairie. But they don't party together. Here's a cactus, see, right there. Kind of blurred, but it's a cactus all right. And here you have what is a pretty convincing orchid, and some zinnias over here next to a couple tulips. Not likely, man. Not likely at all. Different soils, different times of year. Maybe, possibly, in a hothouse somewhere, but not any garden. They are all like that. None of these flowers would grow together at the same time in the same place. Here's an apple blossom. And right here, she's painted a marigold. I'd say it's a fantasy garden, but it's more like a nightmare. Is she trying to be funny? It's not funny. It's kind of, well, sicko. I hate to say that, but it's not right."

I felt my pulse quicken. My first pair of expert eyes had been Aurora's. Now I had my second. Someone who could talk like a normal person. Well, almost like a normal person. "Look at this." I handed him the printout of the garden site home page. He read it slowly. I curbed my impatience.

"Is this a joke? This has to be somebody's idea of a joke, right?"

"I don't know. I want you to tell me."

"Same problem. All wrong."

"Wrong flowers?"

"Wrong information."

He reached for a book from the shelf behind him. It was large, heavy and worn. He opened it at random. "Here, see? This is the legend."

☼ ◊   Z9 – 10 H12 – 9   ↕93in (03cm)↔1ft(3m)

"The little sun there means what kind of light you should plant in. It will be full, or filled in to varying degrees. Get it?" I nodded. "That little drip shape means the amount of water, the Z indicates what zone. See, they are called plant-heat zones. Pretty standard coding. They have numbers and colors. So for each plant you can tell by the number and color what part of the country they'll do well in. What zone. See? The map, here—" He flipped to an early page in the book, "...is colored to match. Then you have these numbers that tell you what time of the year to plant, how deep and how far apart. But the numbers here... on this Web site it's all gibberish. See, you've got hardiness zones, heat zones, all the symbols mean something. But these symbols...I don't know, this outfit needs a new webmaster or something. Somebody who knows something about flowers. This is garbage. They must get a shitload of e-mails from people who planted something and watched it die. There should be a law against this. This is criminal, man." Chris felt about plants the way some people feel about puppies.

"You are absolutely right. Thanks, Chris. Thank you very much. You can have this, if you want," I said, indicating the painting.

He almost said no, then caught himself. Something for nothing is tempting, even if you don't just love the something. "Sure, thanks. I'll put it up at Halloween."

I thought, *Thank you, Aurora. Thank you very, very much. I'm sorry about what Dora did. We'll deal with her, I promise.*

Chapter 20

I rang the precinct, and then ducked into a health food store and bought an extra-large strawberry/soy shake and into Starbucks for a large light coffee. Juggling my containers of hot and cold, bitter and sweet along with the paper in my hand, I walked to the station.

I waited for Olive to tell me to be careful...she'd just had our dry cleaning done, and for Hester to complain about how she would look with stains on her jacket and why did I have to wear the black one again. But they were silent. Instead, I heard the eerie sing-song of Bethy-June and Sula. *Snow White and Rose Red pricked their fingers to death they bled.*

"That's cheery, kids. I'm on it. We don't need to rush. Leo isn't even there yet."

"You cracked it, eh?" Rudy had smacked his gum in my ear when I called.

"No, but I think I found something he can crack it with. Maybe. I don't know."

"I'll call him. Come on in. Bring your own coffee."

"Got it covered, Rudy." I'd come to a bench outside a

pastry shop and sat. Now that I knew what I was *not* looking at, a garden site, maybe I could see what was there. I'd stared at the numbers. If they didn't mean what they were supposed to mean, what *did* they mean? What kind of code—no—codes *hide* meaning. *Hide in plain sight.* Lance must have been telling me I was not looking at a code. Lance and his stories and metaphors, Aurora and her pictures. Why couldn't people just tell me things, straight out? The only thing I got straight up was the bitching of the two divas. Everybody else was cryptic, poetic or mute. I sucked up the last of my smoothie noisily and tossed the waxy container into the tall city trash basket next to my bench. Sipping my coffee, I stared at the numbers again. Maybe it wasn't in the numbers. But then, why change them? Why not use real heat zones and planting information? The numbers had to mean something. I couldn't see it. Did the flowers themselves mean anything? The choice of one flower over another? But why change the numbers?

Nothing is hidden.

Then why couldn't I see it?

I tossed my empty coffee cup into the trash. I went into the pastry shop and bought another cup of milky coffee and a croissant. I waited for Hester's protest. Again, it didn't come.

I walked my thoughts, my Web page and my brown paper bag to the precinct.

"Rudy."

"Shiloh." Chew chew.

"He back yet?"

"On his way."

"Can I go up?"

He nodded as he picked up his ringing phone.

I sprinted up the stairs and found my way to Leo's desk at the back. Jimmy Stokes was not here. The officers who were, just nodded as I went by or were too absorbed in their work to pay attention to me.

I unpacked my coffee and croissant at Leo's desk and munched and sipped and thought and studied the damn page. His computer was on. I wondered...I punched in the URL for this Web site. There was the Web page, same layout. Different flower, different numbers.

You're doing this wrong.

"Where have you been?"

You need to think like a pervert.

Oh, Hester. That's your job.

Hester and Olive were back, nattering at each other, but they were right. I had to look at this from a different point of view. I'm a pedophile. What do I need to know? I need to know where a child is, when, who to contact... No...all I'd need is a phone number and a date and time to call.

Oh, cripes. So simple. Stupidly, brilliantly simple.

I smacked the table and made an *agghh* sound that jerked heads up. Leo was walking toward me down the aisle, Feeney right behind him. If the newbie had had a tail, he'd have been wagging it. Leo said, "Whaddya got?"

I jumped out of his chair and slapped the paper with the flat of my hand.

He sat down. "What am I looking at?"

"A Web site."

Feeney leaned over his shoulder. "For flowers, or gardens."

"Yeah, it says Flowers and Gardens, Feeney. This one of Burkes' sites?"

I said yes.

"Our lab checked—"

I cut him off. "But nobody in your lab is a flower expert. They know computers and porn sites. This is no garden site."

"What is it?"

"It's a message board. For pedophiles. It tells him who to call for details on a vulnerable child."

He stared at the page.

"I didn't see it at first either. I was looking for something complicated. But it's not. See those numbers and letters there?"

☼ ◊   Z9 – 10 H12 – 9   ↕93in (03cm)↔1ft(3m)

"Forget the letters and symbols. They don't mean anything. They would mean something on a real site. But this isn't a real flower site. Ignore them. Just read the numbers. Backward."

"Looks like a phone number. Two numbers left over."

"Time."

"Huh?" Feeney grunted.

"The time they should call. And look at this." I pointed to Leo's computer screen. "I opened this just now. Different day, different flower. But read the numbers backward. A phone number."

"It's not the same number," said Feeney, perplexed. Leo looked skeptical.

"*Strangers on a Train*, Leo, *Strangers on a Train*."

"What the hell…"

This time Feeney got it first. "It's an old Hitchcock movie, Lieutenant. These two guys—strangers—meet on a train. They get to talking and discover that each has a problem that could be neatly solved by a little murder. Only they don't want to get caught. So they make a deal. They'll each do the murder for the other one. They think it's the perfect couple of crimes, because the murderer has no connection to his victim, and they'll each have an alibi for the victim they are connected to. Right?"

He was eager for a little pat on the back, and I gave him one. Not literally. "That's good, Feeney."

He beamed.

"I think that people in this network exchange information on where and how to get children. So the children that they know are always taken by someone else, completely unrelated. A total stranger."

Roses are red violets are blue roses are red violets are blue

"We have to shut this down." Feeney reached for Leo's phone.

"No!" Leo and I yelled at him at the same time.

"*We* are going to call these numbers. We'll pick off these bastards one by one," said Leo.

Feeney asked, "Will this lead us to Anna?"

Roses are red violets are blue violets are blue violets violets violets!!!!! The chanting was loud, insistent and incessant inside my head. "Get your lab to find…"

"How you holding up?" Leo cocked his head and tried to

look into my eyes.

"I'm fine, Leo. Find the site that the kidnapper accessed. The one that—" The word stuck in my throat, "*advertised* her. You don't have to go back farther than April third."

"April third?" the newbie parroted.

Roses are red Violets are dead "Stop it!" I said out loud. Feeney was about to open his mouth again. Leo held up a hand to stop him and waited.

"Not you, Detective Feeney, sorry. That is Anna's birthday. That was the day of her party."

Leo asked, "Soooo, how will we know which site refers to her?"

"Find the day when the flower on this homepage was a violet."

Feeney was slow. "Why is that…"

"Because," Leo was now on board, "she was wearing those goddamn overalls with a goddamn sign on them…TAKE ME." Leo swore more richly under his breath as he got the lab on the phone. "Harry! Leo. Tell the girls and boys that nobody goes home till I have a name and address. … The Keating case. … Yeah, I know, but you're gonna do it again. I'm putting Shiloh on the phone. She's got an idea and I want you to follow up on it and get me some names. … Five minutes ago!" He handed me the phone.

I explained what the lab needed to look for and why. Harry wasn't balking at the job, but he had a point, "There could be hundreds of hits. How are we going to know which ones are pervs and which ones are just people surfing for flower sites?"

Violets are blue that's the clue blood is red roses are dead I rubbed my forehead. "Leave out the names that are obviously women. Then, I don't know. Get them all and we'll have to sort it out here." I looked at Leo for confirmation. He nodded.

I was certain they'd find a site in our time frame with violets on it, but if they didn't, I told Harry to call me with what they did find. Leo took back the receiver and barked some more instructions.

She bathed with roses red, And violets blew And all the sweetest flowers That in the forest grew.

Feeney was on the phone bringing in the members of the task force who weren't already at their desks. Today's Web site said the time for the call would be thirteen—one o'clock.

Chapter 21

Within thirty minutes, six detectives had assembled. They were a haggard-looking bunch, all in street clothes, from suits and ties to faded jeans and holey T-shirts, depending on their personal preference and the streets they haunted for information. I'd met most of them. They just nodded or offered a wan smile if they caught my eyes, but no one came over to chat. I was grateful. This wasn't the complete task force. Four were assigned to other cases, including the case of the child found yesterday in the park.

Leo stood before them. Feeney operated a laptop projector. I tried to stay inconspicuous on a chair in the back corner. "It's time for you boys and girls to earn the big bucks the city of New York is paying you." There were a few humorless snickers and some rolling eyes, but the atmosphere was fraught with tension, with anticipation. "We've got this Web site." Feeney clicked a button and it came up on a screen behind Leo, who stepped aside so everyone could see it. "Shiloh thinks, and I think she's right, this is where pedophiles swap information. These numbers down here are a phone number. Read it backwards. The time to call is here." Leo paused to take a question.

"How do we know what time zone?"

"For now, let's assume it is the time zone of the number being called. We can also assume the date is today—whatever day someone opens the site. This is the site we opened up this morning. There is some way—we don't know yet how—they, the webmaster, whoever that is, knows when to change flowers and numbers. We'll worry about that later. Right now we have to find out where this number is and make sure we are the first to call it. Rami and Stuart are working on that."

"Now, two of you are going to eyeball that site every second of every goddamn day from now till we have reeled all these stinking fish in one by one. You people work out your own schedules."

"This won't help us find Anna. Not in time." Detective Celia Chong, one of the better groomed in the task force, was right.

"The lab is getting me a list of names and addresses of hits to the site on the day it referred to Anna."

"How do you know which day that was?" Holey T-shirt. I couldn't remember his name.

"Shiloh is betting that the site that day had violets on it. If you'll remember what she was wearing the day she disappeared— a playsuit with violets smack on the bib."

I remembered now—Holey T-shirt was Jeff something. Didn't bathe too often. Said it gave him an air of authenticity when talking to the lowlifes. He did remember the playsuit. "Spencer Burke bought her that. Should we pick him up?"

"Not yet. He could claim he was an innocent flower surfer and that he got the idea for her playsuit from the Web site. I want more before I go after him. As soon as we get that list, we'll track down every person on it. I think we're looking for someone who has the means and opportunity for a fair amount of traveling, someone who does not live in Manhattan, and someone who was in Manhattan that day, of course."

The chanting of the flower rhyme had stopped, but I felt ill. I was breaking a sweat and my head hurt.

Detectives Felicia Rami and Nick Stuart were still on with the phone company tracking today's phone number. The others got themselves coffee and munched bagels and rolls they had brought with them. Most of them looked like they hadn't slept in days. Still, there was a buzz of excitement at this new opening in the case, a welcome relief from the frustration and hopelessness that had built hour by hour since Anna's disappearance.

"Headache?" Leo stood over me with a cup of coffee in his hand.

"It comes and goes," I said.

"You can go home, Shiloh. We can take it from here."

"I'd like to stay."

"Sure." He lifted his cup in the direction of his team milling around the coffee machine. "They're right. It's going to be tough to pin this on the Burkes."

"Leo, Leo, Leo, do we have to tell you everything? You'll get them with just a little imagination. Fix your tie."

The room was hazy and far away, but I could hear her distinctly and sort of see Leo. I felt like I was in a dream where I couldn't quite get my eyes open. She unbuttoned the jacket and pushed it back and open with her right hand on her hip.

"Dora?"

"You remembered me. I'm touched."

"Maybe you better go and let us do our job."

"Why isn't anybody ever glad to see me? Without us you would still be chasing your tails. Russian mafia? Oh, please! You can get Spencer and Manfred...I talked to them you know. In the showroom. Isadora had to leave suddenly—she wasn't feeling well, she is such a little hothouse flower sometimes—and I finished the job. And you know what I found out in the course of one short conversation with the troll Spencer?"

"Tell me."

"He doesn't know the difference between a pansy and a peony. He wouldn't know a begonia if it sprouted from his ass."

"And how did you determine that?"

"As I said..." She got up and strolled past Leo, pausing to straighten his tie, to perch on his desk. "I just got him into conversation about the lovely flowers gracing his showroom. I pointed to my favorite, the lush azaleas framing the cheese boards, and he agreed that azaleas were his favorites too. He couldn't get enough of azaleas. Only they weren't azaleas, they were petunias. There wasn't an azalea in the place. So I felt him out—metaphorically speaking—about a couple more blooms, and I confirmed that he knows fuck all about flowers."

"And what makes you an expert?"

"I've picked up a few things hanging around Aurora. I pay attention. I'm not just a devastatingly beautiful face. I also tried to talk to Manfred, but he wasn't in the mood. Isadora has so antagonized him that he is not the tiniest bit cooperative. She really is not right for this work, you know. She's just not good at it." Dora frowned and picked off a few crumbs from my breakfast that were still clinging to my lapel. She flicked them away. "You should hire me. Ray agrees that I am good at this. I could schmooze the pants off a snake. Oops, sorry." She giggled. "Shouldn't say the S word." This last was to me, whom she knew was listening.

From behind him, Leo heard, "We've got it, Lieutenant!"

Leo left Dora swinging her leg off the corner of his desk. "Got what?"

Detective Rami said, "That phone number is to a phone booth in Seattle."

"Get me the Seattle police commissioner on the phone. They're Pacific time. That gives them over what? Three, four hours to get organized."

"Four," said Feeney.

Everyone stopped talking and eating while they waited for the call to go through. Leo took it from Felicia Rami's desk. He introduced himself and then fleshed out the details. The plan as I overheard it was simple. The Seattle police would be watching the phone booth. *We* would call the number and make sure we were the first to do so. That was easy, we'd keep the line busy until the guy showed up. Anybody who tried to make a call would just think the phone was out of order. The guy who showed up to wait for a call—the phone would ring and it would be us. The Seattle police would nab him, and we would keep the line busy for a while longer. Any other callers to that number would assume they were too late. After that, the phone wouldn't be answered. Before we knew what any secret perv passwords might be for them to identify themselves to each other and how the webmaster was notified to change the site, we didn't want to set off any alarms. The Seattle police were eager to participate.

A little bing sounded from Leo's computer. "Dora, get off my desk."

"Hester is right, you can be quite rude." She slid off his desk and hovered. He squinted at his screen and hit the print button. "Feeney. They gave us twelve names and addresses. Pass them out. If Shiloh is right, somebody on this list has Anna."

And if I'm wrong, you've just wasted a lot of time. Dora, go now. Thanks for the tip. But just go.

"Oh, all right. I was just trying to help. No need to tattle to Ray. I'm gone."

"Are you talking to me?"

"No. Bye bye, Leo."

I came back, feeling a little dizzy, and apologized to Leo for sitting on his desk. He waved it off. "Haven't seen her in awhile."

"She showed up yesterday. None of us were thrilled to see her, either." I knew Dora had to be listening. "Leo, you have a full plate and I'm not your problem, but I need you to do me one favor."

He looked at me curiously, noncommittally. Leo is unsentimental. There was no guarantee he'd do anything for me just because I was a case that could jerk tears out of old ladies and young detectives alike, or even that I had perhaps given him a good lead. I was getting paid for that and probably more than the city of New York was paying his detectives. He said, "What?"

"If Dora comes back, arrest her, lock her up and call Ray."

"On what grounds?"

"Ray will give you all the grounds you need to keep her locked up for a long time. This is important. She could—hurt this case, and me."

"Anything you say. You look like hell. Why don't you go lie down in the back there. We've got a cot. It's not too full of bugs. We'll call you when we get something. It will take a while to run down all these names."

I passed the malodorous Jeff poring over Feeney's computer screen—they were both studying the violet site—and found my own way to the tiny back room. I wasn't sleepy. I just needed the quiet. I shut the door and lay down.

Feeney woke me up by banging on the metal table next to my head. "We've got him! A dentist in Jersey."

"Where in Jersey? What time is it?"

"A little after one. Nutley. The Nutley police are picking him up now. We're heading out there. Leo wants to know if you want to come along."

"Yes, I think I do." Sometimes I have a gift for understatement. I stumbled after him, embarrassed that he had found me sleeping. When I saw Leo, I said, sheepishly, "Thanks, Leo."

"You still look like something scraped off a New York shoe."

"Always the flatterer."

"Come on then."

Feeney drove. I, Isadora, sat in the backseat. Hester and Cootie had left me. Dora probably had something to do with that. I kept my eyes focused on the blaring colors of cars and buildings and signs, glints of chrome that formed the churning collage outside of the car. I listened to Leo and Feeney as they filled me in on everything they had learned while I was not napping in the back room.

The lab had traced all the hits from April fourth, the day of the violets. There weren't as many as they had feared. Only fifty. Forty of them were women. They were saving that list in case none of the men panned out, although I believed it unlikely that a woman was the kidnapper in this case. Of the other ten, one was a resident of Manhattan; they put him to the side as well. One, named Bobbie, turned out to be female. The dentist from New Jersey was the only one they knew to have been in and out of New York at exactly the right time. The other people were being checked. An insurance broker in Houston. The Houston police had been notified. The owner of a seed and grain operation in Fargo. He was being questioned as well, but Leo doubted he was our man. A retired career army man in Florida. Leo didn't think he was a candidate either, but the Palm

Springs police were picking him up. And so it went. One person they couldn't find but all the others were being questioned by their local police.

After bringing me up to speed on the case, Leo made a couple more calls and conversation died in the car. We were all three tense, excited, fearful of disappointment, of finding her dead, of not finding Anna at all. There was no need to discuss it. My knuckles were white as I hung on to the armrest in the backseat.

The ugliness that was this part of Jersey reeled by the window. Roadside trash by the ton, asphalt, concrete, malls, smokestacks, filth on the ground and in the air. I should have called Ray. But Dora didn't stay, and she did have a tip for Leo. And I had stayed conscious. Pretty much.

Given the wasteland we had just passed through, we turned off into a surprisingly pretty town, powdered with a shimmery green. Well-kept homes of all sizes and varieties. A plethora of lawn ornaments—mostly statues of the Virgin Mary. Splashes of color from spring flower beds.

The car slowed as we pulled into what appeared to be a big cobblestoned square with storybook New England buildings in pink brick with creamy trim, like matching set pieces in a toy village. They were separated by plenty of green space and connected by winding sidewalks. I remembered passing a church and a synagogue coming in, and I saw another steeple shining through the trees several blocks away. Probably more churches here than restaurants. And everywhere old, stately trees. Nice place, Nutley.

We went in the side entrance of the Town Hall. This quarter of the building served as the police station.

Chief Stackmeier looked like an ex-football player who still led a clean, active life. He looked better than Leo, even though he must have had at least fifteen or twenty years on him. He shook Leo's hand and introduced us to two young uniformed cops named Lambert and Russo. Leo introduced Feeney, who also shook hands with the Chief and then, "This is Shiloh. She consults with us."

Hester Hester where are you? Olive? Cootie? Now what?

Stackmeier stuck out his hand. Nobody was there to take it but me. He got the limpest handshake of his life, and I broke into a cold sweat and felt light-headed. He dropped my hand immediately. To Leo, he said, "He has admitted using the site and has a garden behind his house to prove his interest in the subject. He's cool as a cucumber. We haven't turned up the heat. Kept it casual. Thought we'd wait for you." He shifted his weight. "Just so you know, Lieutenant, I know him. He's not my best friend, but—"

"Thanks, Chief. I appreciate it."

"I just hate to think—"

"We don't know he's the one."

Chief Stackmeier nodded.

Officer Lambert had red hair and freckles and looked like Opie all grown up. Russo was an Al Pacino type who would not be long in Nutley. He cast a glittering eye at Leo Gianetti, and on his face I read: *transfer forms*. He could hardly wait to get the hell out of Mayberry. We followed them to the interrogation room.

The Nutley police station was cleaner, brighter than any I had ever seen in Manhattan. It did not have that worn out and beaten-half-to-death-look that such places have in New York. The walls were paneled in light wood and the surrounding woodwork was painted a cheerful pastel yellow. I imagined a sign in their lobby that said, We want to make your interrogation and incarceration experience the best it can possibly be. Have a nice day.

The Nutley officers led us down a narrow hallway, stopping in front of a window into the interrogation room. The sound from inside the room came to the spectators through a small speaker mounted on the wall to the right of the one-way glass.

"Shiloh, come with me. Feeney, you stay here."

The dentist was a smallish, pinch-faced, forty-something man with sandy hair, glasses, manicured hands and a tennis tan. His eyes darted back and forth between Leo and me and then settled on Leo with a concerned, willing-to-cooperate-in-any-way-I-can-officer look on his face.

Leo introduced himself and me. No handshakes were

offered. We both sat down across the table from our suspect.

"We are looking for a little girl named Anna Stern. Ever see her before?" Leo slid a photograph of Anna, taken at her birthday party, across the table.

The dentist looked at it. Shook his head. Looked Leo right in the eye. "I'm afraid I haven't seen her. Is she from Nutley?" His voice was evenly modulated. The voices of Bethy-June and Sula were a shrill *want to leave, take us home getting dark*

"She lives in New York City."

"Why would you think I might know her?" He had a perfectly calibrated smile on his lips. Not too broad—child missing after all—but relaxed, willing to help, friendly. Behind his glasses, his eyes were stones.

...want to leave no more please so scared we'll be good so good home mama mama there is no mama there is no mama Where were Lance, Sugartime? Gatekeeper?

"On April fourth, one of the hits on this Web site..." Leo slid the printout of the home page across the table stopping it flush with the photograph, "was from your computer. I'm a little surprised you used your own computer."

"Why wouldn't I? I was looking for information on some plants I was thinking of putting out back of my house. I hadn't had experience with them before. I wanted to get some tips."

"What plants would those be?"

The dentist blinked and swallowed. Everyone blinks and swallows. The significance is in the timing. "Well, a few things really. Some bulbs. I wasn't sure if I was too late. Maybe I should have planted them last spring. I..."

"What bulbs?"

"Ehhh....Glads. Irises."

"You accessed this site," Leo said, tapping the corner of the paper. "See there, it's a site with a picture of violets on April fourth, and four days later, Anna Stern goes missing from her playground."

"I'm sorry to hear that. What does the Web site have to do with her?"

"This Web site is a message board for pedophiles. The flowers are just...symbols...for children."

"How do you know that?" Amazement on his face. Not feigned. The shrieking in my head got louder.

"Because the information at the bottom there...see the little sun and the little teardrop shape right there?"

He nodded.

"That, if you read it right, is a phone number. Did you call that number from your home phone?"

He emitted a short laugh. "Of course not."

"Where did you call from?"

"I—I didn't call at all." He was trying hard to keep his friendly smile but the muscles in his chin were tightening up. His breathing was getting deeper. Deep, cleansing, calming breaths.

Leo said to the dentist, "Will you excuse us for a moment? Do you want some coffee or anything?"

"No, thanks. Water. I'd like some water, please."

When we closed the door behind us, Leo said, "He's almost good enough to pass a lie detector test. How about the Shiloh test?"

"Not even a D minus."

"How can you tell?"

"I don't know. I've got kids in my head squealing in terror. Hester, Olive and Cootie are either silent or gone. He's too relaxed. Like he has taken courses in it. He's too sure. Too sincere. But that throbbing vein in his forehead is no lie and neither is the spazzing chin muscle. He's scared. He is so scared that you could probably poke him with your finger and he'd start blubbering."

"That's all I wanted to hear. Now I do this alone."

I stood outside the one-way glass with Feeney, Lambert and Russo.

Leo loomed large in that small room with the small, seated dentist. He paced. His shirt had eased itself out of his suit pants during the drive out here and he hadn't bothered to tuck it back in. If I looked like something you scraped off a shoe, Leo looked like what that shoe had stepped in. He began, "Now Sheldon..."

"Doctor Morris," the dentist corrected him.

"Shel—" The dentist winced but said nothing. "—so did you get help with those dahlias of yours?"

"Yes."

"Not from this site you didn't. Where is she?"

"You can't assume that just because I looked at a Web site—a thousand people must have looked at that." A shaft of light suddenly poured through the high western window as the sun came into position for a direct hit, making the sheen of perspiration on his face glow.

afraid of the dark the dark the dark bad in the dark hurts

"Actually, on the day in question, Sheldon, only fifty." Leo leaned in to his suspect and spoke in a very chummy manner. "And going back, you know what we found? You have looked at that site on a very regular, you might say frequent, basis. The site is no good, Sheldon. You wouldn't find anything useful about plants on that site. After the first visit, you'd know that. The only reason you'd go back is to find your next victim."

I turned to Feeney. "Did the lab have time to go back farther than April third?"

"No. Gianetti is making that up."

"And that's not all we have." Leo's voice resonated through the box on the wall next to me. "We have a record of your EZ pass. We know you made a trip in to the city every day from April fourth till the day Anna was taken, and you haven't gone in since. What kind of a dumb bastard uses his EZ pass when he's going to kidnap a kid?"

"There you are, Lieutenant." Nervous laughter leaked out all around his words. "If I were kidnapping someone, would I have used my EZ pass?"

Leo steamrolled over that bit of nervous logic. "We know where you got the fake uniform so you would look like a New York City parks worker."

The dentist visibly wilted.

I asked Feeney, "Do you know that?"

"Nope." Feeney was grinning.

Leo spoke softly, intimately. "Where's the body, Sheldon?"

"There's no body! I didn't kill her!"

Like his namesake, the King of Beasts when he has closed

the gap on the hyena, Leo smiled, "Oh?"

"I mean, I wouldn't kill *anybody*."

Leo kept smiling through his heavily lidded, weary eyes.

"I want my lawyer."

Leo slid the phone toward him and left the room.

"Can you listen in on that call?"

Officer Lambert nodded and headed for the outside office.

"Make sure he only calls his lawyer. Then find out who the lawyer is and give me a traffic jam between wherever he is and here. Hold him up for at least forty-five minutes."

"You got it." Officer Opie was out the door.

Sheldon Morris spent about ten minutes on the phone. We heard nothing enlightening from his end of the conversation. Just where he was, that the lawyer should get there as quickly as possible and was to notify Mrs. Morris. Leo and I waited and sipped coffee that the office clerk, a middle-aged, chunky but solid woman named Cathy brought us in glass mugs. "Anybody take it white?" I nodded and she handed me two packets of powdered creamer and a plastic stirrer. I thanked her. Then I asked Leo, "Is it legal to listen in to a call like that?"

Leo stretched and took a sip of coffee. "Gee. I just am not that familiar with Jersey laws."

Officer Opie came back and took his place beside Russo, Feeney and me. As soon as the receiver had come to rest in the phone set on the interrogation table, Leo was in the room again.

His lips pursed, almost pouty, the dentist admonished, "You have to wait for my lawyer before you can interrogate me."

"Who's interrogating? We're just talking. I'm just keeping you company till he gets here."

The man tried to stand up, and Leo growled the order, "Sit down!" Lion: the hyena killer.

The dentist sat. His veneer of calm was showing signs of wear and tear. Leo continued to prowl the room, his demeanor no longer chummy.

"Can I have some water?"

The hyena's mouth was dry. I could hear it in his voice and see it in the way he was licking his lips.

His pout turned to petulance and he said, "You can't do anything till my lawyer gets here."

The lion stopped prowling and leaned into the hyena, so close he probably felt Leo's hot breath on his cheek. "Let me tell you something about the real fucking world, Sheldon. I can do anything I want. Absolutely anything. What would be a good analogy here?" Leo straightened up and searched the air for his analogy. "Let me think. Oh, yes. I'm the man. And you're the little girl. You're absolutely helpless. You are absolutely at my mercy. No-one-to-hear-you-scream type deal. I can do what I want, any time I want, as often as I want, for as long as I fucking want. You are my little girl."

My knees were shaking. I looked around for a chair. There wasn't one. I had never seen Leo like this. In the few interrogations I had watched, Leo was always strictly by the book. I wanted to leave, but I was also fascinated. Anyway, my legs wouldn't work. The crying in my head was now a migraine, voices indistinguishable from pain. I saw what was happening in the room as if I were looking through a camera lens. I couldn't see anything around it. Just Leo, and the dentist, and the words coming out of the box to my right mingling with the sound of pain in my head.

The dentist licked his lips, and his eyes moved rapidly back and forth. "Isn't there a jurisdiction issue here? Where are the New Jersey police? I know the chief of police. Bernard Stackmeier. We golf together. You may get by with your high-handed thug tactics in New York City, but not here you won't, mister. This is a decent community." The dentist took out a white handkerchief and blotted his face and neck. "Where's Bernie? He'll tell you you can't do this."

"Look, little girl, this is me, doing it." Leo unbuckled his belt.

I leaned up against the wall just to feel something solid.

"What the hell is he going to do?" breathed Officer Russo to my left. "Fuck him or beat him to death?"

Feeney didn't answer. I couldn't answer. The skin around Officer Opie's freckles got a paler shade of white.

"You see, the Chief of Police, *Bernie*, is out. I heard him tell the dispatcher. The other officers are all on coffee break. They won't be back till, well, I don't know when they'll be back. I'm unfamiliar with the Garden State's rules about that. You see, as you pointed out, it's not my jurisdiction."

Watching Leo, Lambert was uncomfortable, Russo was hard-faced, his eyes slits, maybe enjoying the little play in the interrogation room. Feeney looked grim.

The suspect had stopped his face-blotting when Leo unbuckled his belt and, as Leo slid the belt off slowly through the loops, the chair the dentist sat in began to rattle.

"Tell me where she is, honey, or the fun begins," Leo purred.

I finally felt someone who I thought was Hester…if she had had control of the body, we'd be throwing up now.

"We've got you on the Web site. We've got you going to New York every day to scope out the playground while you figured out what you were going to do. We've got a search warrant, and the police are right now going through your beautiful house on Sattherwaite. They'll find that uniform."

Two officers had been sent to Morris's house with a warrant. That part was true.

"Could I have some water please?"

"No."

"I want my lawyer."

"Tell me where she is." Leo folded his belt in half.

"You can't—"

And slammed it down on the table with a *whack*! loud as a gunshot.

Bethy running! Bethy running! Don't. Don't hit. Running to the stairs running up the stairs belt off calls me the bad names behind me closer running to the dark space hiding hiding in the dark space way to the back crouch the big coat smells bad is heavy but I crawl under it he won't see I'm hiding go by go by don't find me I'm invisible I'm not here he's here he's here! the coat is off hurts my arm hurts my shoulder hurts he's pulling me up hard my feet don't touch the floor tight around my chest something tight I can't breathe I kick it gets tighter it's too tight it's holding me up I'm hanging in the dark he slams the door alone dark can't breathe can't breathe I hate him want

to hurt him can't breathe ....
....*I am June. I can be still.*
I know how to breathe hanging.

"Isadora. Isadora. Hey, you okay? I brought you some more coffee. You take it with milk, right?"

I took the coffee that Feeney was holding out to me. My other cup was on the floor, half full and cold.

"I think Leo's going to break this guy. He's got him sweating like a pig."

So was I. I looked at the clock. He'd been in there fifteen minutes.

I hate flashbacks.

Leo's voice was still coming through the box on the wall. I tried to listen to what he was saying as I held my cup in both hands and sipped. Stay here, no matter what happens, I said to myself and all my people. No response.

"...tired of this, Sheldon? I know I am. I'm so tired. But I can go get some rest. You can't. If I quit keeping you company like I'm doing, someone else will be in here keeping you more company. You'll never want for company, Sheldon. So why don't you stop trying my patience. Thin ice, Sheldon old man. That's what my patience is right now. And it's cracking." Leo had been pacing around the dentist like a predator wearing down his prey. "You hear the cracking?" Now he turned and circled close again and said, "Nope that's it, Sheldon. I want to know where she is. I can't kill you, but I can make you hurt in ways no doctor can diagnose."

"Feeney, I'm going out for some air," I said. My voice sounded strange to my own ears.

I was nearly staggering down the hall, and the junior detective followed me. I had a feeling that Leo had ordered him to keep an eye on me, so telling him to leave me alone would only make him more suspicious that I shouldn't be left alone under any circumstances. I collapsed in a chair in the office and sipped my coffee. Feeney casually pulled up a chair and sat next to me. Cathy smiled at us and went back to her work, whatever that was.

"You and the lieutenant have known each other a long

time."

"A few years."

"I know he's not happy, me being his partner."

I didn't confirm or deny. I did not feel like small talk.

"He thinks my old man pulled strings to get me this job, and he did, but he wasn't happy about it. He wanted to use his strings to get me into politics and I wanted to work with Gianetti. He's good. Learn from the best, right?"

I nodded and concentrated on the taste of my coffee and the yellow woodwork and the light bouncing on the shiny linoleum floor. My metal chair was hard, and I tried to stay aware of it against my back and my butt. Stay here. Stay here, I ordered myself.

Feeney was distressingly chatty. "So, what kind of name is Shiloh? Is that your first name, like Cher? Or a last name?"

"It's an acronym."

"Of what?"

"The names of some of my people."

"Oh. Like a pseudonym, or stage name."

"No, it's my legal name. I had it changed in court."

"Well," he said rather softly. "I guess I understand why you wouldn't want to go by your father's name. Hey. Did you hear? Calafano sacked Jimmy Stokes."

"Why?"

"That little scene with you...er...the other..."

"Hawk."

"Right. That was the last straw on a pretty heavy bale. The camel died. But, really, the captain was only going to put him on probation with compulsory sessions with the department shrink, but Stokes lost it. Really lost his temper and made some threats. I don't know what all. So the captain fired him on the spot. Took his gun and his badge. End of story. Lieutenant Gianetti thought his fuse was way too short anyway, and it should have been done a year ago." Feeney sipped his coffee. "But, it's done now."

Lambert and Russo shot through the door, followed by Leo, who barked, "She's in a room in the basement of a public storage facility on Kingsland."

Russo and Lambert had already bolted out the door to their

car.

Leo, still buckling his belt and tucking in his shirt, ordered Feeney, "Take over. Find out everything you can about that site and how they use it—if there are any passwords when they make the phone calls and how the information is changed on the site. He doesn't get water, he doesn't get to piss or call his mama. You don't have much time before his lawyer shows up."

Sirens were already blaring away from the station north toward Kingsland when we passed Cathy on our way out to Leo's car.

She was putting the phone down. "An ambulance is meeting you there," she said to him. "You know where it is? Take a right off Franklin when you get to Kingsland. Half a block down you'll see a big gray building on your right."

The paramedics were just getting out of the ambulance as we arrived. An old man, probably the building manager, was handing keys to Russo. Leo said, "Wait. I think a woman should go in first." Leo looked at me.

Jesus Christ, Hester, where are you? I can't do this! I can't. Where were they? Even Cootie would do. But there was no one but whimpering Bethy-June. I couldn't send a crying child in there. Even Sula was gone. My vision was now restricted to a narrowing tunnel straight ahead of me.

I followed the building manager, who was just a shadow. Leo was right behind me and the paramedics behind him. I didn't feel my legs, but somehow I was going forward, gripping the railing hand over hand to get myself down the stairs. I moved my head from side to side to take in the basement. A fluorescent bulb made the concrete floors and rows of doors to left and right look flat, colorless.

The manager offered me the keys to the last padlocked door on the right. I shook my head. He opened the padlock and removed it. I pulled the door open. A faint fetid smell greeted me. There was a high window in here, so it was dim, not dark. Straight ahead of me under the window was a twin bed with a rumpled pink coverlet. A child lay on top of it.

All my people had left me. Now even Bethy-June was silent. Gone. There was no one to go with me. I, Isadora, approached the bed. I was the only one left to look down at this still silent child.

I picked up her hand. It was warm. She had a strong pulse. She was dressed in an elaborately frilly pink dress. Her face was sticky and tear-stained. Her hair lank. Her hands grubby. Her dress had slipped up, exposing ruffled underpants. I pulled the dress down carefully. "Anna." My voice sounded like it was coming from a squawk box a mile away.

"Anna, we've come to take you home."

She didn't move.

I turned to Leo. "I think she's drugged."

I hoped she had been drugged insensible for most of her incarceration in this grotesque playpen. Not her playpen, but his. No, I did not need feelings. I knew why the others had retreated deep into the gyre.

I backed away from the bed and one of the paramedics stepped up and gave her a quick examination. "Heart's good," he said. "Breathing good too. Yeah, I think she's just doped up."

As he gathered her into his arms, she moaned and moved her head. I tried to take in the small room on my way out. A television was on low, either playing tapes or tuned in to a cartoon channel. A nightlight was plugged into the outlet above the television plug. Scattered dolls and empty candy and snack wrappers and soda bottles littered the soiled indoor-outdoor carpet that covered the cement floor. A full potty chair in the corner.

As we mounted the stairs, Leo was already on his cell phone calling Claudia Keating. "We've got her. We've got Anna. We're taking her in an ambulance to the Nutley Hospital. Yeah. Nutley, New Jersey. She seems—okay. I'll have a squad car pick you and her mother up. Right."

He placed another call to order the squad car he had promised, then he closed his phone with a snap and slipped it in his pocket. "I need a drink. Come with me, Isadora."

We went out and up the street to a neighborhood dive that advertised chicken wings every day and lasagna, all you can eat, on Tuesdays. Leo ordered a Jack Daniels straight up. I ordered a tonic water with lime. The bartender was a woman in her forties, with overtanned skin, ample and visible cleavage, and long nails with silver racing stripes painted over the bright pink lacquer. Word travels fast in a small town. "On the house," she said and left us alone.

Leo called Feeney and told him to get a ride to the bar and pick us up and drive us back to New York. Stackmeier now had official charge of the dentist whose lawyer was threatening all kinds of things but, according to Feeney, was so disgusted with his own client that his heart wasn't in it. Mrs. Morris, when told that they found the child, and where, refused to post bond for her husband.

Relating this to me, Leo said, "Yeah, this kind of thing will really put a crimp in a marriage." Neither of us laughed.

He threw back his whiskey and didn't order another. I downed my tonic. The bar was dark and seemed to be getting darker. I heard myself say, "Now we can get Charlotte."

"I thought you said—"

"I said you couldn't help Charlotte."

"You know where she is?"

"I think so."

"Well, Jesus fucking Christ on a pogo stick, Shiloh! How long have you known?"

"From my first day on this case."

"I've a mind to arrest you right now. Never mind waiting for Dora. How did you know? *What* do you know, anyway?"

"Do you read Sherlock Holmes, Leo?"

"Jesus, here we go again."

"There's one story where the great detective solves the case because of what the dog did in the night."

"Okay. I'll bite. What did the goddamn dog do?"

"Nothing. He didn't do anything."

"That's it. You're under arrest. Are you going to tell me—"

"You need to call Ray. She should be at the hospital to talk to Miriam and to Anna. The kid's going to need a lot of help."

"Why don't you call Ray yourself?"

"I don't have...I'm not feeling..." The spinning began so abruptly that I clutched the bar.

"What are those people doing?"

Leo just smiled at me. The lion's smile. I was the hyena. I had to get to a phone.

But the spinning accelerated and people surrounded me and I couldn't go anywhere.

Chapter 22

"*This is a play. A game.*" *Her voice is reassuring.* "*Ceremonial. Ray likes a ceremony to cement integration. You know. Celebrate it. Mark it.*"

We didn't want to integrate.

"*Of course we do, don't we?*" *She is Mary Poppins, encouraging me to take my medicine.* "*Ray wants this. All of this is just symbolic anyway, you know. Role playing. Psycho drama. You know how she is. Integration begins with a little dying. Rivers to ocean and all that. But we don't really die. You know what she says.*"

She says little rivers to big river.

"*Let's not quibble,*" *she says coldly.* "*Ready?*"

I feel the knife and see the smile dawning on her face and realize the bargain we made—not exactly a bargain—we engaged to play the game where she stabs me and I die. A game.

Too many realities for the mind to grasp come to a point in that smile as she cuts again, deeply, this time—the killing cut, for the blood gurgles like muddy water up through the neck of a slim pipe, warm, spilling over my hands as I try to hold my abdomen together. I lose feeling in my extremities and go light in the head. Blank spots yawn and crescents shimmer in my visual field. I hope Ray can hear me.

Call an ambulance. Game over. I give up. I want to live. I'll tell them I did it so you won't be blamed.

I think of the pain when they will move me and sew me, stick me and fill me with foreign fluids; I'll feel the pain in every part of me, but I'll live, and I feel myself going under and the medics will get here or they won't; I'll wake up in pain, or I won't wake up at all.

People in robes gather, like medieval religious. Someone lets a child run into the room. My bed is slick with blood. My blood this time. The child screams and screams and runs back out. I am angry they had been so careless. My anger floats, disembodied.

I can hear Ray is arguing with a nurse, just outside the door: "You are so appalled at what this child did? You should be appalled at what was done to her! She saved herself. The only way she could. If you can't get your head around that, then get on a different ward. In fact, I'll see to it."

No, that's a memory. That's not here.

I am still conscious, still not on a stretcher. No one is sewing me up. But I am now connected to an IV. Clear, rose-colored fluid drips into my vein. Not enough to save me, just prolong things. Why bother with it, I wonder. Now, Ray is angry. At me. The others are all smiling, watching me die. Dora's smile glitters, the knife still in her hand, though her work is done. I keep bleeding. This can't last forever. I will run out of blood, my veins will fill with rosewater. I'll be dead, but I won't dehydrate. This is wildly funny, but nobody laughs.

In the thickening dark, I go over it all again, how I got here, and I feel no regret. We found Anna and the one who took her. I won't be able to get them Charlotte. They will never find her without me. But I am not afraid to die. It will be a relief.

The spinning accelerates to a whirlpool sucking me down into cold black and evil. I don't mind dying, but I will not go THERE. Ray would not want me to go there. The place worse than death. Dora has the knife and the cold glittering smile. She can kill me, but she can't make me go there.

I say, "No." I look into her eyes. Basilisks, I always thought they would be. To look into them would be to surely die. But now I look, straight, without flinching, and they are just eyes like my own, and I say, I am the firstborn.

She drops the Poppins face and hisses, "Are you sure about that? The firstborn is dead. This is something they and your precious dyke shrink are afraid to tell you. The firstborn is dead. You are just a shell for the rest of us. I am the strongest. I deserve to keep it."

Little river to big river. I am the big river. I am the firstborn. I am not the one to die or even pretend to die.

"Go back."

Dora's smile falters.

"Go back," I say again, with more strength than I should have left, given the soaking bed, the blood dripping everywhere. It is always like this. So much blood everywhere. Blood fills my mouth, my nose, eyes and ears. I drown in it, choke on it. "Leave me in peace."

The room is darker, the robed figures now only shadows. How long does it take to die?

Saturday

Chapter 23

I heard my name from a distance and wondered from which side someone would be calling me. There was no one on the other side I cared to see, assuming there *was* another side. I had never really accepted that there was. The voice was getting closer and clearer, and the room was getting lighter. There were fewer people. *Is this death?* "Is this death?"

"You are alive, Isadora." My name again. And again, repeated patiently, like someone tugging a line so as not to hurt the fish on the end of it. "Isadora. Isadora."

Now, I recognized the voice. "I'm bleeding, Ray. No one will help me. There is always so much blood."

"You aren't bleeding. There is no blood."

The room came back in pieces. Now the robes were white. *And now only one. And it is not a robe, it is a white coat. Ray is sitting on a straight-backed chair close to the bed to my right, leaning in toward me, her elbows on her knees. She looks tired, worried, not angry. They did take me to the hospital then. They must have changed the rosewater for blood. The pieces fill in around Ray and the doctor standing over me on my left. Yes, this is a hospital room.*

"Isadora, you are not bleeding. You were hallucinating."

"Did I die?"

"No, you had a psychotic episode. You are safe. You are not bleeding and you are not dead."

I still feel the cuts and the warmth of my own blood flowing.

I licked my lips and brought my fingers to my tongue, just to check. No blood.

"Isadora, look at your arms."

I was in a hospital gown, a sheet pulled up to my waist. Gingerly, not wanting to disturb the IV connection, I lifted my left arm, but there was no IV, nor in my right arm. I looked up and saw no bottles or IV bags hanging anywhere. The doctor managed a weak smile. She was fresh-faced, terribly young. She reached for my arm but Ray shook her head and she dropped her hand. "Look at your arms, Isadora." I pulled up my sleeve and saw my skin, unmarked. But Dora hadn't cut my arms. She cut my stomach. I lifted up the sheet and used it as cover while I pulled up the papery gown to reveal my midriff. No cuts. No blood.

"She'll be all right now. Could we be alone, please?"

Baby doctor did not seem at all reluctant to leave. When the door closed behind her, Ray said, "Forgive me, Isadora. It was too soon. I thought you could handle it. But, of course, you did handle it. You brought Anna back to her family. Isadora, you were brilliant. I just wish the toll for you had not been so high."

"Not so high. I didn't die."

"No, you didn't die." She unclasped and reclasped her hands in a quiet gesture of triumph and relief.

"Ray, if I hadn't…"

"Hadn't what, Isadora? Tell me what happened."

"Dora tried to kill me."

She didn't say anything and for once I could not read her face.

"Could she? If I hadn't come back, would I have died? Would she have been the only one left?"

"I don't know. I would never have rested till I got you back."

"What if I weren't…here anymore to get back? She said we were integrating and at first…but then I knew she was lying. She said the firstborn was dead. Has always been dead."

Ray studied me thoughtfully. She was not in her usual suit, but a silk shirt and blue V-neck sweater. A bit casual for her for a Friday. Ray dressed expensively, impeccably. She said as soon as she got money she spent it on the most expensive clothes she could afford, because she was tired of people mistaking her for a cleaning lady.

The door opened and Leo stuck his head in. "I hear she's back."

Ray nodded to him to come in and he did, closing the door behind him.

"What happened?" I asked Leo.

He stood at the foot of the bed, looking even worse than the last time I had seen him, except he was wearing a clean shirt. Maybe he kept an extra in his car. "You started crying and fell off your bar stool. I knew you hadn't had enough tonic and lime for that, so Feeney and I hauled you out to the car and brought you here."

"Where is this?" The taste of blood was almost overpowering. I checked my tongue again with a finger. Ray noticed, but didn't say anything.

"The Nutley hospital."

"Is Anna—"

"She's just down the hall," said Ray.

"How is—"

"They want to keep her here another day. She's dehydrated. I brought Georgina with me."

Georgina Dobson was a child psychiatrist. She specialized in abused children. Ray brought her in a few years ago to work with June, Bethy and Sula. Because of their sessions with her, Bethy and June had fused. Sula and Bethy-June still saw her once in a while.

A plump woman in a flowered dress walked in. "Hello. How are you?"

"More embarrassed than anything," I said to Georgina Dobson.

"Speaking of..." Ray smiled at her and said, "Lieutenant, this is Dr. Dobson."

She nodded at Leo. "We met in the cafeteria this morning." She came to the left of my bed and smiled warmly down at me.

Georgina is about sixty-five with snow white gramma hair, she calls it, blue eyes that really do twinkle, and a gramma smile. "You did a wonderful, remarkable thing. Come in and talk to me about it sometime. Not therapy. We'll just chat over a pot of tea."

"Sure," I said.

She squeezed both eyes in a double wink, smiled at Ray and Leo on her way out. Anna was in the best of care.

I raised my head to focus on the disheveled lieutenant still poised awkwardly at the foot of my bed. "I'm sorry Leo. You shouldn't have to take care of me."

"Cops get wounded on the job, kiddo, and we take care of 'em. Don't apologize. You did good."

I tried to pull myself up to a sitting position. Ray pushed the button to raise the head of my bed. "How long have I been here?" The window seemed to glow rather brightly behind the closed blinds. "What time is it?"

"Nine o'clock."

"But..." I looked at the window.

"Nine o'clock in the morning."

"Oh, good grief! Where are my clothes? I have to go. I have to talk to Claudia."

"Are you going to tell me what's going on?" Leo took a step forward. He was grinning at me. "I'm only the officer in charge. If I could just get a clue."

"Drive me back to New York and I'll tell you."

Ray gave me a stern look. "I'll check you out if you promise me two things. One, you will come to my office tomorrow morning at ten o'clock. We have some work to do."

"Tomorrow is Sunday."

"Then, make it eleven."

"Okay. What else?"

"Eat something. Leo, get her something she can eat in the car." Leo nodded. "Are you going to stay with her for awhile?"

"As long as she lets me."

"All right, I'll check you out. On my way down to see Anna."
Ray patted the bed next to my hand and left the room.

"I'll eat." The blood taste was gone from my mouth. I usually couldn't eat till I'd had some strong coffee to wash it out. "Where are my clothes?" I asked again. I didn't feel like throwing off the sheet and exposing my bottom, but before I could insist that Leo leave as well, we heard a timid rap on the door.

Leo opened it to Miriam, who spared just a glance for the lieutenant. Word traveled fast that I had come out of bo-bo land, wherever the hell I'd been. Well, it was hell. The hell that can only be created with help from a person who wants you dead. The bad bitch and I had a showdown coming. It was time. Miriam, looking positively rosy, came close to the left side of my bed and reached for my hand. Hester was back and at the ready, offering her hand with the graciousness of at least a duchess. Hester loves this stuff.

Miriam clasped Hester's hand in both of hers, brought it slowly to her cheek and held it there, reverently. Then she placed her hand back on top of the sheet and without a single word, turned and left.

"Russians! You gotta love 'em!"

"Hester?" Leo asked.

"Yep. A little worse for wear, I must say. *What* a freak show! Leo! Is that a *blue* shirt? Solving a case makes you really push the fashion envelope. Well, gent, you need to leave the room so a lady can get her britches on. Where are they? My clothes? Let me get dressed already!"

He left grinning and Hester went to the closet. The only thing in there was a brown paper bag. She looked inside and wrinkled her nose.

I suggested, *Why don't you let Cootie do this. He won't care.*

"Oh, brilliant. The little grubmeister is good for something."

Cootie dressed and swaggered out. He found Leo and Ray in the hall engaged in low-voiced conversation. "Yo! Law*man*, Ray-*man-adana*. The chicks want to get the show on the road, and I am your trav ling com PAN yun."

Ray waved us off saying, "I'll take care of the paperwork. You go ahead. But tomorrow, eleven sharp."

"Right. See ya."

Leo and Cootie made their way down a couple of hallways following the EXIT signs to an elevator, past the reception desk and out through the glass doors to a parking lot.

"Cooter! Are you going tell me what the hell is going on?"

Cootie was behaving remarkably well, listening to me instead of charging ahead with his own agenda. He didn't even demand a Coke. He felt bad about losing his grip along with everybody else.

"Yeah, Lawman, but you gotta, like, give her a little slack."

"Like, I haven't?"

"Well, I'll tell you, but she's gotta handle something first. You're going to have to sort of, like, wait in the lobby."

"Wait in what lobby?"

"First, her lobby. She needs to go home and change clothes. The chicks aren't like me. They don't like grubbing it."

"You look fine. Feeney got there as soon as she hit the barroom floor and we picked her up right away. Five second rule, you know."

"I know. It's a chick thing. Never put something on again till it's been washed, ironed, disinfected, autoclaved, nuked and Simonized. If you get my meaning."

"Yeah. Sure."

Cootie was never reluctant to eat and made no protest at all when Leo stopped at the first deli he saw on his way out of town. He came back to the car with a bag full of sandwiches, chips, coffee and Cokes, and three packages of Sunny Doodles.

Chapter 24

Leo dropped Cootie off at our apartment. I think he was glad to be rid of him. Cootie had talked his arm off and littered his front seat with sandwich wrappers, cellophane and empty soda cans. But now Leo knew what I knew and why I had to talk to Claudia. He didn't like the scenario Cootie narrated for him, but he understood it.

As soon as I stepped into my apartment, I felt it. An anxiety that was almost overwhelming. More like a feeling of dread. I did not want to dwell on it or let it control me, so I forced myself to the phone, called information and got the number for the Heartwood Buddhist Center. I dialed it and asked to speak to the Abbess.

When I hung up the receiver, it was suddenly clear to me what I was reacting to. I had had the same feeling in the asylum when they put me in a room for the first time with one-way glass and I sensed people watching me. The realization came too late. Before I could turn around my world went dark.

We all woke up, but it was Hester who felt the hard, cold floor beneath her and the bag over her head, tape over her mouth, her hands tied behind her back and her feet bound—not for the first time, but the first time as an adult. Except for the sore spot on the back of her head, she didn't seem to have any other bruises. She wiggled around and sat up. Conditioned not to make noise, knowing that would only bring on greater pain or a longer time tied up, locked up or whatever was being done to her at the moment, she kept still and waited. Hester had the body, but we were all there except Hawk—and Dora, whose habit is to take to the gyre at the first sign of real trouble. Her coming out with the snake was an anomaly, born out of a desire for self-preservation. She didn't want to end up at the bottom of the well drowning in a couple feet of fetid water. So we owe her that one. Olive was the first to speak. *What the hell is going on here?*

I assume that's a rhetorical question, I said.

More or less.

Hester was trying her wrist bindings to see how tight they were. They were tight. She tried to loosen her feet, but they were tied securely as well. Then she lay back down on the floor and rubbed against the bag on her head. It was porous, but still, it was not so easy to breathe with her mouth taped. Again, we'd been here, or somewhere similar to here, before. It then occurred to me with a shock that I, Isadora, had not been here before. I had always been pushed back into the gyre, and one of the others had come forward. In that realization, I had a new respect and sympathy for my alters. They could all feel it.

If we get out of this one, I'll be nicer to all of you.

Thanks Isadora.

More Coke?

Sure, Cootie.

Since Hester couldn't talk, she thought, *Can I dye my hair red?*

As a fire engine.

Well, that is something to live for.

Our internal banter ceased as we heard a metallic sound. A click. And then a muffled voice: "You are going to stay here till you admit that you're a fake."

Huh? We all kind of said that in unison. Hester made audible grunting sounds. Two huge hands lifted the bag up above her nose and tied it there so her eyes were still covered. Then the tape was ripped off her mouth.

"Ow! That hurt!"

The voice said again, "Start talking. I have a tape recorder here. When I get the truth on tape, I'll let you go."

Don't say anything, Hester.

Wasn't planning to.

There's something odd about that voice.

It's a recording. That was Lance. *The person who is here doesn't want us to recognize his voice, so he recorded instructions disguising his voice.*

But we know who it is, don't we? Cootie thought he knew, but wasn't sure.

Sure. Don't tell him we know who it is.

Why? Afraid of hurting his feelings?

Noooo, if he knows we know who he is, he might kill us.

Oh.

Hester said, "We're sorry you got canned, Jimmy."

Hester! What are you doing?

Getting on his good side.

I don't think he has one.

Hester started again, "We were really sorry when we heard—"

"There's no *we* you freak! Stop playing movie of the week and just tell the tape recorder you are faking this whole load of crap. Calling you in on special cases. What a load of crap."

He seems fond of that expression. 'Load of crap.'

"Why do you think we're faking?" Hester used her warmest, friendliest tone.

"I saw Sally Field do the same shit in a movie. Then somebody told me that was bogus. Never happened. Any of it. Some shrink trying to sell books."

Well, that was true. And we'd heard it all before. So had Ray.

"But, why should we fake it?"

Hester was being remarkably reasonable.

"I know what you are. You were a bad kid who got away

with killing her old man. That's all. And you have to keep it up or they'll put a murder rap on you. A lot of kids get knocked around and they don't kill their parents. They wait till they are old enough and they leave home."

"Is that what happened to you, Jimmy?"

"What?"

"Did your old man beat on you?"

"He was tough. I was a kid who needed a tough dad. Some kids do. I turned out all right."

"Is this all right? Look at what you're doing here. Think like a cop for just a few more minutes."

No answer.

"Anyway, we were locked up a long time, so we didn't get away with anything."

Still no response.

"Jimmy, since I already know who you are, could you take this bag off my head?"

There was a long silence and then a shuffle, and the bag was jerked rudely off her head, almost ripping her nose and ears off. "Ouch! Geez, Jimmy, what's the point?

"You will never break Isadora. She is not even here." Hester knew I was not in the gyre. But I saw where she was going with this. "Jimmy, unfortunately, we are what we are. No fake. No game. You can't break us because each of us was born in a dark closet, in ropes and gags, down wells and in acts of rape before we could speak. There is nothing that you could even imagine that we haven't already sheltered Isadora's mind from. So if you are after her, you won't get her. And if you do something to us, chances are, more of us will be born. You can't make us say or do anything."

"If I put a bullet in your head, you're dead." We heard the hammer go back on a gun. We all hate guns.

Hester took a deep breath. "You raise a good point. All right, you've got us. I'm a fake. A big old fat fake. There. Can we go now?"

"No, say it like yourself. Not your put-on character."

"I am saying it like myself. Oh. You want me to say it like Isadora." Hester cleared her throat and tried to say it like I'd say it, but she can't imitate me any more than I can imitate her. She tried. She still sounded like Hester.

"Do it, bitch, or I swear I will blow your head off!"

The Company was in a panic. We all knew if I took the body, under these circumstances, I couldn't keep it. I'd black out. I thought it was a miracle I was still out of the gyre. I felt a sort of mental pushing and shoving and Olive was on the floor. Maybe she thought she could sound more like me. She did, in a way. Her voice was lower. Unfortunately her face is quite different.

"What do you care if I'm a fake or not? So I'm a fake. Who cares? I've done time in a cell. A cell in an asylum isn't better than a cell in a jail. Believe that."

Jimmy was not saying much, but he was sweating and breathing hard. His agitation was full of rage and frustration. He lifted the barrel of his gun to the wall above Olive's head and fired. Olive jumped. "Are you going to kill me, Jimmy?"

He cocked the gun again.

"Would you do me a favor? Kill me if you must. It's not much of a life, living in her head. I can admit to that. But, I'd like to have sex first."

Are you nuts? What are you doing?

Trust me, came back a whispered thought.

Jimmy Stokes was as surprised as we were, because he lowered the gun for a minute and stared at her.

"I never get any. Isadora has a *thing* about it, as you might imagine, so the rest of us are supposed to live her meager little life. I can't hurt you. I have no weapon. Just untie me and we can have a little fun before I...well, kiss you goodbye. It's no trick. You have the recorder on, so people will know it's consensual. And then if you don't shoot me, and we don't press charges, then no foul. It's your way out, and my way to a little satisfaction. What do you say?"

Jimmy put the gun on a high shelf. He came to Olive and untied her legs, warily, expecting her to kick, but she didn't. Was she waiting for Hawk?

No! Olive. Not again. Not again! Don't let Hawk...

The Company shushed me, for a change, as he gingerly untied her hands, again, ready to shove a fist into her mouth if she made a suspicious move. She didn't. She laid back down, flat on the floor, and gave a good imitation of Dora at her most appalling. Jimmy unbuckled his belt and unzipped his pants and lay on her and started moving himself around on top of her. My panic was rising to a white noise in my head. I thought I was going to explode. Then Olive slipped her right thumb under the neck of his shirt on his right and crossed her hands, slipping her left thumb under the left side of the shirt neck and just raised herself up, her forearms closing like a scisors against his neck. Her movements were so swift and easy, he didn't see it coming. Neither did we. In seconds the blood was cut off to his brain. He was out cold. She held her arms tight against the arteries in his neck for a moment or two longer. Then let go and heaved him off her.

Olive! How did you know to do that?

"Ray showed me once," she said, brushing herself off. "That's the classic Judo choke. Now let's find a way out of here. I don't know how long he will be out."

Shouldn't we kill him?

I think we should just run.

I wonder where we are.

"I don't know. Let's find stairs and a door or an open window."

The basement was not large, and we quickly found a stairway that led to a service entrance. Olive pushed through the door and was met by Leo Gianetti pointing his gun at us. Feeney, on the sidewalk to our right, suddenly took a flying leap and pushed Olive down on the sidewalk as two shots rang out. One shot smashed the windshield of the car parked at the curb, passing through the air where we had just been standing, and the other shot ended in a grunt and a heavy thud.

"Get off me, Feeney. You're a married man." Olive was once again pushing a man off her.

Leo was standing over Jimmy Stokes's inert body. Olive went to his side. "I thought Feeney said the captain took his gun?"

"This is another gun."

Leo was shaken, and breathing hard. "Stupid son of a bitch. What the hell was he up to? Are you all right? We were just about to bust in there when you busted out."

"I'm fine. Is he dead, Leo?"

"I didn't aim to wound him. He had a cocked gun in his hand."

We were all afraid he was going to have a heart attack right there. Olive tried to get his eyes off the dead cop and on to her. She touched his sleeve. "How did you know where to look?"

"Who are you?"

"Olive."

"Have we met?"

"No. Nice to meet you, Lieutenant."

"Ehhh…"

"How did you find us?" she asked again.

"His partner…ex-partner told us he moonlights as a night watchman here and has the key." Olive turned and looked up. We were looking at some kind of warehouse. The river was to our right. "What street is this?"

"We're in the teens."

"How did he get me here?"

"He must have just taken you out the back to his car. You're probably missing some blankets that he wrapped you up in, or a rug. When you didn't come out I went in and found the phone knocked off its table and you gone. I put two and two together and it came up Jimmy Stokes."

"You're not a detective for nothing, Detective. Excuse me—Lieutenant."

"Feeney." Leo's voice was not in its usual whip-cracking register when he spoke to his junior officer. It was low, flat.

"Yes, sir." Feeney stepped forward, his voice low as well.

"Make the call." Leo handed Feeney his gun, butt first. Feeney took it, sadly.

"We've got to get back. What time is it?"

Leo eyed me carefully. "Isadora?"

I looked down at the blood spreading in a dark, warm circle on Jimmy's chest. *It's just blood Isadora. It doesn't MEAN anything. You don't live in some primitive tribe where drinking blood means that you take on something of the enemy, or the animal…it's just a biological substance that you destroyed in your stomach and pissed away in a few hours. It's gone. And you didn't exactly drink it. You were trying to keep from choking on it. But it doesn't matter. It's gone. And there is no meaning attached to it.*

"Isadora?"

Ray's voice faded and Leo's voice held me in the moment. I raised my eyes to him. "I've got to see Claudia. What time is it now?" More wasted time because of…well, no, this time was not my own system chaos that delayed us, but the nutcase lying still warm and dead at my feet. I would shed no tears for him, but for Leo, I said, "I'm sorry you had to do this, Leo."

He gave a little shake of his head, not quite an all-in-the-line-of-duty-ma'am gesture, because I knew killing a fellow officer would have its ramifications, both officially and in his own head.

"What time is it?"

He checked his watch. "Two o'clock."

"I really need a shower before I see her."

"I'm coming in with you this time. Even if you turn into a head of cabbage. You aren't going into your apartment alone." He turned to Feeney who was closing his cell phone. He said almost gently, "Those strings I'm always ragging you about Feeney, if you can pull a few to keep them off my ass till I finish this thing today…"

"Yes, sir." Feeney's expression betrayed no feeling about the request.

"Tell the Captain I'll be in as soon as I wrap this up today. In just a few hours I imagine."

"It was a good shoot, Boss. I'll tell them that."

"So will I," I said.

Leo nodded but said no more.

Leo, as good as his word, came into my apartment with me, gave the place a thorough check, and then seeing I was really uncomfortable with his presence there—only Ray had ever been in my apartment—left.

I stepped out of the shower, dried off and pulled on some clean clothes, the first things I grabbed, which turned out to be a purple shirt, black pants and black jacket. I took a deep breath and called Vin.

"Hey, Miss Thing!" he said. "You did it! I swan—"

"Vin, are you at the apartment?" He said he was. "Is Claudia there?"

"In the next room. I'm fussin' in the kitchen."

"Who else is in the apartment?"

"Nobody. The boys are kickin' a ball around in the park with their Uncle Mike. Miriam is still in Nutley. How are you? I heard you—"

"I need you to do something for me. Lieutenant Gianetti and I will be there in a few minutes."

"Well, sure I'll take care of that." I had the feeling that Claudia had just walked into the kitchen. I told him to meet me in the lobby and not tell her I was coming and to not let anyone else upstairs. He didn't ask me any more questions.

Chapter 25

Leo was drinking coffee out of an **I Love New York** paper cup. He'd had plenty of time to walk to the corner deli and back. He was leaning against his double-parked car, his tie loosened around his neck. The late afternoon breeze was whipping his too-long hair around his head. He had had some sleep the night before. He had told Cootie, when he could get a word in, that he had stayed at the hospital with me till Ray got there. Then he and Feeney drove back to New York. Leo had come back to Nutley alone in the morning. Hence, the clean shirt. It was probably a clean suit too, but all of Leo's suits were the same. Dark gray. Goes with the badge, he always said. Most of his shirts were white. Hester was right, Leo in a blue shirt constituted a fiesta.

We got in his car. "Leo, you put cream and sugar in that didn't you?" Hester eyed his light, thick-looking brew. "You don't pay any attention to me, and when you are hooked up to a heart monitor and it starts flatlining, I will be there to say I told you so, Leo. I told you so."

"Something to look forward to, Hester. How you doin' after the…"

"The train wreck? The mental train wreck that was Isadora's breakdown? If she let us do more, it wouldn't have happened. Olive and I tell her, but nobody listens. She has to do it all herself and that's what happens. Train wreck!"

You abandoned me, I reminded her. She squirmed a little and was quiet, but it didn't last. "Sugartime could help, but she won't." She was talking to me more than to Leo. "She minds the little ones, but then so does Lance. Why do they get so much attention? Why don't they just GROW UP? Or go away. You know, on that ONE SINGLE POINT I agree with Evildora. On everything else, well on everything else she's a homicidal sociopath. But still."

"Actually, I didn't mean that. I meant your kidnapping and near murder by Jimmy Stokes."

"Oh, that. We had that under control. We were escaping when you found us, weren't we?"

"He was about to shoot you in the back."

"Oh, yes. Well, it all worked out," Hester finished vaguely.

Hester, you little twit! Olive was almost screaming in her head. Leo just killed the man. Unusual for Olive to take the sensitive role. These were unusual times.

"Oh, I'm sorry, Leo. Are you going to be in trouble?"

"There will be an inquiry. Isadora will have to be questioned. Will she be okay with that?"

"As long as they don't do it in an elevator or a cab, she'll be fine."

Leo had to smile. A little. "Feeney will take care of things till I get back to the station. Then a little hell will break loose, I expect. I have a good record. They'll put me on administrative leave, send me to the department shrink. It'll be all right. Eventually."

"Did you ever kill anybody before?"

"Never even fired it at a human being. Just target practice."

"Well, we are very glad you practiced, Leo. Very glad."

He smiled again.

Hester was quiet after that. Unusual times, indeed.

Leo waited till we were out of the car and I was back before he asked, "Are you sure you want to do this by yourself?"

"I don't think she'll talk to anyone else. I hope she will talk to me."

Vin had been leaning against the building smoking a cigarette and chatting with Victor. When he saw us he ground the cigarette out with his foot and met us halfway. "What's goin' on? Hi, Lieutenant. Guess I'm not a suspect anymore, huh?"

I heard the phone ring just inside the lobby door. Victor ducked inside to answer it.

Leo just shook his head. He'd never seriously considered Vin Parrish a suspect anyway.

"I need to talk to Claudia," I said. "Alone. It might take awhile. Can you kind of stick around here and make sure we aren't interrupted?" I addressed myself to both Leo and Vin, who looked surprised that Leo agreed to be consigned to waiting in the lobby with him.

"Does this have to do with Charlotte? Is she…" Vin looked about ready to cry.

"Lieutenant Gianetti will explain."

I sprinted past Victor and took the stairs.

The Jack Russell began to bark as soon as I hit the bell. Claudia opened the door. "Oh, I tried to—Bungee, hush—I tried to see you at the hospital when I went out with Miriam, but they said you were…uhm…I'm so glad you're…are you all right? Please come in."

While Miriam had been like someone come back to life, Claudia was hollowed out. Ghostly.

"I owe you the balance of your fee." Her voice was thinner, even breathier than before. "Vin made his special Mississippi mint tea. Please come into the kitchen."

I sat down at the table and watched her open the refrigerator door and take out an oversized pitcher of sparkling tea and two glasses from the freezer. There was a tremor in her hands that I hadn't seen before as she filled the glasses and then set them on the table. "I'll get my checkbook."

"Sit down for a minute, Claudia."

With some hesitance, she sat.

"You're a good mother. I respect you." I sensed her constricting, pulling back, shutting down. "I know what you did." Her hands found a grip on the tea glass. "I've known *what* you did. I just didn't know why, until yesterday."

Her face went perfectly expressionless, reflecting mine, I supposed. Her tremored grip on the glass tightened, the ice rattled. She was close to bolting, but both of us knew she had no place to run. I continued softly, carefully, and slowly.

"I know you can't tell me, so just listen and I will tell you, and then it will be all right. No more bad things will happen. I give you my word. You trust me?"

She nodded and stared blankly at the table. "He warned you not to tell, and you told. And that person, the one you loved best, died. And he told you over and over that it was your fault, and that if you ever told anyone ever again, someone else would die."

She brought the rattling tea glass to her lips and just managed to wet them without taking a swallow. "*You* didn't tell me. So nothing bad will happen. I promise you. I know how these things work. You were very good at not telling me anything. Someone else did."

Her eyes grew wide with panic. "Nobody knew. Who told you?"

My gaze fell to Bungee, in his usual place by her side, regarding me warily. "He did. He didn't bark. Nobody gets in or out of this apartment, or comes to the door, without him making a racket. So, I concluded that no one had." She frowned, puzzled. "No one had come to the apartment to take the baby. So, if she was missing, as she clearly was, she hadn't been taken from here."

Claudia let go of the tea and dropped her hands to her lap. Her eyes closed, in resignation or relief. I couldn't tell which.

"Everything after that just confirmed my theory. You said you put the buggy in the closet because you couldn't bear to look at it. But everything else that was Charlotte's was still out. That nursery is like a shrine, a memorial to your lost child. When I saw the buggy I knew why. You didn't want the police to see it and get any ideas. It's the old fashioned kind, with the top that rolls halfway over the bed to keep it shaded. Keeping a child in shadow. You left with a baby and returned with a doll. A lifelike baby doll. I saw it in the nursery. Victor had no reason to look closely or be suspicious. You returned the doll to the nursery. Waited forty-five minutes and called the doorman first, just to make sure he was clueless."

"Just the buggy?" she uttered in a near whisper.

"When I left you on Wednesday, I walked around the block and found the Heartwood Buddhist Center. They have signs all over their gates, but one sign on the door at the west end of the portico I found particularly interesting. SAFE HAVEN. There's a turnstile inside that second door. You place the baby in the basket, and turn it and ring the bell—a system as old as monasteries and convents everywhere in the world. And in New York the Safe Haven law guarantees that there are no questions asked. It was your only chance to save her, to make sure she was out of his reach. Then, that night, Lance told me a story."

"Lance?"

"One of my alters. He communicates mostly in stories."

"What story?"

"The story of Moses. Which is really the story of a mother who saves her infant by giving him up. The first time I met you, you were grieving—that was no lie—but not in the same way as Miriam. You weren't in shock. You were not confused. You had no anxiety. Just profound and simple grief. Charlotte was in a good, safe place, just not yours anymore. Then I had to ask, why would you feel so desperate that you would give away your baby? I knew it wasn't that you felt you couldn't take care of another child without your husband. You have financial resources to get all the help you need. When I asked you if your uncle or your father had ever abused you, you didn't say 'no.' You said, 'They never laid a hand on me.' Until yesterday morning, I was confused by that, because I knew you were telling me the truth, but I also knew what you had done. And I felt the presence of another person with us there, and I assumed it was your husband. I assumed his memory would have been strong in your bedroom. But it wasn't him, was it? It was your father, commanding your silence. I understand now. We found the Web site. You heard about that? He didn't molest you, did he? He gave you to other men. That's why you have nothing in your closet the color of flowers. He used to dress you up in flower colors. Even back then, the network had its code. Before the Internet, they still styled themselves as a garden club."

"His little *daisy*." She almost choked on the word. "He would never have molested me. Incest is so…aesthetically repugnant. But he had no qualms about—" Her hands clasped together, formed a single fist that she pressed against her forehead as if to keep it from blowing apart.

Then she rose, trembling from head to foot, picked up her chair and carried it across the room. Lifting the chair by the back and swinging it like a bat, she smashed the china hutch causing an explosion of blue-and-white porcelain.

Bungee leapt straight up in the air, yelping. I grabbed his collar and scooped him out of harm's way. I stepped back ready to duck if anything came our way. What pieces weren't demolished by the impact of the chair, she began smashing individually. Once in my arms, the terrier stopped barking. I was afraid to let him down because of the broken china, so I carried him to the family room and shut him in. When I came back, I found Claudia on her knees, bent over, her head almost in the rubble of shattered Delft, crying with two fists held over her heart.

I knew there was no comfort in sympathy. I squatted in front of her at a little distance. "We can get her back and put him away for the rest of his life." I pulled a handkerchief from my pocket. "Your hand is bleeding."

She let her hand bleed and used the handkerchief to blow her nose. She sat back against the counter. "Sleepovers…he took me on business trips and left me with—friends. When I told him bad things happened to me at night, he said I was just having nightmares.

"When I got older, I knew I wasn't dreaming. The things that were happening to me at these sleepovers were horrible, but real. So I told my mother. He'd told me not to ever tell anyone, but I told my mother. Two days later, she was dead. It was my fault. And if I ever told again, someone else would die. Just like you said. He told me over and over. And after awhile, he didn't have to tell me. I never got his voice out of my head."

"You've never told Vin. I'll bet you never told Dan."

She shook her head.

"None of this is your fault. Not then, and not now. You wanted someone to find out. You hoped I would find out. I did. But now, you will have to tell. You won't be telling, really. I've already done that. Gianetti knows. He is downstairs right now, telling Vin. But you will have to confirm it. Can you do that? You must do that."

"They can't arrest him without—"

"Yes, they can, but telling them is for *you*. If the secret is out, he has no more power over you. You'll be free, Claudia."

Except for a brief time when her husband was alive, terror and helplessness had been her two constant companions. These were the members of HER company. I much preferred mine.

Limp as the Raggedy Ann in the nursery, she sagged against the hutch. "Why? Can you tell me why? Does he get money?"

It dawned on me then that her *why* was not existential. She did not know what her father got out of giving away his little girl, her nanny's little girl. "He's part of a ring of pedophiles. They provide children for each other. They have to provide a child every so often or they somehow get excluded from the ring. We haven't worked out the details yet."

She looked at me with a reservoir of horror I wouldn't haven't imagined she had. "You mean he does to children the things that they did to me?"

I nodded and she threw up a pool of bile in the rubble at her knees. She heaved and heaved till there was nothing to draw up. I soaked a towel in cold water, wrung it out and handed it to her. She buried her face in it and slid back, away from the sticky mess.

I reached for the wall phone and called Leo's cell. I told him what had happened and that Vin should be prepared for the state of the kitchen.

Claudia didn't have the energy to move. I met them at the door and led them back to the kitchen. Leo surveyed the place and just shook his head.

Vin knelt gingerly beside her. "Hi, sweetheart."

"Oh, Vinny. I gave away my baby!" She sobbed loudly, this time. He sat down beside her and drew her head onto his shoulder. "I know, honey, I know. We can get her back now."

"What if she's already gone? What if they—"

"I don't think things happen that fast. We'll get her back." Vin looked at me, gripped by a sudden anxiety that he was wrong. I nodded a confirmation and he relaxed again, his arms encircling the weeping Claudia.

Leo was in the living room on his cell phone telling Feeney to bring Spencer Burke in for questioning.

Claudia had stopped crying, and Vin scanned the kitchen with a big grin on his face. "Look at this MESS!"

"Can we move in with you?" Claudia asked, blowing her nose on the towel.

"You want to live in my old rat trap?"

"It's not *here*."

He considered that for just a moment. "Well, sure. Why the hell not? At least till we find a bigger place. But," he said, his gleeful eyes surveying the room, "you're going to have to learn to clean house, girlfriend, and I'm gonna need to get a *real* job."

Chapter 26

Spencer entered the station with the air of the invited guest, smiling like a VIP, looking spiffy in a blue suit, sparkle-white shirt and navy bow tie. He walked with his usual forward sloping posture, his head bobbing a greeting to all he passed like one of those plastic dogs in a rear car window. I have to say this for the NYPD: they are not much impressed by very important people, and less so by self-important ones. Whether or not Spencer even noticed that no one genuflected or even smiled back, I couldn't tell.

Leo rose from his seat at the back of the room as the officer led Spencer through the obstacle course of chairs and desks. "Thank you for coming in, Mr. Burke." Leo did not offer his hand.

"Anything to help, Lieutenant." Spencer bobbed in my direction and Feeney's. He got no response from either of us.

Leo said, "Let's go somewhere we can talk. Would you like some coffee?"

Spencer held up a hand, "No, no thanks."

Leo led him back to the main interview room. Spencer

was still acting like he was here to discuss a new business deal instead of as the prime suspect. Leo would make that clear soon enough. I declined to follow. I didn't want to reprise any of my walks down flashback lane. But I didn't leave the station either.

"Aren't you going?" I asked Feeney.

"No. Leo likes to work alone at this stage. The captain and a couple other detectives will be watching if he needs anything. He never does. He'll crack him if anybody can."

"If anybody can."

"You don't think he'll do it?"

"I don't know. Did Leo tell you to keep an eye on me in case I do a Linda Blair?"

He was apparently familiar with *The Exorcist* because he laughed with some embarrassment. "Not in so many words. He means well, you know. You...you're important to him. I don't mean as just a—"

"I know."

"You want some coffee? Not the crap we have here. I'll send out for some. We have plenty of time. I don't think this guy is going to fold as easily as the dentist."

"Light, with cream."

Does the word cholesterol mean nothing to you?

Hester, for God's sake!

For once, the bickering of the divas was reassuring. All was normal in my weird world.

Feeney picked up the phone and spoke to Rudy downstairs. In ten minutes a clerk brought us our coffee and a bag of rolls. Feeney paid him, then made himself comfortable at Leo's desk. Between bites of his Danish, he asked, "Are you a mind-reader?"

"Who said that?"

"Nobody, exactly."

"I don't read minds in the way you're afraid I might. I don't read thoughts. I often read intentions. Sometimes feelings. Right now, I can tell that you don't really want to be here. You'd rather be in there watching Leo. But you don't want to leave me either. You are still trying to prove yourself to Leo. That's very important to you, and you will do as you're told, and you are also very curious about me, because you can't quite believe what Leo has told you, and you can't quite believe your own eyes. So you want to try to figure me out on your own, but at the same time you really want to be in there observing Leo, because you want to be as good as he is."

He flushed but didn't say anything.

"I can often tell when someone is lying but not always why they are lying."

"How do you do it?"

"To me it's just obvious. I read body language. I pick up what people are feeling. Ray says there's not a word for me. I'm not really an empath."

Feeney took another huge bite and chewed hungrily, keeping his eyes on me. "A real empath takes on another's feeling like a chameleon takes on a color. I don't feel the feeling. I just know what it is. For me, it's like reading a book. Or looking at numbers. They either add up or they don't."

Feeney swallowed. "Whatever it is, it works. That's the main thing."

"Nothing I do holds up in court."

"Doesn't have to. It points us in the right direction."

I didn't feel like talking anymore, and to his credit, Feeney read my body language as I leaned back, watched the comings and goings in this room, and sipped my coffee. He turned his attention to some paperwork on Leo's desk. I closed my eyes.

Listening to all the sounds in the room, not filtering anything out, not giving one sound any more importance than any other, I could shut off my thoughts. The voices, raised or low, drawers closing, doors opening and shutting, phones ringing, chairs scraping, papers rustling. The Company was quiet. I listened to the room as if it were music.

Several times in the next couple of hours, Feeney got up and went somewhere, always coming back after a few minutes. Once he came back with fresh coffee. I accepted it with thanks and took the last pastry in the bag. Hester was there, disapproving, but she didn't say anything. I ate the pastry and drank my creamy coffee with satisfaction. In the last few days I had consumed more coffee than I had in the previous six months. Hester would, when this case was over, enforce a strict detox regimen. I wasn't looking forward to the organic brown rice, broccoli and green tea that I knew was coming.

Heavy footsteps coming directly toward me caused me to snap open my eyes. Leo was headed for his desk and he didn't look happy. Feeney got up in a hurry. Even he could read Leo's anger and frustration from several feet away. Leo collapsed heavily in his chair.

"He didn't crack. He didn't change his story. He never got defensive. He knows we don't have anything on him, so there is no way he's going to talk. That showroom crawls with customers, sales reps—cleaning staff. Everybody had access to his computer and he knows it. And plenty of people accessed that flower site who were only looking for flowers. He knows that too. Without evidence, all we have here is coincidence. And the Teflon sonofabitch isn't going to be convicted based on the testimony of a daughter who looks like a grief-stricken widow with postpartum depression. And he knows that too. You know how confident he is? He never asked for his lawyer. He is very concerned for his daughter, by the way, very forgiving. He understands what strain she's been under."

"I'll bet." I had noticed that while Leo didn't have his gun back, he was still in charge of the case. Feeney must have strings indeed.

"I'm going to let him stew in there for a while before I go back in. Besides I need to take a piss and have a cup of coffee. Want anything?" He asked me, not Feeney.

"No." Leo thrust a hand into his pants pockets and brought out a handful of change. He studied it, and Feeney asked, "You need coffee money, boss?"

"Yeah, loan me a buck and I can get one of those apple things. I like those apple things they have in the machine."

As Feeney handed him a dollar I said, "What you need from Burke—I'll get." I surprised myself. I hadn't intended to be more than an observer going forward. But once it was out of my mouth, it sounded like a good idea.

"How? You can't wear a wire. You can't even wear a watch."

"I don't need to wear a wire in there."

"You'll fuck up our intercom."

"There will only be one of us present at any given time."

"Can you promise that?"

"I can't guarantee it, but I predict it."

"You can't hurt him."

"Do you care?"

"Not as much as I should. Goddamn it, Shiloh. You hurt him, it'll all be there on tape. You know everything in interrogation rooms is recorded. That miserable piece of shit is not worth you getting into trouble. And if we have it on tape that you tortured a confession out of him, I won't be able to smooth it over. And then they'll throw the confession out anyway. We'll get him another way."

"How?"

"I don't know, goddamn it. I don't fucking know!" He picked up something at random on his desk and threw it down again. Feeney, for once, didn't flinch. "I have to take a piss."

Feeney and I watched him go.

Without a confession, Claudia will never be free. She'll never get her daughter back.

Hester sounded serious for once, and for once, she was right.

Let Hester talk to him. She likes rats.

Olive was agreeing with Hester and giving her the stage? Maybe...

I got up and told Feeney I had to go to the ladies' room. Which I did. It was also time for a Shiloh & Company meeting.

"Hester, if things start to go south, you'll let me take over."

Isadora, if things go south, you'll go souther. You know you can't handle this. Let us do it. If things go bad, I'll let Olive take over, okay?

"Fine by me. Can you handle this, Olive?"

Don't be ridiculous. I get a fair price out of Robin Bartholome—the biggest skinflint in the art world. Not to mention getting us away from Jimmy. I can do anything.

She had a point. "Okay, let's do it."

The Lawman won't like it, offered Cootie.

No, but he'll be watching, and if things get out of hand, he can charge in like the cavalry. He'll like that.

"Another good point, Olive. You're on, Hester."

Hester looked at herself in the mirror. She took the lipstick that I'd promised to always have there, out of the blazer pocket, filled in her lips and used a little to add some color to her cheeks. She put water on her hands and fluffed up her hair and pushed the left side behind her ear.

When she returned to Leo's desk, she tore a sheet of paper off his notepad and scribbled on it, folded it in half and showed it to Feeney. "Deniability." He looked blank. She sighed in frustration. "What you don't know, Detective, Leo can't blame you for. I'm going home. Got it?" She stared meaningfully into his eyes.

"Sure. You're going home."

"When Leo comes back, give him this note." She tucked it deeply into his suit pocket.

The junior detective squirmed. "Sure."

Hester walked away. Instead of taking the door out, however, she ducked down the hallway to the interview room, flashing her incandescent smile at the officers posted outside the door. "Hey, Krupkies, how are you?"

They laughed. "Hey, Shiloh. What's up?"

"Leo's giving me a crack at our subject while he takes a break."

They nodded, and Hester went in.

"Hello, Spencer. I'm Hester."

She pulled out a chair and sat across the table from him, keeping her big smile and bright eyes fixed on him.

"Hello. You're Shiloh...what..."

"Spencer," she chided him, "you were told what we are before you met us. Did you think it was a joke? Some therapist's way to a book deal?"

"No, I'm sorry—Hester, you said...?"

He was scrambling to get his own smile back as he readjusted himself in his seat.

Hester folded her hands on the table top in front of her. "Okay, sweetie. Talk to me."

Spencer Burke wasn't used to being called sweetie. He was

speechless.

"You should talk to me or you might get someone else in the Company, and none of them like you. But I don't have any issues. I'm just me, Hester." She propped her chin on her hand, elbow on the table. "So tell me about this Garden Club. Oh... did Leo tell you? They found the one who took Anna, and they found Anna."

"Yes. No. I already knew. Yesterday, Michael called. My daughter's brother-in-law...the priest... We are all so relieved."

"I'll bet."

"And I'm more than willing to help. More than willing. But I've told them everything I know." He rubbed his forehead, perplexed. "I don't know why they are so fixated on me."

"You don't."

He shook his head and shrugged.

Hester smiled and shrugged back. "You fit the profile."

"What profile is that?"

"The profile of a perv."

More vigorous head shakes. "No, no no." He uttered a congenial little chuckle. "They won't find anything in *my* life. I've led a quiet life—a good life." Spencer was under no obligation to talk to her, but he babbled on. "I don't smoke. I don't drink. I don't gamble. I've provided well for my family. I've given my fair share to charity. I...I donate blood."

"I'm growing fonder of you every minute. Keep going."

"I've never hurt anyone."

"What about your daughter?"

He sighed hugely, exchanging his helpful, slightly hurt smile for the mask of self-disappointment. "I could have been a better father. After her mother died, I tried my best. She never wanted for anything. But I—"

"You gave her to other men to use."

"That story." He shook his head sorrowfully. His head seemed to have its own separate battery pack. "I don't know where she came up with that. She stayed over with friends occasionally when I was traveling, but nothing ever happened. This is just her being upset and depressed. You see, she had nightmares as a child. To her they seemed real. I should have taken her to a therapist. I admit that. That was my fault. I thought she would get over them. Grow out of them. I didn't think she'd remember them."

Hester kept smiling. "Claudia remembers you blaming her for her mother's death and telling her—no—*programming* her to never tell. And she never has. Isadora figured it all out."

He kept that head shake going and the smile on his face. No sign yet that his batteries were wearing down. "No, no, you see that's all part of her nightmares. Of course small children feel guilty when a parent dies. They all do. I tried to tell her it wasn't her fault. I didn't do enough, that's clear. I take full responsibility."

I knew that by now Leo would have come back, yelled at Feeney, read Hester's note:

Dear Leo,

Let us have a try. We can't make it worse. Don't yell at Feeney.

Love,

Hester

and would be outside to watch her every move. She knew it too and changed her tack, leaving her chair and circling to perch casually on the side of the table, speaking in an even friendlier, disarming manner, her hands clasped loosely on her lap. "Well, you can understand why the police are interested in you, can't you? You are a well-positioned man with artistic sensibilities and tastes and the means to indulge them. In that, you must admit you do fit the profile. You can't blame them."

"No, I know they are just doing their job. But you understand it is difficult to be called in here and questioned again when I've already told them all I know." He played for her sympathy and she responded.

"I do understand. And that's why I wanted to talk to you. I think they've been very heavy-handed with you and are missing an opportunity to…" She paused while he waited hopefully, expectantly, "…avail themselves of your expertise in this affair." She had found a phrase right out of one of Lance's novels, and Spencer, who probably didn't read those kinds of novels, released a genuine smile, like a mouse who thinks the cat has just extended the paw of friendship.

"We need insight into the workings of the mind of a man of your class, your sensibilities. Could you help me with that?"

"Yes, certainly, I'll try." His eyes welled with modest confidence.

"Because as you and I both know…" She leaned toward him a little, casting a quick glance around the room, mentally cursing the turtleneck I made her wear and wishing she had some cleavage to show, lowering her voice, indicating that what she was about to say, she wanted to be below the range of the mikes. Of course, the mikes in the room were sensitive enough to pick up a whisper, which she was well aware of. "As you and I both know, the police—they try with their profilers and all that, but they're, you know, so blue-collar. They can't really know… I thought you could help us develop a better, more refined profile of the man we're looking for. The person who took your granddaughter—"

"Do you think it was the same man who took Anna?"

"Do you?"

"Oh no, not the same kind of person at all. She's too young."

"Too young for what?"

"Too young to fit the profile of the group you're talking about."

"Is she? We only profiled the kidnappers, not the children."

"I just mean…"

"We're looking at many other people."

"Of course, I'll be happy to help. Any insights I can offer…"

"Good. Thank you." Hester rose and circled the room slowly, still casual, still amiable. "You see, your average perv knows he's a perv. These guys, these fellows in the Garden Club think they are epicures. Let's say—hypothetically—a man with your sensibilities wouldn't consider himself a monster. Would you?"

"Of course not."

She sat on the edge of the other side of the table. Spencer readjusted himself so he could look up at her comfortably. "You would consider yourself a gentleman with special tastes."

"I would imagine so, yes."

"You would." She nodded, taking a moment for reflection. "*I* would imagine that all of the members of the club come through personal referrals only. Wouldn't you imagine that?"

"Yes. Yes, I would." He nodded in hearty agreement.

"You make every effort to keep a certain kind of person out and only let in a person of discretion, affluence no doubt, and of course, patience. And most importantly, a person who you know will play by the club's rules. Am I right so far?"

"Yes, yes. Absolutely."

"So, I have to wonder what went wrong with the dentist. It was a dentist, you know, who took Anna. What do you think went wrong with the dentist?"

"I don't know." Spencer puckered his forehead in deep thought. "Perhaps he didn't return Anna as soon as he would have, ordinarily, because of all the attention brought on by the disappearance of Charlotte."

"Yes, that certainly makes sense. A missing child belonging to a nanny would not draw the same attention as the missing child of a wealthy Upper West Side family…"

"Yes, taking Charlotte was certainly a mistake."

"A mistake?" Hester's voice was like whipped cream.

"For the club, no doubt. It doesn't seem to be their profile to keep a child for more than a few hours, or at most, overnight. I imagine all the children are returned promptly. I'm just offering an insight here. A possible insight."

"Yes, that's good. This is just what I hoped for. We are getting somewhere here."

"Do you think they are getting this?" He gestured toward the mirror, which he knew was a one-way glass.

"I'm sure that they are. So you are saying that the rules of the club would mandate—can I say 'mandate'? Or 'suggest'…"

"Mandate, I would expect."

"The rules of the club mandate that a child be kept only a few hours…one could then simply assume she wandered off or something when she turns up again on her own."

"Yes, yes and they are always returned unharmed."

"Unharmed?" Hester reflected on that word. "Unharmed.

Oh, you mean, what happens to them in a few hours in the company of one of these gentlemen, would not hurt as much as say—a vaccination…or a fall from a swing." Her voice remained smooth, one reasonable person in dialogue with another about a subject on which they might disagree, but striving all the same to see the other's point of view. "Is that what you mean?"

"If you put it like that, it—"

"And, if the child isn't kept, it isn't really kidnapping, is it? It's just borrowing. A child goes for a little visit, spends a little time in the company of one of these gentlemen and before you can say 'Bob's your uncle' she's returned. Is that how you imagine it is?"

"I suppose so, yes."

"And the children are all so young, they can't really describe what happened to them or where they've been, or who took them, and there's no physical evidence, of course. I'm sure these gentlemen are all very conscientious about that. No bruising."

"Bruising? Oh, of course not! Nothing like that."

"Yes, nothing like that, and no DNA, but even if there should be, if someone slips and is careless, it's untraceable to anyone the child knows, or anyone known to the family of the child. Because she was borrowed by a complete stranger, someone who probably lives miles, maybe hundreds or thousands of miles away. That's really the point of the club. Don't you agree? To match gentlemen with children who cannot be traced to them by any means. Am I right?"

"Yes, I would think so."

"And, really, like you say, none of them are really hurt. All these beautiful, borrowed children." Hester's voice had become more soothing, rhythmic, hypnotic. "All these beautiful, borrowed children. Little children. Little flowers. Beautiful little flowers. Vulnerability and beauty create desire. It's only natural, don't you agree?"

"Oh, yes. We are born sexual beings. Freud proved that. Children are sexual beings," he replied, lulled by her voice, intoxicated by his own memories. His face relaxed, his eyes took on a faraway glaze as he looked at her and said, "You must have been a lovely little girl."

Hester had time for only a moment's regret and wistful thought, *Just when I was getting somewhere*, before she went hurtling into the gyre, the rest of us were steamrolled, and Hawk was lifting him up by his shirtfront, kicking his chair over, pushing him against the back wall and snarling through her teeth, "Children are not plants!"

"Hester..!"

"Do I *look* like Hester?" She bounced him against the wall, keeping her hold on his shirt. "Now you tell me why your daughter gave up her own child."

"What?"

"Pay attention," she snarled again and rapped him once more against the wall. Her arms were long and he flailed his own, shorter arms uselessly, like a cartoon figure. In Hawk's fire, he was straw. "In spite of everything you did to her, Claudia is stronger than her mother was. She protected her daughter. She gave her away."

"She what?"

"Are you deaf? Charlotte is where you will never get your hands on her. Now you tell me exactly what you did, because I am tired of talking, and if you don't, I'll kill you."

"The police...are watching this."

"I'm sure they're enjoying the show."

"You can't kill me in a police station."

"If they were concerned about your nasty ass, they wouldn't have let me in here in the first place."

He stared at her, speechless.

Hawk whispered, "The first time you kill, they say, is the hardest. The second time, it's easier. But I confess, the first time I killed somebody, it wasn't that hard."

"You killed somebody?" he warbled in fear.

"It's a fond memory. Now, speak to the microphones. Loud and clear. Enunciate. What you did, or I will kill you. I have nothing to lose. You see, according to some experts, I don't even exist. Tell me first what you did to Claudia."

He said nothing. She released his shirt and her hand closed on his throat like a mouth, her nails dug into his flesh like teeth.

Now, he couldn't talk and he stank of fear. He could breathe but only enough to stay conscious. I knew if he didn't start confessing, she would kill him slowly, painfully, and he'd be conscious till the very end.

"Tell me what you did." She released the pressure enough so he could take a breath.

"I didn't do anything." She closed on his throat again and shook him. And gave him a breath.

He gasped, "I had to. I owed the club. I couldn't find anyone else and my time was running out. Everyone in the club has to supply information, or a child at least once a year. That's the rule! She wasn't hurt. She was too young to even remember."

She squeezed tighter, cutting his air off. His arms flailed uselessly, pawed at her arms uselessly. "How many times?" She allowed him a breath.

"Not many—only a few times—"

"Now, what did you do to Anna?"

She eased her hold again, just enough for him to get a deeper breath to speak. "I just supplied the information. For the Web site. That's all."

"Louder."

"I supplied the information."

"And someone called you?"

"Yes."

"Louder!"

"Yes! Someone called me."

"And you gave them Anna's schedule and told them she would be wearing a certain outfit?"

"Yes."

"Thank you," Hawk growled and, shifting her position slightly, placed herself in the line of sight between his face and the observers, she began her deadly squeeze of his throat, watching silently as the life drained from his face.

He's on me so heavy my hands pinned to my sides weak against his strength helpless...................................... I am Hawk I strike my teeth sink into his neck a sickening crunch tear and bite again deeper and rip he has not even screamed blood fills my mouth must swallow to breathe I shut my eyes and bite deep and tear his throat out…blood spouts like a fountain over me fills my mouth up my nose in my ears. I choke try to spit but I must swallow or choke he has thrashed and twitched bruising me but is quickly still I am drenched in what I did not swallow tides of his blood the sheets are slick with his blood my hair my nightclothes I will never get the taste out of my mouth the smell out of my nostrils the devil's blood my father's blood.

Then, a hand slipped over hers, and a dark, molasses voice crooned, *That's enough now sweetheart. Let it go, honey. This is not for you. Let it go, baby.*

Hawk let go. Spencer collapsed on the floor, gasping and choking and clutching his throat. Sugartime left. Hawk stayed.

Leo barreled through the door muttering *shit shit* realizing he might be too late. Feeney was right behind him. Hawk lifted her eyes from Spencer, wheezing for air on the floor, to Leo.

"You're Hawk," Leo said, relieved that he still had a live suspect.

"You're Leo."

"Nice t'meet ya."

"I doubt it."

Leo yelled through the open door, "Somebody bring the bastard a glass of water. Feeney, take his statement. Hawk, come with me."

Leo and Hawk paused outside the room and watched as Feeney tossed a yellow legal pad on the table and helped Spencer get to his knees, then into the chair. Spencer was rasping, "She killed someone. Did you hear her?"

"Old news."

An officer came back with a paper cup full of water, set it in front of Spencer Burke and left. Feeney placed a pen on the pad.

Feeney watched Spencer down the water, then he pushed the yellow legal pad and pen toward him. "Start writing."

"Be quiet. You get used to it."

"Are you talking to me?" Leo eyed Hawk.

She shook her head. "Why do you need the statement if you heard everything?"

Leo was trying not to smile. "We couldn't hear a thing. It was all static. But he doesn't know that. He'll just reiterate on paper what he thinks we got a recording of. And sign it. It's a beautiful thing, a signed confession. Anyway, you always need a signed confession." He almost sang it. "Can't go wrong with a signed confession." Then, seriously, he said, "You could have gotten yourself and me in deep shit in there."

"Could have. Didn't." She sounded disappointed. "Go back to the gyre."

"Who are you talking to?"

"Isadora."

"Can I talk to her?"

"No."

"Why not?"

"She can't speak right now."

"Why the hell not?"

"She's…howling."

"What in God's name for?"

"She remembers."

Monday

Chapter 27

We all wanted to sleep off what Olive had wrought Saturday night. She doesn't do it often, but when she drinks, she puts herself in a stupor and gives the rest of us hangovers that can last for days. The memory that came to me as my own, after all these years, came to the rest of the Company as well. No one blamed her for getting drunk as a sailor with shore leave on payday. We were all right there with her for every swallow of sweet, potent Kentucky bourbon. Fortunately, I'm the least affected by her binges, but I still didn't feel too steady. I would have welcomed a day-long nap. I didn't need to be there for the denouement of my cases. I hand over the information, whatever it might be, and then I disappear, usually with a check in my pocket.

But I was the only one Claudia wanted with her, so there we sat, on a hardwood bench outside one of the many small courtrooms in the main courthouse building where criminal cases are heard. A drab environment in which to spend a sunny Monday morning.

Where are we?

Well, good morning, starshine, Hester drawled sarcastically.

Thank you so much for giving us all a headache.

Yeah, don't rag me anymore about my Coke.

Sorry, Cootie, it's been a tough week.

Really? Next time things are too much for you to handle, just go to the gyre and stay there. Hester didn't really blame her, either, but couldn't miss an opportunity to claim the upper hand. Olive seldom felt contrite enough about anything to let that happen.

Please, don't lecture me now, Hester. I'm sorry. Where are we?

We're at the courthouse.

What for? They never let Isadora testify.

No testimony required. He pled guilty. Pled? Pleaded? Whatever. It's just a matter of setting a date for sentencing and making sure he's locked up in the meantime.

He's rich. He'll make bail.

Maybe not. Claudia's uncle has to sign off on any big money...they don't keep quantities like that outside a joint account of some kind, which requires two signatures unless one of them is dead. Manfred is alive and kicking and won't let loose of a penny.

That's interesting. Do you think it's a cover for his own involvement?

He went off like a Molotov cocktail when he heard what Spencer has been up to all these years. He threatened to kill him with his own hands. Leo was a little half-hearted in telling him it wasn't necessary.

Weren't we supposed to see Ray yesterday? Did we...?

We cancelled.

Because of me? Ray must have been furious.

No, we had other things to do. And she wasn't furious at all. She's still feeling guilty about Isadora's breakdown. Hester snickered. *We can get mileage out of that for a long time. Oh, and we told her about the memory-thing...you know. I don't think she believed us.*

So what did you have to do yesterday?

Claudia asked Isadora to find out about her uncle.

As Hester recounted our Sunday to Olive, I revisited my phone conversation with Claudia. "My uncle says he didn't know," she told me, "and that if he had known, he would have stopped it. You can tell if he's lying or not, can't you? I just want to know if my kids still have a granduncle. And he wants to take care of Anna and Miriam. Wants them to move in with him and Phoebe. I told her she could stay in our apartment for as long as she wanted to. But she doesn't want to live alone, and she didn't want to come with us. I don't blame her. The boys and I packed our suitcases and moved down to the Village with Vin on Saturday night."

"I'll go see him. Will he talk to me again?"

"If he doesn't—that's my answer isn't it?"

"I suppose so."

I felt like sleeping, but I went to see Manfred Burke.

He lived in a building overlooking Gramercy Park. I didn't call first. The doorman buzzed upstairs and announced me.

Manfred surprised me by answering the door himself, inviting me in with a nod. As always, he was impeccably dressed in matching beige slacks and long-sleeved shirt and a tan and maroon argyle sweater vest. He was wearing leather slippers instead of shoes.

He offered me a comfortable chair and sat on the sofa facing me. All the furniture, whether painted or upholstered, was white. Color and pattern were supplied by a rich maroon oriental carpet and flowered wallpaper.

"I only want to ask you a couple of questions. Claudia sent me."

"Yes, would you like something? A drink?"

Oh please God no drink, Hester almost wept.

"Or some coffee? Or tea? Or we have cranberry juice. My wife drinks cranberry juice. I should have bought stock."

I declined everything. He didn't look happy to see me, though he wasn't hostile. I got right to it. "Did you know what your brother did to Claudia when she was a little girl?"

"I have no brother! He is dead to me!" He began to cry bitterly. "I should have. Shouldn't I? Shouldn't I have known? Why didn't she come to me? Why didn't she come to me?"

He cried into a large handkerchief and blew his nose. He took off his glasses and wiped his eyes and put his glasses back on.

"Did you know that he abused other children and was part of a network of procurement?"

"If I had known any of it, wouldn't I have killed him? I swear to you I would have killed him. Or turned him in. No, I would have killed him."

"Thank you, Mr. Burke."

I left him crying on the sofa and let myself out.

Back home, I called Vin's home number. Claudia answered. "Your uncle didn't know. I think he would enjoy a visit from his grandnephews."

"Was Miriam there? Anna?"

"I think he was alone."

"Thank you. I'll call Miriam. They'll be good for each other, I think. He is already paying for Anna's therapy."

Hester was finishing up her account. *And you should have seen that apartment! It looked like an old Russian whorehouse!*

Olive still wanted to know, *Why is she here?*

She just wants to know the minute he is taken off to the slammer so she can go pick up Charlotte. She isn't going to bring Charlotte back till she knows he is in jail and is going to stay there. It's a THING. She wouldn't even tell the police where the baby is. Leo wanted us to tell, but we wouldn't, Hester said smugly. *Client-detective privilege, don't cha know!*

Is there such a thing?

There is now. Leo didn't push it. Claudia didn't do anything wrong.

Where is Leo?

In the courtroom. He promised to come out and tell us as soon as they haul the sonofabitch off.

Like Faust to hell.

Lance, you here too?

Wouldn't miss it. It's epic. It's Homeric. Biblical.

And we know he's going to be hauled off to jail, now, today?

Well, if the bro won't pay and the confession stands, chimed Cootie.

The lawyer tried to talk him out of his confession, but I guess being abandoned by his family… We are just waiting for the word and then off we go.

How's she doing?

How does she look?

Claudia, sitting next to me, unaware of the cacophony of voices in my head, looked thin as a wraith, white as paste. Her eyes were fixed downward, her hands knotted in her lap. Even after her outburst in the kitchen, even after her statement to Leo and a two-hour conversation with Ray, she wasn't convinced that her ordeal was over and her daughter safe. And, she was still, probably, waiting for someone to die.

A few yards down the hall a table was set up with coffee and pastries and bottled water and juices. I decided to get a cup of coffee and something sweet. As I stood up, Claudia said, "Don't leave."

Even though we hadn't said two words to each other all morning, my presence was somehow holding her together, since Vin and Michael Keating were both back in the small Village apartment with the boys. I sat back down and fished in my pockets. I found a half-roll of antacids. I shook them out into my palm and ate them all.

Sorry, Isadora, muttered Olive. *I owe you one.*

The door to our right swung open and Leo burst out as though flung from a slingshot. "They're taking him out. No bail. Sentencing next week, but he'll get the max."

Claudia who had been locked up tight started to cry again. Different tears this time. More like irrigating waters to a parched field.

Leo stood over her and said, "You don't have to worry about that old man anymore. He is going to die in prison. You have my word on that. And the judge's too, if I read her face at all."

"Was he smiling?" she asked, without raising her head.

"That smile washed out of his face like cheap ink running off a page. I think reality has finally sunk in for Spencer Burke."

As it was for Claudia. She turned to me. "Did you call them?"

"Yes. They're expecting us." I had called Ray, too. She was ready to meet us there. Wouldn't miss it for the world, she had said.

Now Claudia couldn't get out of that building fast enough. I had no time to bid Leo goodbye. I just saw him grin as he watched us take off down the hall to the elevator, which was too slow. Claudia hit the button again and again, and once we were on it she fairly danced in place as we were lowered to the ground floor.

Fortunately, we had no trouble hailing a cab. I was afraid if we had been passed by she would have chased it down like a terrier. I got in first, and as she slammed the door shut behind her, she barked directions to the cab driver about where we were going and the fastest way to get there. I realized that people really are like their dogs and that, for the first time in my life, I had just ridden in an elevator, and for the second time in my life and the second time in three days, I was riding in a cab. I had no time to contemplate these new developments because Claudia fairly yipped, "Can you call Vin? He has to meet us there."

"I don't have a cell phone."

"Oh." She dug hers out of her purse and handed it to me and rattled off his number while I pressed them into the tiny keyboard. The little phone felt like a toy in my hands.

Why can't we have one of these?

Because after we carried it around for thirty minutes it would stop working.

You don't know that, Olive.

It's an expensive experiment if it didn't work. We don't need one as long as we have a quarter in our pocket.

Vin answered before the first ring had finished, and before I could finish my sentence, he let out a whoop that rattled my eardrum. I asked him to call Ray and gave him the number.

I handed the phone back to Claudia.

"Do you think she'll remember me?"

What I knew about infant memory probably did not apply to this situation, but—why not? I said, "I'm sure she will remember you."

The cab driver was speeding up the Westside Highway and, as we turned off on Ninety-sixth Street, she handed me a wad of bills and directed him to the Buddhist Center. She had the door open almost before he came to a complete stop and was opening the gate while I paid the fare. I didn't wait for change, but sprinted after Claudia, through the gate, up the walk and through the big wooden doors.

We found ourselves in a small, cool foyer with a glossy linoleum floor.

Oh, this is a good place. See the pretty statue.

To our right, a small standing figure looking like a child with shaven head in a monk's robe, carved out of smooth luminous stone greeted us. The plaque on its wooden pedestal identified it as a Jizo, protector of children.

It's so pretty.

Yes it is, Sula. Yes it surely is, crooned Sugartime.

Opening the door had rung a bell, which still echoed. We were soon greeted by a young woman in tan slacks, black sweater and stockinged feet, who came through an archway at our left.

"My name is Shiloh. I called this morning."

She smiled broadly. "Oh yes! Ani is expecting you. My name is Laurie. I'm a volunteer here. Come with me."

We followed her through a door to the right into a small room. Against two walls stood portable metal coatracks hung with a few jackets and sweaters and beneath them, in untidy rows, a number of pairs of shoes.

Laurie directed us, "Take off your shoes, here, please."

Thank God you wore decent socks.

Laurie showed us through a curtain into what seemed to be a meeting room. "You can wait here." I thought Claudia might explode if she had to wait another moment.

A few metal chairs were set up, with more folded in rows along one wall. The shiny wood floors reflected the light pouring in through the tall windows. At the front was a raised platform, with a smaller fabric-covered platform in its center. Dark orange drapes covered the back wall. As I turned to my right, Bethy-June and Sula *oooohed* in wonder. There was an alcove lined with fabrics in brilliant colors and designs. On a many-tiered altar was a larger-than-life-sized seated golden Buddha, glowing in the reflected lights of innumerable candles and oil lamps.

Laurie was gone. Without ceremony, a woman in robes of tangerine and maroon entered through a part in the drapes. A smile was on her face, a bundle in her arms.

Claudia, who had been silently streaming tears since we entered, emitted a sob and held out her arms.

The infant was bright-eyed and a little chubby. The nun placed the baby, swaddled in a multicolored striped blanket, in Claudia's arms.

At the same time I heard a commotion in the coatroom. Vin, Ray, Michael Keating and the two boys had arrived. I heard Vin say, "Y'all be quiet now." Laurie laughed, "They don't have to be quiet. Your mom is in there."

They all charged through the curtain and there ensued a lot of hugging and crying and jumping up and down, and not all the jumping was done by the two boys. Ray looked over them and smiled. She doesn't smile often. When she does, she dazzles. The Catholic priest and the Buddhist nun shook hands warmly. Vin, who had ordered the boys to be quiet, was hooting *I swannee!* over and over again.

I stepped back, out of the way. Now that they were here, I wanted to exit as quickly and quietly as possible.

Hester protested. *You're going to slink off like John Wayne at the end of that movie? The one where he does all the work and doesn't get to stay for the party?*

I don't like parties.

Well, I do! Let me stay.

No. This is a family thing.

Well, I'm not ready to leave yet. And Ray's here. She's not family. Look at that Buddha! Look at those colors! Can we get a Buddha? I want to get a Buddha.

Oh, for heaven's sake, Hester. Olive, when it came to parties, agreed with me.

Well, it's beautiful. It's peaceful.

Who's going to clean up all the wax?

You are.

I was just turning around to slip out past the family reunion and almost knocked over the nun who was quietly, smilingly, waiting behind me.

"Uh, sorry. Hello."

"Hello." She was small of stature and a bit stocky. Her hair was cropped to about a quarter of an inch all over her head and the color of pewter. Her skin was lined, a little rough, a bit jowly, her eyes a very warm brown.

"You are the one who called."

"You are the abbess?"

"Yes. You can call me Ani. You are Isadora. But you are also... Shiloh. Isn't that right? You are all Shiloh."

When I looked into her eyes I felt embraced by a kindness that I never dreamed could exist. I felt Hester beginning to weep.

"You are welcome here," she said. "Come back anytime."

I felt an overwhelming urge to do just that. I wasn't sure why. Perhaps just to bask in the alcove Buddha's golden glow.

Then the abbess said, as if enjoying a private joke, spreading her hands in a fan-like gesture to include all of us, "You will join your selves and find no self at all, and then you will be happy. I promise."

I had no idea what the hell she was talking about, but I knew she was telling the truth. This woman was all about truth.

Then she said, "Life can really be a pisser, can't it?"

She laughed, and I, Isadora, laughed for the first time that I could remember.